UNDER THE SUNS OF SCORPIO . . .

To those unfamiliar with the Saga of Dray Prescot all that is necessary to know is that he has been summoned to Kergen, an exotic world orbiting the double star Antares, to carry out the mysterious purposes of the Star Lords. To survive the perils that confront him on that beautiful and terrible world he must be resourceful and courageous, strong and devious. There is no denying he presents an attractive yet enigmatic figure. There are more profound depths to his character than are called for by mere savage survival.

Called to be the Emperor of Vallia he, with the Empress Delia and their blade comrades, is slowly guiding the island empire from its Time of Troubles. They must all look to the future which is dark with the threat of the Shanks, the Fishheads, raiding from over the curve of the world. The terror of the Shanks lies over all the bright lands of Paz; but at the moment more immediate perils beset Prescot. He has often been at cross purposes with the Everoinye—the Star Lords—during his tumultuous career on Kregen: now he is whole-heartedly with them in their desire to stamp out the unholy cult of Lem the Silver Leem.

Down in the island of Pandahem Prescot and his comrades, having burned a temple or two, must now press on and open a fresh campaign against the Silver Wonder. Life is not so simple as that, particularly on the horrific and fascinating world of Kregen where, under the mingled streaming radiance of the Suns of Scorpio, the unexpected is always to be expected.

ALAN BURT AKERS

The Adventures of Dray Prescot
are narrated in DAW Books:

TRANSIT TO SCORPIO
FIRES OF SCORPIO
MAZES OF SCORPIO
DELIA OF VALLIA
MANHOUNDS/ARENA OF ANTARES
ALLIES OF ANTARES
BEASTS OF ANTARES
REBEL OF ANTARES
A LIFE FOR KREGEN
A VICTORY FOR KREGEN
LEGIONS OF ANTARES
etc.

TALONS OF SCORPIO

by
DRAY PRESCOT

As told to
Alan Burt Akers

DAW BOOKS, INC.
DONALD A. WOLLHEIM, PUBLISHER

1633 Broadway, New York, NY 10019

The Pandahem Cycle
MAZES OF SCORPIO
FIRES OF SCORPIO
TALONS OF SCORPIO
MASKS OF SCORPIO

FIRST PRINTING, DECEMBER 1983

1 2 3 4 5 6 7 8 9

DAW TRADEMARK REGISTERED
U.S. PAT. OFF. MARCA
REGISTRADA. HECHO EN U.S.A.

PRINTED IN U.S.A.

TABLE OF CONTENTS

1	Pompino's name affronts him	7
2	The Devil's Academy	19
3	We sail for Bormark	28
4	The instructive history of a zan-talen	37
5	Aye	47
6	The Lady Nalfi hides in the Chunkrah's Eye	53
7	Twayne Gullik	61
8	Concerning the traitress Ros the Claw	65
9	How a blood-stained switch changed hands	73
10	Of the power of the Lemmites	80
11	How the Great Lio spread	90
12	Of the Pied Piper of Port Marsilus	99
13	The Little Sisters of Impurity	106
14	Strom Murgon puts on a show	113
15	Dafni	122
16	Mindi the Mad	131
17	A Rose between two thorns	141
18	Of the spitting of Ros Delphor	154
19	Sheathed Talons . . . ?	162

CHAPTER ONE

Pompino's name affronts him

"It's very simple, Jak," Pompino said as he leaped nimbly ashore. "All we have to do is recruit a few more rascally fellows and go across and bash this Lord Murgon Marsilus. Then we burn all the damned temples of Lem the Silver Leem, sort out who marries whom—and go home."

"Simple," I said, and jumped up onto the jetty after my comrade. Always difficult that—for me to remember not to shoulder forward and be first out of the boat. The twin suns glittered off the water, gulls circled and screeched above, the air tasted like best Jholaix, and we were off to burn another temple.

Pompino started along the jetty, striding out, arms pumping, chest and head up, red whiskers flaring. I looked after him, and then down to the boat where the rest of the rapscallions who had wangled shore leave were tying up and jumping out onto the wet stones. Our ship, *Tuscurs Maiden*, lay in the roads, canvas furled, and those poor wights detained aboard hanging over the gunwales with faces like grandfather clocks.

To either side of this little seaport town of Peminswopt the red cliffs stretched, serrated, flecked with shadings and tonings of rust, orange and ruby under the light of the suns. We had made landfall within the enormous curve of the Bay of Panderk and here we were in the Kovnate of Memis. Our destination, the Kovnate of Bormark, lay to the west. I started off after Pompino. He was the Owner, the man who owned a fleet of ships, and his men knew him and would follow to keep him out of trouble.

With Pompino the Iarvin on the rampage, trouble was a natural and inevitable occurrence.

7

He headed toward a line of broad-leaved sough-wood trees shading a walkway beyond which rose the walls of the outer town. Much activity went on here as the sailors and fisher-folk went about their business. The smells of tar and pitch mingled with the sea air. A long string of curses rose from a ramshackle shed where tarred nets hung. Someone was in difficulty in repairing their nets. Pompino took no notice. He strode on for the land gate situated alongside the water gate with its portcullis of black iron.

Lofting over the town the fortress of Peminswopt reminded anyone careless enough to let it slip his mind that reivers and pirates might at any time roar in to do all the unpleasant things that folk of that ilk are prone to. This fortress reared up, strong and well-positioned. From those battlements accurate volleys of rocks, darts and flaming carcasses could shatter an unwary attack. Trouble was—the pirates operating here in North Pandahem were just as crafty as renders operating anywhere else. I followed Pompino, aware of the men at my back, and—I admit—comforted by their presence.

If Pompino insisted on burning the temple to Lem the Silver Leem here—a sound and righteous thing to do, seeing that the adherents of the Silver Wonder indulged in murder and torture and baby-sacrifices—the ensuing fracas would need the ready weapons of our comrades.

His reddish whiskers abristle and his foxy Khibil face shrewd, Pompino halted in the shadows of the arched gateway. A string of calsanys passed, each one loaded down with straw-packed boxes, their tails tied to the neck-rope of the one astern.

"Before we start, Jak, my throat is—"

"Aye. And mine."

As we stopped—and only for a couple of heartbeats—a sinewy brown hand reached out between two of the calsanys and groped for the wallet hanging on my belt. I looked down with interest, always fascinated by the ways in which differing people go about earning their living. This one was smart and quick. The steel knives fastened to the inside of his fingers would have snipped through the thongs in a trice.

Pompino said: "The rast!" and snatched at the lean wrist. He gripped it, tugged and a bundle of gray rags flew out between the animals. The restraining rope caught around the wretch's neck and hauled him up. He gargled.

"Look out for the calsanys," I said quickly. "You know what—"

"I know what they will do if they are upset."

Pompino hauled the thief upright, disengaged the rope, and, taking an ear betwixt finger and thumb, ran the snatch-purse a few paces along the wharf. The fellow twisted in Pompino's grip; he did not produce a weapon.

"By Diproo the Nimble-Fingered!" burst out the cutpurse. "You're mighty quick, dom!"

"To your sorrow, you forsaken of Pandrite!"

"Leave off! I need that ear."

"As you needed my friend's wallet?"

"I've three wives and ten children to support—"

"More fool you. Where's the Watch?"

Now the thief looked alarmed.

"You wouldn't hand me over to the Watch? I'm a poor man. Renko the Iarvin I'm called and—"

I thought Pompino would burst a blood vessel.

"You're Renko the *what*?"

But the fellow babbled on. "Kov Memdo is mighty fierce in these latter days after the wars. You wouldn't—"

"Renko the *what*!"

My comrade's apoplexy was a wonder to behold. Pompino the Iarvin held onto Renko the Iarvin's ear, and bellowed purple of face into that imprisoned organ.

"The Iarvin—" Renko babbled. He squirmed and twisted lik a caught fish.

I stood aside, very serious, very thoughtful as the last of the calsanys trotted past. I wouldn't laugh. No, by Vox, even though my insides pained as if about to explode.

"How dare you bear that name!"

"Why—wha—? Leave off my ear, dom!"

Now these Kregish nicknames are a jungle of meanings in themselves. They contain more than one allusion to the quality and attributes of their bearers. To translate them faithfully into a language of Earth one would need to use a considerable quantity of definitions. Iarvin, for instance, means—inter alia—a smart fellow, someone who is sharp, bright, clever, nobody's fool, impeccable—and there are more shadings. Pompino lived up to his sobriquet. Few girls bear the Iarvin as a nickname, for the meanings run differently for them, and the nearest, I suppose, would be the lueshvin. So, now, the two Iarvins glared, one at the other, and slowly the thief of that name understood what the Khibil of the same name was after.

"You wouldn't hand me over to the Watch, dom? No—of course you wouldn't—"

Cap'n Murkizon, enormous as a barrel, black as a thundercloud, stormed up. I told him what had happened, for he and the others with him could see plainly enough what was going on.

"Aye, Jak. Clever, these folk. Tied himself alongside a calsany and waited until he could reach a likely victim." Here Cap'n Murkizon's eyes squeezed shut and tears started. "But, by the black armpit and flea-infested hair of the Divine Lady of Belschutz! Horter Pompino is no likely victim for a trick like that!"

"He's the Iarvin."

Brick red of face, brilliant blue of eye, sprouting hair every which way, Cap'n Murkizon glared about. He cocked his massive head up on that barrel body. He stared at the soughwood trees.

"Watch?" he bellowed. "Watch? When there's a tree with a suitable branch handy! Now, thief, you may thank whatever ancient ship's captain it was who brought the first soughwood tree all the way from distant Havilfar. How could he know that one day, when the trees had grown so fine and tall, they would serve to save a wretch from the Watch?"

Renko the Iarvin grasped instantly what this dynamic bundle of a man meant.

"You wouldn't—for a wallet? By Diproo the Nimble-Fingered! Are you then all stark mad?"

"Aye," said Quendur the Ripper, standing easily at Murkizon's side. The smile on Quendur's face would have filled a shark with horror.

The Kregan way is often an odd way. The spirit of Yurncra the Mischievous must have caught at us. The minor pantheons of Kregen are filled with spirits and demons who move men and women to willful, wanton and reckless ways.

"Where is the rope?" demanded Cap'n Murkizon.

"A seaport always has rope aplenty," observed Larghos the Flatch. He stood close to Murkizon. These two had formed a close friendship since the time Larghos had dived into the sea to save Murkizon. Now Larghos looked about with his Bowman's eye.

"No, no, horters!" yelled Renko the Iarvin. "You would not!"

Just how long Pompino would allow this charade to play I could only guess. The game was growing cold to me. This poor devil Renko, seeing the faces of the seamen around him, devoutly believed they would hang him high from a branch of the sough-wood tree. I stepped forward.

Like the others, I wore simple sailorman's clothes, blue trousers cut to the knee, a blue shirt and a red kerchief around my head. A rapier and main gauche swung at my sides from the broad lesten-hide belt. Only Pompino was dressed with great magnificence, as befitted the Owner, and Captain Murkizon wore a shiny black coat much decorated with gold, his axe swinging from a thong at his belt.

"Renko," I said, "how true is it that you have three wives and ten children?"

He jabbered, and spittle ran. Pompino eased up on his ear.

"I lied, horter, I confess, I lied! I have but the two wives, and but seven children, as Pandrite may smile on me!"

"He's more likely to laugh at you, you great buffoon!" Pompino, for all his talk of going home, had little back in South Pandahem to draw him apart from his pair of twins.

One of the crew swung up with a length of rope; but Pompino had wearied of the farce. He let Renko up. He stuck that fierce Khibil face close into Renko's.

"Now listen to me, you great heap of useless garbage. When you chose to steal from us, you chose the wrong victims. By Horato the Potent, you imbecile! You might have had your hand cut off!"

"No, no, horter! Had I known, I would not—"

"That's what Pantri the Squish said when the needleman explained to her," said Murkizon in his coarse way.

The others guffawed at the reference to the old story of unexpected consequences. This Renko the Iarvin squinted up at them, and, in truth, they wore the appearance of a cutthroat band of ruffians well enough. They'd elected to follow the Owner, they and the others of the crew of *Tuscurs Maiden*. Pompino had explained sufficient to them to justify completely this mission of burning the temples of Lem the Silver Leem, although—for obvious reasons—he could not explain all.

Now Pompino pushed Renko a little way off and glared at him in a most baleful fashion. Renko was all skin and bone, scrawny, with lank hair and the frightened face of a denizen of the stews. His clothes, mere rags, hung on him.

I said: "Do you worship any particular gods hereabouts, Renko?"

At once he was on the defensive, as any sensible person is when questioned too closely by strangers over matters of religion.

"I swear by the potent majesty of Havil the Green," he said, a little truculently. The answer was safe. Havil the Green, one of those all-purpose major godhoods, is worshipped all over the continent of Havilfar and the island of Pandahem. That folk tend to hunger for the more personal worship of a closer god gives rise to the untold numbers of minor religions and cults abounding on Kregen. This is human nature when the chief god cannot sustain all a person's spiritual longing.

Pompino caught my eye. In the partnership we had forged through a number of interesting adventures I was still perfectly happy to allow my comrade the lead. He nodded with his mind made up. He advanced on Renko with what the thief took to be a renewed attempt at hostilities.

"Renko, the crawling nit upon a ponsho fleece! What d'you know of the Brown and Silvers?"

Renko jumped as though branded.

"Nothing, horter! Nothing—"

"Speak, ninny, or—"

"They took my little Tiffti, my little girl. She went with them for sweets and candies and she never came back. And I was beaten, one night, by men—"

"All right, Renko," I said. "You needn't go on."

This was the pattern. The vile adherents of the Silver Wonder, clad in their robes of brown and silver, sacrificed little girls in the most horrific rites. They believed that what they did reflected glory upon them and stored up wealth in the paradise to come. We happened to believe differently. So far we had been able to do precious little to make the other side see our point of view, and, as I said to Pompino, burning a few temples would make little difference. But, it was a start.

"Can I go, horters? My family are starving—"

That might be true, it might not be. I fingered out a golden deldy with the face of a King Copologu on one side and a proclamation on the other suggesting that Copologu the Great was responsible for wealth, health and happiness. Where his kingdom might be I wasn't sure, somewhere down in the Dawn Lands, probably. I tossed the golden coin to Renko.

The gold did not wink a glitter of splendor in the air. A shadow fell about us and a chill gust of wind rattled between the pillars of the archway. Clouds piled in, shadowing the glory of the Suns of Scorpio.

Captain Murkizon said: "B'rrr!" And, then: "Are you letting this miserable specimen go free, Horter Pompino?"

"His punishment is being what he is," observed my comrade, twirling his whiskers and obviously enjoying making a profound statement of eternal truth.

Renko the Iarvin snapped up the golden deldy and it disappeared into his rags. He shivered. He was, in truth, a sorry specimen, and I felt for him. Not everyone, on Earth four hundred light-years from Kregen, as on that marvelous and difficult world itself, can be a hero forever swashbuckling about with a sword.

"Be off with you!" bellowed Pompino.

No doubt Renko imagined these rogues would repent of their leniency and produce the rope instanter. He ran. He scurried off along the quay and vanished into the throng of folk all preparing for the coming rain.

"He'll empty a few pockets before he goes home," quoth Pompino. "But that is no affair of ours. Hai, fanshos! Are you for this wet we promised ourselves?"

So, laughing and ahurrying against the rain, we took ourselves off. Through the gate the streets presented a cobbled, close-set, pointy-roofed-houses impression of huddlement. We found a swinging amphora and a sign that read The New Frontier, and in we went.

Someone wanted to know what the sign might mean, and Cap'n Murkizon rumbled out, with a reference to his Divine Lady's anatomy, that this brave new frontier was off across the ocean in the continent of Turismond, where many nations had established ports and trading stations. The ale passed and we quenched our thirsts and watched the rain sparkling on the cobbles.

The landlord, a cat-faced, bright-furred Fristle, came over with a fresh jug. He wore a spotless blue and yellow striped apron.

"The new frontier did very well for the kov," he told us, pouring carefully. "His father, Kov Pando na Memis, made a fortune over there in Turismond. The dowager kovneva, the

Lady Leona, brought the young kov back home and now he lives in great style.'' He wiped the lip of the jug with a clean yellow linen cloth. ''Of course, Kov Pando being in the army had to go and get himself killed fighting those Pandrite-forsaken rasts of Hamalese. The wars, they spoiled everything.''

''They're over now—''

''Aye, thank all the gods. But we hear tales of those Shtarkins who raid and burn. No coasts are safe, it seems, these days.''

He had his worries, we had ours. That is how the worlds roll on. We drank and waited for the rain to stop and took little notice of the company in Fandarlu the Franch's The New Frontier.

Cap'n Murkizon, anxious to put right what he considered a slur upon his honor, wanted to know more about the plans to burn the accursed temple here in Peminswopt.

Pompino explained enough, and little at that.

''This hateful cult of Lem the Silver Leem—'' and he kept his voice low—very low ''—appears in different guises from country to country. The king here, this flat slug of a King Nemo the Second, supports the religion. It is spoken of a little more openly, and more people know of the Brown and Silvers. But they like to keep their secrets. They use passwords and secret signs. And they torture and sacrifice little children.''

Murkizon drank ale, and his fists clenched on the jar. He said nothing.

Quendur the Ripper, raffish and reckless and almost a reformed character, said: ''When I was a render adventuring for my own profit and leading a band of bloodthirsty pirates, we never did that. It would not occur to any civilized man.''

''Draw your own conclusions.''

Larghos the Flatch poured more ale and pushed the jar across to Murkizon. ''Civilized people might think to raise a Great Jikai against this evil cult.''

''Many do not believe what they cannot grasp. The secret powers of the Leem Lovers are great; men and women disappear in the night, others are assassinated. The followers of the Silver Wonder have friends in the highest places. The jikai against them is difficult—''

Murkizon looked at the jar Larghos pushed across, down at the one in his fists and saw that was empty. He exchanged the jars, drank, wiped his lips, and said: ''Anything worth doing is difficult. This is not anything like the fight against the

Shanks." He clamped his heavy lips shut. No one said any more about that fight, in which Murkizon had been absolutely in the right to suggest we should not fight, and when we had fought he had taken his part right royally.

Outside in the rain a file of soldiers wended past, hunched in their capes. Their flag hung wet and shining. This was the flag of Tomboram, a solid blue with the symbol of a quombora, a fabled beast all fangs and spits of fire. Tomboram utilizes the system of having a simple national flag which is differenced by each sub-use, so that the Kov of Memis charged the blue with a silver full-hulled argenter, and Pando over in Bormark where we were bound had a golden zhantil emblazoned in the center of his blue flag. This is an interesting tradition of a number of nations on Kregen. I looked at what trotted along after the soldiers.

Sleek and shining in the rain, the lethal forms of werstings appeared to undulate like a river in spate, so close their backs were packed. Black and white striped hunting dogs, werstings, vicious and trained to hunt and kill. Yet they have only four legs, and not over-large jaws or fangs. The pack humped along, chained together, and led by their Hikdar, who carried his switch tucked under one arm.

"Werstings," said Quendur. "Now those I do not like."

"Out in the rain?" said Pompino. "Some poor devil is for the chop, then, that is sure."

The landlord, Fandarlu the Franch, came back to our table. He looked after the last of the werstings, loping along with tucked-in tails, and made a face. When he offered to refill our jars, we refused, for the rain was easing and the first hints of ruby and jade across the street gave evidence that the twin suns of Kregen, Zim and Genodras, once more deigned to smile upon the world.

"Thank you, landlord," said Pompino, standing up. "Here is the reckoning." He put a handful of coins on the table. The others nodded and smiled, pleased that the Owner had treated them. We went outside where the air held that freshly scrubbed after-rain tang. Water ran in the gutters. People began appearing on the street. A few birds climbed away from the eaves where they had sheltered, heading out for the fish quays. They were gulls and small birds, not saddle flyers.

"A nice place, The New Frontier," commented Pompino as we walked along. "Clean and respectable."

I felt like stirring Pompino a little. Now the landlord's

nickname of Franch means a fellow who thinks a lot of himself, and is able to prove it. It is not in the same category as Iarvin. So I said: "His nickname suited him, no doubt. Perhaps they are all cut from the same cloth hereabouts."

He stopped and glared at me. He took my meaning. Then he laughed. Pompino Scauro ti Tuscursmot, called the Iarvin, can laugh as only a Khibil can. For Khibils are a mighty supercilious folk, highly hoity-toity in their ways and when they laugh they relax from that high posture and let it all roll out.

"And there," he said when he stopped laughing, "is the fellow we need." He nodded his head.

Indeed, there was the man. He strutted along the street pompously, swinging a golden-headed balass cane. His clothes ballooned splendidly, laced with gold and silver, wired with gems. His hat glistened, the arbora feathers flaring. A few paces to his rear trotted along a Brukaj, patient, docile, carrying a satchel which no doubt contained all the fussy necessaries this puffed-up personage required from time to time.

The object which unmistakably told us that this was, indeed, the man we required was pinned to his lapel. A small silver brooch, fashioned in the form of a leaping leem, and with a tuft of brown feathers setting it off.

"They are more open, up here," I said.

"They are safe, the cramphs. If you do not know what the silver leem and the brown feathers mean, then you do not matter. And if you do know, then you had best walk small and keep a still tongue in your head, otherwise you're likely to find yourself in the gutter with a slit throat."

"Aye. You have the right of it."

Murkizon said in his thunder-growl voice: "Shall I twist his arm a little?"

"When we are safe from observation. And the poor Brukaj slave will have to be attended to."

"I," said Quendur the Ripper, who had once been a pirate, "will treat him with great courtesy."

We followed this glittering popinjay in an unobtrusive way among the growing crowds. His slave carried the furled-up rain-shedder, a kind of umbrella, over his shoulder, and looked miserable. The popinjay himself carried a multi-colored kerchief in his hand, with which he made much gallant play to passing ladies and acquaintances. He also carried strapped to his waist a rapier and main gauche. For all his dandified looks, he'd be able to use the weapons. On Kregen weapons are carried for a purpose, and those that carry them are expert in their use. Those that are not are dead.

As the suns shone down and we dogged our quarry, I qualified that thought. Not everyone on Kregen is a roistering rapscallion of an adventurer, and, in addition, there are those who carry weapons and who have only a modicum of skill in their use. Usage and custom dictate where the twain shall meet, if they do, and how they shall conduct themselves.

"He is making for the zorcadrome, I believe," said Pompino. "The thought of a fine dainty zorca saddled to support that bulk offends me."

"You are right, and you are wrong."

"What, Jak? What in the name of—?"

"You are right to say he is no zorcaman, despite they are sturdy and strong and always willing. You are wrong to say he is going to the zorcadrome. Look. That is his destination."

The fellow we followed in our unobtrusive way lumbered up the steps of a building that gave no indication of its use. It was simply a three-storied structure, one of a row in this street, with a fantastical array of pointed roofs and toppling spires and chimneys. The slave Brukaj followed and the door closed after him.

"How long is the ninny going to stay in there, wherever he is?" demanded Murkizon.

Before Pompino had time to speak, I said: "Well, I for one, do not intend to hang about to find out."

They looked at me. To give my comrade his due he grasped my meaning before the others. Larghos the Flatch started to say: "What, Horter Jak! Giving up so soon!"

Pompino broke in. "And I am with you!"

"Good," I said, and wasted no more words. Across the street, dodging a smart carriage drawn by freymuls, up the steps and a thunderous tattoo on the door I gave Pompino no chance to dart in front. He was at my side as the door opened.

A small Och woman—and Ochs are small in any case—turned her head up to regard us. She wore a decent black dress and a yellow apron and her hair was covered in a white lace coif. Pompino spent two heartbeats staring vacantly down the brown-varnished hall with its side tables and vases of flowers before he looked down at the little Och lady.

"Yes?" Her voice held the timbre of a saucepan struck by a carving knife.

"Ah . . ." said Pompino.

He stared at me with the same vacant look.

I said in as cheerful a voice as I could manage: "Pray pardon, madam. Is Horter Naghan Panderk at home?"

The name just jumped into my head—Naghan as one of the more common Kregish first names, Panderk for the bay of that name.

She looked me up and she looked me down. Her nose wrinkled just a trifle.

"There is no one here of that name."

I looked suitably flabbergasted. Pompino picked it up at once.

"Surely there must be, madam? This is where he lives."

She shook her head and made shooing motions.

Maybe Pompino had picked up more than he ought to have done. Maybe this place was not a house where people lived at all. As though confirming that notion a hulking great Chulik of a fellow hove into view along the passageway. His yellow-skinned face and the upthrusting tusks at each corner of his mouth bore down on us, together with his beetling brows and his thin lips and his iron armor and his sword.

Perfectly normal to have a watchman, a sensible precaution in a chancy world, of course—but this fellow bore down with so evident an intention of picking us up by the scruff of our necks, of smiting at us with his sword, of doing us a mischief, that the normality of the custom vanished instantly.

He wore brown and silver favors, and that condemned him in our eyes.

"Out!" he roared. "Schtump!"

"Now this," said Pompino, and he spoke almost gratefully. "Is more like it!"

At that instant the terrified scream of a child rocketed up through the house, bounced along the corridor in a shriek of agony.

"Devil's work!" yelled Pompino.

Together, shoulder to shoulder, we charged past the little Och woman and slap bang into the raging Chulik beyond.

CHAPTER TWO

The Devil's Academy

If the famous Watch of Peminswopt of whom Renko the
Thief was so scared had chanced by just then and seen a wild
bunch of ruffians breaking into what seemed a private house,
they would have taken us for reivers, criminals, bandits. That
piercing scream proved otherwise.

The little Och woman toppled sideways, unharmed as we
crashed past. Pompino dealt with the Chulik in a summary
fashion. The man was unready for such a swift and headlong
assault, and he went down soundlessly.

We roared on along the passage.

"Down there!" yelled Pompino and we clattered down the
blackwood stairs leading off at a right angle at the turn of the
corridor. The others whooped after us. A vague orange glow
from the edges of a door at the foot of the stairs abruptly
bloated into brilliance. The door smashed open as Pompino
put his foot to it. We all rushed through. The room beyond
held four more Chuliks in iron armor and wearing brown and
silver. Their weapons glistened in that orange light.

They did not hesitate. They launched themselves at us in a
feral onslaught designed to smash us instantly, with no questions asked. Pompino yelled, Cap'n Murkizon's axe whistled
about, Larghos switched his sword forward. Quendur simply
slid down and along the polished floor on his seat and skew-
ered upwards. A nasty trick—dangerous, of course; but then
that was Quendur the Ripper, reckless and swashbuckling. I
joined them and in a trice the Chulik guards were overpowered.

"They were not guarding that entrance for nothing," quoth
Pompino. His sword indicated the curtained doorway at the
far end.

The shrill and agonized scream broke out again, ending in a ghastly bubbling wheeze.

"Hurry! Before we are too late!"

The curtains whisked aside.

Pompino used his sword to open the drapes; what we saw beyond convinced us that swords would have to be used for a grimmer purpose before we were done with this place.

"The Devil's Academy!" Pompino's words summed up that scene. The man we had followed was in the act of dressing himself in clothes suitable for what went forward here. His assistants, meek, frightened, pallid men and women, fussed over him, oblivious of our entry. The room's lamps shed that orange light upon the cages and the basalt slabs, the racks of knives and saws. For a foolish moment I thought we might have stumbled upon a surgeon's operating room; but I saw no signs of tar barrels, and Kregans do not operate in quite that way. The man in the blood-stained smock over his brown and silver looked up. His fingers ran with blood. The girl child upon the slab would not live, not now. The saw in the man's fingers was a single bar of crimson.

He shouted: "Who are you?" And, then, quickly: "Guards! *Guards!*" For he saw our swords and understood what they meant.

The man we had followed struggled to get either into or out of the smock his attendants fussed with, and he, too, screamed for guards. It was quite clear what was going on. As Pompino said, this was the place where the priests of Lem learned their butcher's trade.

We were too late to save the child who had screamed and so brought us here; we could try to save the four other children, three girls and a boy, penned in the iron cages against the walls. Their hands and feet were bound, and they wore blindfolds and were gagged. We did not think it was from concern over their feelings that they were thus blindfolded.

The half-dozen or so younger men in the ubiquitous brown and silver standing goggling to one side must be the acolytes, the trainees. Here they were taught the finer arts of sacrifice.

With a shout of pure horrified anger, Pompino threw himself forward. The others followed, yelling. This, I thought, was what the Star Lords wanted us to do, eradicate Lem the Silver Leem, root and branch. I gather that here on this Earth there have been discovered recently something over two hundred sub-atomic particles, including leptons, and things called glues which hold, or appear to hold, quarks together within protons. I'm pretty confident that the Star Lords know of many more sub-atomic particles if there are many more to know. These sacrifices were being divided and sub-divided, like atoms, into sub-atomic, sub-human, particles. If this was Lem's idea of scientific research, then the Star Lords had our whole allegiance in putting a halt to it. So, nauseated, I dived into the fray, and my prime object was not revenge but to get the four children safely out of it.

The flash of sword flickered in a most particular and sinister fashion in that pervasive orange light. My comrades rushed upon the adherents of the Silver Wonder. I turned toward the cages.

As the clangor of the fight broke out at my back I looked at the cages. The iron bars bulked each with a heavy full roundness that told of strength sufficient to hold not only children. Leems would be kept penned there when required. The bolts were shot home, the locks clumsy and intricate. To one side two angerims gaped upon the scene.

Sharp-toothed are angerims, all hair and ears, and as a race of diffs who are not Homo sapiens they are an untidy, messy lot. Staring at me they backed off, holding their mop and broom up as though they were weapons.

"Just give me the keys," I said. For the key ring at the taller of the two's waist spoke eloquently.

"Keep off!" screeched one angerim, his hair sprouting everywhere, half-concealing his brown breechclout.

"Run!" yelped the other.

They threw down the mop and the broom and started to run toward a small door set abaft and to the side of the cages. Opaz alone knew what maze they'd disappear into if they escaped through that exit. I sprinted after them.

In their mad flight they kicked over a metal bucket containing bits and pieces. The floor stained red and slippery. I jumped. They almost reached the door when I realized this was no way to get the keys.

Instantly, I yanked out my old sailor knife, poised, and threw.

The broad blade pierced the thigh of the taller angerim and he toppled over, screeching. His companion did not wait about but simply wrenched open the door and leaped through with a long wailing cry. In a heartbeat I reached the fallen diff, saw that he would live if he reached a needleman in time, and took two things from him—one the key ring and the other my sailor knife.

The noise spurted up as Pompino and his crew sorted out the problem of the Leem Lovers. The third key fitted the lock and the first cage swung open.

The best plan would be to open all the cages first and then to release the bonds and the blindfolds. To do it the other way around would see the first child running screaming every which way, probably to fling himself in the way of a sword.

Each cage opened with its own individual key. A neat touch. Remaining on the clumsy iron ring three keys promised other doors in this place it might be worth the opening. I glanced over my shoulder. The acolytes had either run or been cut down. The two chief butchers, the instructors, must have attempted resistance, for the body of one still clutched in one half-severed hand a broken sword. The other vomited out his life over the corpse of the child.

From the distant end of this unpleasant chamber the guards at last appeared. A group of half a dozen or so Rapas rushed into sight. Predatory, beaked and feathered, their vulturine features convulsed with killing fury, the Rapas hurled themselves at Pompino and his men. No doubt they intended to avenge their paymasters.

Cap'n Murkizon let his booming roar lift over the noise.

"Hit 'em, knock 'em down and tromple all over 'em!"

This he proceeded to do with great gusto.

Confident that all was well, I returned my attention to the cages and the children.

If you wonder why I, Dray Prescot, whom my companions knew only as Jak, did not roar into a knock-down drag-out fight, but, instead, opened cages, then you profoundly misunderstand my nature. A fight is a fight; there have always, it seems, been fights and, no doubt in the nature of man and woman's inclinations, there always will be fights. That does not mean a fellow has to hurl himself headlong into every one that comes along if there are more important tasks at hand.

Like now.

Freeing the children was easy; calming them down was an enormous task.

Only two were apim, Homo sapiens, like me. One girl was a Fristle Fifi, sleek and charming and graceful in her feline way, her fur a glorious honey-colored softness. The lad was a Brokelsh already with his coarse black body hair abristling everywhere, quite unlike the swagging growths fringing an angerim.

I'd half a mind to keep their ankles hobbled up; but after I'd spoken to them in a manner more brusque than I really cared for, they quieted. Their eyes, round and glistening, regarded me as though I was a fabled devil from Gundarlo or Cottmer's Caverns. I tried to smile for them.

"You will all go home to your parents—" And, of course, that was the wrong thing to say. At that, they began to cry. The picture was obvious and ugly enough. So, to repair the damage, I told them that as soon as the nasty men had been dealt with we would find a new home with many sweets—in fact, I said, embroidering, "We will find you a home right next door to a Banje shop!"

A Rapa blundered past with half his beak missing and his feathers bedabbled a brighter color than their usual green-gray. I merely watched him as he struggled to reach one of the other doors in this place, for the Devil's Academy was well-provided with exits. Larghos the Flatch, sweeping his sword in a slashing cut very suitable for a Bowman to use, helped the Rapa on his way. I held the little Fristle Fifi's hand, and the other children clustered around. Their eyes remained large and round and glistening.

The noise quieted. The stink of spilled blood rasped in the close atmosphere. Pompino came over, looking as though he was halfway through a chore.

"Fire, Jak," he said. "Now we burn the accursed place."

"And hope the temple is handy."

"Too right, very handy, to be consumed also."

Larghos said: "That Rapa—he must be dying; but he dodged off. He could raise the alarm."

"Then settle him, lad, settle him!" boomed Cap'n Murkizon. "By the nit-infested armpits of the Divine Lady of Belschutz! Don't waste your sympathy on these cramphs!"

Larghos ran off, swirling his sword. Murkizon trundled along after. They were forming a right partnership, that pair.

Quendur the Ripper said: "I am glad Lisa the Empoin is not here to witness this." He shook his head, raffish, reckless yet trying to reform.

"If she had been here," Pompino told the ex-pirate, "she would have been more merciless than we mere men."

"Oh, aye. That is sooth."

I cocked an eye at Pompino. The Khibil brushed up his

reddish whiskers. No doubt he was thinking of his wife, who nourished ideas above her station, and with whom Pompino no longer got on. A startling confirmation—a re-affirmation—in the coincidence of the actions of Pompino's wife after a fight and what next occurred, a confirmation only that human nature is human nature, gave me a feeling of helplessness in the face of that very same human nature. Cap'n Murkizon returned to the chamber yelling with merriment. He fairly golloped out his glee.

Following him walked Larghos the Flatch, his head bent a little to the side and over the sleek dark head of a naked girl who walked close to him. We all stared.

"A cloak!" bellowed Murkizon. "To cover the Lady Nalfi!"

Quendur leaped to one of the less distorted bodies and whipped off the brown tunic. The silver hem was only lightly bespattered. He took the garment across, saying: "Until we can find something better for the Lady Nalfi."

Larghos the Flatch took the tunic from Quendur. I noticed the officious way in which he acted, taking the tunic, fussing, handing it to the girl. She was in the first flush of womanhood, firm and rosy, with bright eyes in which a pain easily understood clouded the blueness. She lifted her arms and slipped the tunic on, shivering.

"Thank you, jikai," she said in a small voice, speaking to Larghos. He was acting as though he'd received a thirty-two pound roundshot betwixt wind and water, so we all knew his business was done for.

"The Rapa?" said Pompino, brushing aside what went forward, anxious to get on with the purpose.

"He led me to the Lady Nalfi," said Larghos. He spoke through lips stiff with some emotion we again envisaged as being all too easy to understand. "I cut him down. And a rast of a Chulik tried to bargain with us over the Lady Nalfi—"

"Standing holding her!" roared Murkizon. "But she didn't stay held long."

"She just took his dagger from his belt and slit his throat." Larghos gazed fondly at Nalfi. "A brave act for a naked girl in so perilous a position."

She lowered her eyelids and leaned against Larghos.

"I—I had to."

"Do not think of it, my lady, if it pains you—"

"No, no. It is not that. Just—"

Pompino burst over all this. "Find combustibles. Pile them

up. Let us burn the place down and leave, for, by Horato the Potent, the stench is getting down my gullet!''

As we busied ourselves over this task, I reflected that the adherents of Lem the Silver Leem hired mercenaries of a reasonably high quality. Also, while it is said that Chuliks and Rapas are hereditary enemies, this is not strictly and invariably true. Of course, some Chuliks and some Rapas are always at one another's throats, just as there are misguided apims who are hereditary enemies—here on this Earth just as much as Kregen, more's the pity. But an employer will hire on mercenaries from many different races, and they will serve alongside one another for pay, and not quarrel overmuch. This system, as I have indicated, works to the employer's advantage in that there is less likelihood of plots against him or her from the ranks of the paktuns taking pay.

The combustibles were set, the children and the Lady Nalfi drew away to a safe distance, and Pompino personally set the first flame.

We had seen no sign of the Brukaj slave who waited on the man we had followed here, and I, for one, could entertain a hope that he had escaped. Slaves are controlled, and do not always believe what their masters or mistresses believe.

Flames ran and crackled and laughed gleefully to themselves. Smoke began to waft in flat gray streamers, filling the place with a soft veil, hiding the horrors.

Retracing our steps up the blackwood stairs we encountered the little Och woman at the top, wringing her hands, crying.

Some of us were for cutting her down where she stood, there and then. Others of us, though, counseled mercy as we could not know the full story and there was certainly no time to wait to find out. Pompino shouted alarmingly, and the Och woman ran off, throwing her apron over her head. The rest of us, the children and the Lady Nalfi, came up and we headed for the front door.

Now even on Kregen in a civilized city a cutthroat gang of rascals with blood-spattered clothing and blood-reeking swords will claim attention if they attempt to march down the High Street. We halted on the steps, staring about.

The Lady Nalfi in her soft husky voice said: "I know a way. The back alleys. Come, quickly.''

Agreeing, we trooped down the steps and cut into the side alley between this house and the next. Murkizon trod on a gyp which howled and scampered off with his tail between

his legs. Nothing else untoward occurred as we hurried along
the alleys, past the backs of stores and houses, and so came
out to a place where three alleys met. Here stood—or rather
leaned—a pot house of the most deplorable kind. Only four
drunks lay in the gutter outside. No riding animals were
tethered to the rail. The Suns shone, the air smelled as clean
as Kregan air ever can smell clean.

Pompino looked at Nalfi.

Larghos held her close and it was clear he would not
relinquish her.

"If we clean off the blood—"

Pompino nodded. So we all went at the pump outside the
pot house, sluicing and sloshing. Larghos eyed the four drunks
calculatingly; but Murkizon told him that their clothes were
far too ragged—and alive—for the Lady Nalfi.

Speaking in a solemn, careful way, in almost a drugged
fashion, Larghos the Flatch said: "I shall see to it that the
Lady Nalfi is dressed as befits her, in the most perfect clothes
it is possible to find. Such beauty must be dressed in beauty."

Nalfi did not reply; but her blue gaze appraised Larghos.
He swelled with the importance of the task he had set himself.
Pompino caught my eye, and smiled; I did not respond. Not
all marriages are made in Heaven, and not all end in Hell.

When we were cleaned up we set off still keeping to quiet
and less-frequented ways down to the docks.

Confidentially, Pompino said to Cap'n Murkizon: "Captain.
It would be best if you asked Larghos, quietly, what he
knows of this Lady Nalfi."

Murkizon leered; but agreed.

The sea sprung no untoward surprises, sparkling pale blue
with that tinge of deeper shadows past the rocks, which, in
their furry redness sometimes looked perfectly in place and at
others oddly out of keeping. Gulls flew up squawking as we
walked along the jetty.

"Thank the good Pandrite!" exclaimed Pompino when we
saw our boat was still moored up. Looking back over the
spires and pinnacles of the close-pitched roofs we could see
no sign of smoke. Murkizon expressed himself forcibly on the
subject of fires, and when, icily, Pompino requested that he
make himself plain, the bluff captain shut up.

But we knew what he was on about. Pompino had set the
fires. We had all seen them burning, beginning to ease their

way aloft. Why, then, had the godforsaken building not
burned down?

Not until we had pulled almost up to *Tuscurs Maiden* and
the watch, hailing us, prepared to receive us aboard, could
the first wafts of smoke be seen over the city.

Pompino merely gave the smoke a single significant glance,
and leaped up onto the deck. That glance spoke more eloquently than any "I told you so!"

Standing on the deck I said to Pompino: "I know a man, a
fellow by the name of Norhan the Flame. His hobby is
throwing pots of blazing combustibles about."

"Aye, Jak. A handy fellow to have along now."

"Down in Hyrklana, though—I think, for he was moving
around the last I heard."

"Don't we all?"

The breeze indicated a fair passage, the vessel was in good
heart, if a trifle stormbeaten, and she'd been careened and
scraped at Pomdermam. Over on the shore the smoke lifted
and people moved about on the jetty. Two other argenters
like *Tuscurs Maiden* lay moored up. Well, being North
Pandahem craft they were not quite exactly the same as our
vessel which hailed from South Pandahem.

"It is reasonably doubtful, Pompino. But there is a chance
we were observed. Therefore we may be followed."

"We may, indeed."

Climbing onto the quarterdeck Pompino radiated energy.

"Captain Linson," he said to the master. "While I do not
profess to understand the tides and the winds as sailors do,
and while it is true that I merely own the ship, I would like
you to take us to sea and toward the west at this very
moment."

Pompino, it seemed, had been learning that owners could
not order their ships to perform evolutions like soldiers on a
parade ground. His heavy-handed way with Linson, who was
sharp, cutting, and with every instinct set on making a fortune
from the sea, simply made the master even more indifferent.
Linson was a fine sailor, knew his own mind, took enormous
delight from tormenting Captain Murkizon, and was prepared
to obey orders if they did not conflict too much with his own
desires.

"We are able to sail at once, Horter Pompino. I made
certain arrangements when I—ah—observed the smoke."

"Did you now, by Pandrite!"

As Cap'n Murkizon and I sailed as supernumeraries, we had no direct part to play in getting the ship to sea, apart from hauling on and slacking off and running. This sailor activity pleased me for reasons Murkizon, who had been born on Kregen as had everyone else as far as I knew, could never understand. As for Murkizon, that barrel of blow-hard toughness ached to eradicate the imagined slight upon his honor.

The Lady Nalfi and the children, escorted below, were safely out of it. I caught Pompino's eye as the canvas bellied and was sheeted home, and the ship began to come alive.

"Linson could see the smoke before we could, as he was higher."

"Aye. Devilish smart, is our master, Captain Linson."

"Aye."

Tuscurs Maiden heeled, took the breeze, and in a comfortable depth of water headed out past the Pharos. A few small craft bobbed here and there. The lookout sang out.

We rushed to the aftercastle.

"May Armipand the Misshapen take them!" burst out Pompino.

With shining oars rising and falling like the fabled wings of a bird of prey, wedge-prowed, hard, a swordship pulled after us, her bronze ram bursting the sea into foam.

CHAPTER THREE

We sail for Bormark

We stared aft as that cruel bronze rostrum smashed through spray after us. The oars rose and fell, rose and fell, beautiful in their way, derisive of the agony entailed in their hauling. Pompino stamped a booted foot upon the scrubbed deck.

"Now I am growing heartily sick of this seafaring life, Jak! I thought buying a few ships and trading would turn an honest ob or two, in between serving the Star Lords. Yet it seems an honest sailorman's life is bedeviled every which way he turns.''

Somewhat drily, I said: "They are probably not pirates, Pompino. No doubt they are some of the Seaborne Watch of Peminswopt. They would like to ask us some questions.''

Pompino eyed the pursuing craft meanly. She foamed along, yet I fancied that once we left the shelter of the cliffs she'd feel the bite of the sea and the thrust of the wind. Once out into the offing we should outrun her, if the breeze held.

"This Kov of Memis runs a tidy province, I'll say that for him.''

"Do I detect a hint that our own young Kov Pando na Bormark does not?''

"Ask his mother—''

Involuntarily, I glanced down as though, foolishly, I could see through the solid planking of the deck into the aft staterooms. Sprawled on a seabed down there Tilda—Tilda of the Many Veils, Tilda the Beautiful—would no doubt be drinking with a steady regularity from any of the splendid array of bottles provided. Never fully drunk, always a trifle lush, the Dowager Kovneva Tilda presented us with a sorry problem. We knew that the Star Lords, superhuman, almost immortal, unknowable, as I thought then, wished us to cleanse the province of Bormark of the Leem Lovers. We had burned a temple in the capital of Tomboram, Pomdermam, and now we had burned the Devil's Academy in Peminswopt, in Memis. Next along the coast in the enormous curve of the Bay of Panderk lay the stromnate of Polontia. I had not yet made up my mind if we should stop there or make directly for Bormark, at the western frontier of the kingdom of Tomboram.

The pursuing swordship foamed along. Long and lean like all her class, she presented only that wedge-shaped bow and the wings in their shining splendor, rising and falling, rising and falling. Faintly, borne across the breeze, the sound of the drum reached us.

"They mean to catch us.''

I made up my mind. As Pompino the Iarvin considered he led our partnership I had to put the decision to him tactfully; this was accomplished easily enough by spelling out our alternatives. Pompino nodded decisively.

"Captain Linson!'' he called. "We steer straight for Bormark!''

Linson nodded, dark and smooth and as sharp as a professional assassins's dagger. *Tuscurs Maiden* responded to a delicate helm, a trifle of canvas management. She headed directly for the open sea, bearing boldly out across the Bay. Soon the swordship was going up and down like a dinosaur in a swamp.

"Hah!" shouted Pompino, filled with childlike glee. "They do not like that, by Horato the Potent, they do not!"

"I," I said with firmness, "am hungry."

"And I. Is there time to eat before—?"

"He won't catch us now. And his oarsmen will have shot their bolt soon enough. Poor devils."

By this time in our relationship, Pompino knew this was no idle remark. He agreed, commenting on his previous remarks about the plight of oarslaves. He had been made well aware that my face was firmly set against slavery.

Sharp set, we went below.

"Of course," said Pompino as we entered his stateroom, "there remains the problem of the Kovneva Tilda."

"She expressed the firm desire to return home to Bormark. Our way lies in that self-same direction." The table was spread with excellent promise, and I addressed myself as much to the viands as to Pompino. "And Pando will not be long away from his estates, not with the trouble he has brewing there."

Biting into a succulent vosk pie, well stoked with momolams and greens and with a gravy poured from the tables of the gods themselves, I realized how fatuous that remark was. On Kregen, wonderful, horrible, fascinating, trouble is always brewing—if it is not already here and hitting you in the back of the neck.

"Did you follow all that rigmarole of the love lives of these folk?" Pompino spoke around a leg of chicken that dribbled gravy into his whiskers. This he wiped away at once with a clean yellow cloth. Khibils are fastidious folk.

"Most. It is not an unfamiliar pattern—"

"Oh, agreed. I meant how can we turn it to our own benefit?"

Sharp, too, are Khibils, especially those dubbed the Iarvin.

I speared a momolam and lifted it. *Tuscurs Maiden*, in Limki the Lame, boasted a cook to be prized. In this, Linson merely emphasized his own approach to the important things of life. I squinted at the momolam, the small yellow tuber glistening and delicious and aching to be tasted.

"Whoever supports us in opposition to Lem receives our support in their amorous designs? Is that it?"

"Aye. Probably."

"Too simple, my friend."

"Nothing is simple where you're concerned, Jak."

I placed the momolam into my mouth and shut my eyes and chewed. Pompino was right, confound it!

I wondered what would chance if the Star Lords despatched Pompino to Vallia to sort out a problem for them and we met up. I'd have a deal of explaining to do then, by Vox!

He waggled his knife at me.

"Your young friend Pando, the Kov of Bormark, is a rascal and yet a very very highly placed noble. He means to have his own way with this girl and to Cottmer's Caverns with his cousin Murgon."

Refusing to be drawn into a wrangle about Pando's character I said: "The Everoinye have commanded us to go and burn Lem's temples. So this we do. We are going to burn as many temples as we can find in the kovnate of Bormark. Young Pando is the kov. A great deal of his property is going to be burned up when the temples are destroyed. What, Pompino, do you think the young rascal of a kov will say to that?"

Pompino laughed and threw his gnawed chicken bone into a silver waste dish.

"Why, Jak! He will roar and rage. But the temples will be burned!"

"Humph," I said, taking refuge in that silly sailorman's noise when he has nothing to add that makes sense.

So, after an interesting space in which Pompino fussed over selecting a wine that pleased him—a light Tardelvoh, of all things—I had to say: "Yes. Pando is determined to take the girl, this Vadni Dafni Harlstam, to wife. This will not only increase his estates, for her vadvarate marches with his kovnate to the south, it will infuriate his cousin Murgon—"

"It may destroy him!"

"You think so? He struck me as dark and dangerous—"

"Oh, aye, he is. But I read him as a man to be broken rather than bend."

"With all the delays that have bedeviled us it's a racing chance Murgon will reach Bormark before we do. As for races, I wouldn't care to wager on which cousin will get there first.''

Thinking of Pando and his mother, Tilda, I was of a mind that Murgon could bend or break so long as he failed in his dark designs. In this I was woefully adrift, as you shall hear.

I could not tell Pompino that over the years I'd had agents in Pandahem to keep an eye on Pando and Tilda, and they had failed me. The reason for their failure, at the time, was easy to understand, what with the turmoil of the Wars and the struggles against poor mad Empress Thyllis of Hamal and the devil wizard, Phu-Si-Yantong, known as the Hyr Notor. In those dread days men's and women's lives were cheap. We were clawing back to the light of the Suns, now, and life was resuming something of order and civilization; we still had a long way to go.

So—this meant I was not in possession of the full facts. Ahead all was murk and uncertainty.

Patting my lips with a yellow cloth, I stood up.

''I'm for a spell on the quarterdeck. I need the breeze in my face for a time. You'll join me?''

''Later. If we are to avoid the Stromnate of Polontia and head straight for Bormark there are arrangements in the bills of lading and the accounts I must make.'' He cocked a bright eye up, mocking and yet serious. ''We great shipping magnates have our work, as well as these tarry sailors.''

''Hah!'' I said, not particularly convincingly, and went up on deck.

A great deal had to be thought about, and much of what I had to contend with was, of course, completely unknown to my kregoinye comrade Pompino. We headed straight across the Bay of Panderk in the days following, shipboard routine continued, the breeze blew, the Suns of Scorpio shed their mingled lights across the waves, and if a fellow had had no other thoughts in his head he might well have enjoyed an idyllic period. We sighted no other sail until a morning of crimson and jade and hurling wind, with *Tuscurs Maiden* bowling along under all plain sail, hard braced, heeling on the starboard tack, racing along—well, racing along for a stumpy argenter.

''You'll get no damned renders in this weather,'' exclaimed Cap'n Murkizon, bristling, grasping a ratline. He stared off across the tumbled sea. ''Up by the Hoboling Islands you'll find 'em creeping about, pirating honest sailormen.''

"You've experience of the Hobolings, Cap'n?"

"By reputation. I heard that once they sent a fleet to fill the oceans down to Tomboram. That was a time ago, now. They've not repeated that kind of raid, to the glory of Pandrite the credit."

That was a most serious statement from our Murkizon.

Carefully, I said: "I heard a chief pirate was Viridia the Render. Does the name mean aught to you?"

"Only as a render leader. She fought better than a man, I am told." Before he or I could continue this hazy conversation the lookout bellowed. For want of anything better to do and the desire to know, I scampered up to the cross-trees and wedged myself and stared at the distant speck bobbing on the horizon rim.

The breeze blustered past and the ship gyrated as any ship will on almost any board and the old sailorman's trick of holding the glass steady enabled me to center the sighting.

She was no pirate. She was a Galleon of Vallia.

Satisfying myself that she was on an interception course, I shinned down the backstay and found Pompino on the quarter-deck with Captain Linson. Both looked grave.

"A Vallian?" Linson rubbed his chin. "We cannot outsail her, then."

Pompino huffed up; but he had to accept that when it came to sailing ships, the Galleons of Vallia were the finest sailing these seas—apart always from the damned Leem-Loving Shanks from over the curve of the world, blast their eyes.

"The days of enmity between Pandahem and Vallia are over," I said. "By Chusto! Those days are dead and gone!"

Both men swiveled to regard me. I realized I had spoken with some warmth. The subject was close to my heart, as you know, and I was wrapped up in schemes for the future when Pandahem, Vallia and the other land masses of Paz must cooperate against the Shanks.

"I picked up rumors in the Captains' Saloons, here and there," remarked Linson. "Not all Vallians share the friendship for Pandahem proclaimed by their new emperor."

I said: "There has for many seasons been friendship between Vallia and Tomboram."

We spoke lightly of Pandahem, which is an island cut up into kingdoms and kovnates, when each nation was an entity unto itself. Just how much truth there was in my last observation I still was not sure; maybe that was just a pious hope.

"Well, Vallian galleons have pirated ships of Tomboram, along with all the other nations of Pandahem. I think," said Linson in his hard way, "I shall prepare for any eventuality."

"Of course."

No captain was going to risk his ship through lack of preparation.

"You think, Jak," said Pompino, "we should run up the flag of Tomboram? Of Bormark? This will safeguard us from the Vallian?"

"It should."

I could hear that infuriating quaver of doubt in my voice as I spoke. By Vox! Hadn't these idiots grasped essentials yet? My idiots of Vallia? Pirating each other, which is what it came down to, how did that help us against the greater foe?

As though further to emphasize the difference between a Vallian galleon and an argenter of any other seafaring nation, the breeze slackened, backing, and *Tuscurs Maiden* although sailing well lost a deal of her speed. Not so the Vallian. He came on at a great rate, and it was now transparently plain that he was, indeed, steering an intercept course.

Linson eyed the other craft meanly.

"If he means to fight, then we can accommodate him."

This idea dismayed me. Of course, from the first moments I'd realized that as a member, supernumerary, of the ship's crew, I would expect to fight her enemies. Those enemies were seamen of my own nation. Before I believed that I had to cling to the belief that seamen of Vallia no longer preyed on the seamen of Pandahem. But—some still did. I knew that. It was no good blinking at facts. If that galleon over there, foaming along with the bone in her teeth spuming white, all her canvas drawing, was in truth a pirate—why then I, Dray Prescot, Emperor of Vallia, had better keep that fact very quiet. Very quiet indeed. A gang of cutthroat renders would as lief string up the emperor as spit at him—they'd more than likely spit on his corpse. My Delia had experienced something of this dilemma in her brush with the Sisters of the Whip, when to be acknowledged Empress of Vallia would have brought not instant obedience and protection but chains, the whip and a death in torment.

The crew took up the positions they occupied at action stations without the usual rush and scurry. The drums did not beat, the trumpet remained mute. Quietly, fingering their weapons, the men and women of *Tuscurs Maiden* stood to.

Up on the forward platform our varterists waited around their ballistae. The forward boarding party, the prijikers, kept close, waiting for orders. Weapons were held down, inconspicuously out of sight of the Vallian. Captain Linson nodded as Pompino finished speaking to him, and issued orders.

Very shortly thereafter, the blue flag charged with the golden zhantil rose above our decks. We sailed under the flag of Bormark of Tomboram. How would the Vallian react to that?

Itching with impatience to know the outcome of the puzzle I took a glass up to the crosstrees again. The galleon neared. She was a splendid craft, one of the new construction we had put in hand after the Times of Troubles. She would be able to range *Tuscurs Maiden*, outsail her, riddle her. As to her crew, well, the Vallian sailorman is a fearsome foe upon the sea, as I knew and joyed in. If it came to a fight, the Pandaheem were on a losing wicket.

The circle of the spyglass roved across the approaching vessel. She was splendid! Soon I could discern the features of the men upon her quarterdeck. I did not recognize any—but at this range I could easily be mistaken.

I thought one man looked remarkably like Ortyg Fondal, and another like Nath Cwophorlin, both capable ship-officers of the old emperor's navy; but I could not be sure.

The glass carried my gaze forrard and picked out the superior gros-varters of Vallia arranged on the forecastle. I stared. One man leaped into focus. His lean body was bare to the waist and his buff breeches were cut off at the knee. He wore a close-fitting leather cap, and there were not one but three red feathers sporting there. I could visualize the thin streak of black chin beard under his jaws, the lean eager look of him, the broken nose. Well, Wersting Rogahan had served me well and fought for Vallia; but he would just as easily fight to line his own pocket with pickings from a Pandaheem as not. I had to hope. Wersting Rogahan would listen to me if I spoke, that was certain.

I switched the glass back to the quarterdeck.

A man climbed up out of the aft cabin, and stretched, and looked across at us.

I felt a suffusing tide of relief. Upright, strongly built, lithe, the figure of the captain of the Vallian moved purposefully to the bulwark. He stared at us, and an outstretched hand was instantly filled by a telescope. He raised the glass to his eye. I felt like waving, and did not. I kept still and small, for Insur ti Fotor, with whom I had fought the Shanks, would recognize me wearing my old Dray Prescot face. He wore a trim naval officer's uniform, with a little gold lace, just to let folk know he was the captain. For since my Delia had had him promoted to ord-Hikdar, he had climbed past the ninth and tenth grades of Hikdar, and was now a ley-Jiktar, into the fourth grade of Jiktar. He ran a taut ship; a single glance showed, unmistakably, all the marks of a vessel and crew on the top line, thrumming with energy and spirit. I counted Insur ti Fotor as a friend, and so I breathed again. *Tuscurs Maiden* would not be attacked and sunk by Vallian renders.

Trade was reopening between the two islands, and Insur must be here with his fine ship as protection for Vallians against pirates of any nation. That was why he sailed down on us, to reassure himself that we were honest merchants.

That could be left to Pompino and Linson. I could make myself scarce. The relief was intense. The thought of having to fight Vallians had been unpleasant for a variety of reasons. I decided to stay in my perch aloft as the formalities were observed.

At Captain Insur ti Fotor's side a fellow lifted a speaking trumpet to his lips. He was a Womox, and his own horns were nearly as large as the horn used to fashion the trumpet. He bellowed, his words rolling out flat and booming, magnified across the water.

"You are a prisoner of war! Heave to!"

Wersting Rogahan's forrard varter let fly and a rock hummed fearsomely across our forecastle.

"Heave to or I'll sink you!"

CHAPTER FOUR

The instructive history of a zan-talen

A second rock hurtled dangerously low over our deck. Wersting Rogahan was a remarkable shot with a varter, and could split the Chunkrah's Eye at tremendous distances. A horrific thought occurred to me in the chaos of the moment—how would a shoot-out between Wersting and our two varterists, Wilma the Shot and Alwim the Eye, turn out? Impossible! I could not let that happen!

Captain Linson bellowed furiously.

"Prisoner of war? Prisoner of war! The Vallian is mad!"

People scurried about the decks, confusion held them all, and the sudden powerful smell of the sea reached up to me in the crosstrees, blowing all the aromas of the ship away.

"You said we could not outsail him!" screeched Pompino. The breeze blew words about like gulls over a cliff. Wilma and Alwim looked aft, ready for the signal to loose.

The Womox bellowed again.

"Heave to! Strike your colors!"

"Never!" raged Pompino. He had drawn his sword and he waved it—somewhat foolishly—about his head.

Over on the Vallian's forecastle, low enough in the sleek galleon build, Wersting's crew was hard at it rewinding the gros-varter. The next rock would not skim harmlessly above our heads. The next shot would crunch sickeningly in, to gout a fountain of splinters into bodies, to smash and rend, perhaps to bring down a mast.

It seemed to me in the midst of this madness there remained but the one thing left to do.

In that old foretop-hailing voice that had cut through more than one gale in Biscay I yelled down to Pompino.

"Heave to, Pompino! Buy some time!"

"You wouldn't surrender, Jak!"

"No. But we must find the explanation—"

"We can pulp that damned varterist on their forecastle!" shrilled Wilma the Shot.

"Belay that, Wilma!" If Linson refused to obey the order to heave to, if Pompino's proud Khibil blood got the better of him, we'd all be pulped. "Just heave to!"

Fiery whiskers flaring, Pompino glared up. He stuck his hands on his hips. His chin jutted.

"You're up to some deviltry, Jak!" he howled.

"Aye. Fighting won't save our necks now."

The two vessels eased close alongside running sweetly, and the galleon shortened sail to reduce her way and so pace the argenter. She creamed along, handled superbly, and the snouts of her varters and the arms of her catapults bore upon us. Her flags were of Vallia—the new Vallian Union of the yellow cross and saltire upon the red field—and the crimson and pale blue of Ovvend. The symbol of the kovnate of Ovvend down on the southwest coast of Vallia is a galleon. That is fitting.

For what seemed to me a damned long time the ships sailed together and the canvas all about me drew strongly. With a rat-tat of the drum and a shrill of calls accompanied by the slap of bare feet upon planking, thankfully, *Tuscurs Maiden* responded and lost way, her canvas fluttering as she first backed her main tops'l and then gathered her canvas in. No doubt Linson had performed the evolution in this manner as a sign to the hostile ship's captain that he did so under pressure.

Whatever the reason, the argenter lost way and soon we rolled sluggishly as the galleon, matching us, paced along side.

Men clustered at the falls of a longboat over on the galleon's spar deck. A boarding party would come fully armed and ready for trouble. Now, it was all down to me. . . .

The water looked a long way down.

That was the quickest route.

Once, I had dived into the Eye of the World, the inner sea of Turismond. That had been a longer dive, far longer; I took a breath, readied, and dived.

The water came up like a brick wall.

Deeply under, with the water thick about me, turning palms upward and so planing around and rising, rising. . . . The blueness turning from indigo through the lightening colors until the silver sky above my head broke into a bursting dazzlement. My head popped up. I felt fine, strangely enough. Instantly, suspecting the worst, I drew a breath and dived again, twisting as I went down.

I'd been right.

A vicious scaled form flicked for me, tail thrashing. Jaws opened and rows of needle-teeth gaped.

The old sailor knife, well-greased, slid from the sheath over my right hip.

If this Opaz-forsaken Styrorynth thought he was going to gulp me for his lunch he would have to be persuaded of the error of his belief. He was infernally quick and lethal in his own element. Accounted a superb swimmer and diver though I may be, I'd only have the one chance against him.

He swooshed in, mouth wide, needle-teeth ready to clench upon this tasty tidbit. Sliding down and under him, foaming in his pressure wave, I managed to avoid that rat-trap mouth. The knife scored along his underside and the water fouled. Without waiting to hang around I kicked hard—not for the surface but in a direct line for the dark shimmering hardness ahead that was the galleon's keel.

The Styrorynth rolled away aft and no doubt those little fishes upon whom he preyed would swarm up to feast. Swimming strongly, feet churning, I went clean under the galleon's keel. Before I surfaced I checked—as far as was possible—to see no other predators of the deep waited to seize me in their jaws.

For the distance I could see underwater with that shimmering silver sky dancing above my head there appeared to be no further danger. No danger, at least, from that direction. When I broke the surface and looked up not a single face peered over the bulwarks upon me. The galleon rolled gently. Well, they had no doubt seen a man fall from the argenter and vanish into the sea. They knew what manner of beasties lurked below the surface. They might cast a cursory look down; they would hardly expect to see the self-same man surface on the other side of their ship.

I hollered.

Three times I sucked a deep breath and dived, knife in fist, warily watching, and three times, seeing nothing, I surfaced and shouted.

On the last time a shock of hair showed over the bulwark

above me and thick voice said: "Whey-ey! Where'd you come from, dom?"

"Throw down a rope and I'll tell you."

"Oh, a rope—oh, aye."

Moments later a coil hit the water by my head and I seized the end and was hauled up over the side, streaming water. I had the sense to stuff the old sailor knife away. It was clean enough from the sea water.

On deck a shake of the head and a few blinks, snorts and shakes set me up to face the perils ahead.

The owner of the shock of hair was Brokelsh, and his nose was a mere flat sponge. He goggled at me.

Over on the other side men clustered, staring at *Tuscurs Maiden*, who rolled listlessly beyond. I said: "Thank you for the rope, dom. I'll do the same for you one day," and headed straight for the quarterdeck ladder.

The Brokelsh shouted after me: "I'll remember that, dom. Make sure you do, too. My name is Bango Barragon, from Ovvend, so remember it when the time comes."

I did not laugh although, by Krun, his shock of hair and his squashed nose and his manner were enough to make a fellow split his sides. I put a hand on the rail of the ladder and a boarding pike came down thwack! I jumped. I looked up and my face must have shone a very nasty glow.

"You nearly had my hand off then, dom!"

"Aye," quoth the fellow at the head of the ladder, clad in leathers, brass-studded, and with the crimson and light-blue banded sleeves of Ovvend. "And if you try to come up here without an invite I'll have your head off, by Vox!"

A few sailors and a couple of Pachak marines came over to stare at me, dripping water on their deck. They held weapons; they were in no wise scared of me, of course; just curious and cautious.

"Tell Captain Insur ti Fotor I wish to speak—"

"*Tell* the Capt'n, is it, now! A civil tongue in your head might keep that object upon your shoulders."

A young lad with a flushed face looked over the quarter-deck rail. I did not know him. He wore a helmet of silvered iron flaunting the feathers of Ovvend. He would be a noble youngster training up in the galleons so that one day he, too, might command one of the sleek sea greyhounds. He could be a fop, a ninny, an autocrat of sadistic humor; he could be a stout-hearted lad ready to learn his trade. I stared back at him, and then yelled: "Captain Insur ti Fotor! If you value your hide, lad, jump! Fetch him!" And, then, I used the word to make 'em leap about. "Bratch!"

He flushed even further, tightened up, opened his mouth—saw my face—and bratched.

The guard at the head of the ladder tried to hit me over the head with his pike. You couldn't blame him, really. I dodged, took the pike away, so that he fell down the ladder on his nose. A Pachak lifted his upper left arm; his comrade stuck out his lower left arm. In another moment they'd all leap on me, and I had no wish at all to fight them, all at once or one at a time.

"Insur!" I bellowed at the top of my voice.

Now Insur ti Fotor's family name—it was Varathon—had been scarcely used by us. He'd always been known as Insur ti Fotor, for Fotor was a tidy little township of Ovvend and Insur Varathon came from one of the chief families there. So, all I could do was bellow out: "Insur!"

Give him his due. He did not hang about. His face appeared over the rail, beside and higher than that of the middy's. He saw. At once he shouted: "Send that man up here. Handle him gently."

The guard sat up rubbing his nose, which did not bleed much.

"Your pardon, dom," I said. "It was your nose or my head."

He sneezed red.

"We'll see, dom, we'll see."

Up the ladder with the two Pachaks at my back I went. Insur turned away, glaring at the middy.

"Please return to your duties, Hikdar Varathon!"

"Quidang!"

The lad scuttled.

Insur simply shouldered on to his aft cabin, shouting to his first lieutenant: "Do nothing until I tell you!"

"Quidang!"

At the carved companionway entrance, Insur half-turned, still not looking at me. "You may return to your duties, Pachaks. My thanks. I will take charge of this man."

"Quidang!"

The Pachaks trotted off and I followed Insur down into his cabin. He waited with the handle in his fist, and he slammed

the door after us. Then, at once, he bowed, and said:
"Majister."

I took his hand.

"My thanks, Insur. That was splendidly done."

"If I say I am amazed—flabbergasted—to find you here. . . ."

"You would match the pleasure I feel in meeting you again."

He motioned to a chair, and so I had to sit down, otherwise he'd remain standing, half-bent, forever. "Well, Insur, tell me all about it."

He sat down and instinctively poured parclear. The sherbet drink fizzed and sparkled in the glass. "I will tell you everything, majister. But—what? I am bereft of words."

"First of all—you did right to keep my identity safe. Second: What is all this nonsense about taking the argenter from Tomboram a prisoner of war?"

He straightened.

"It is hardly nonsense, majister." He wouldn't mince words. "The Opaz-forsaken devils bear heavily upon us. We strive to thwart their designs, but—"

"Press? Designs? What are you talking about? Is not Vallia at peace with Pandahem? All the nations of Pandahem—well, perhaps with the exception of the Bloody Menahem."

"No, majister. Not so."

I gaped. Then I said, harshly, "Tell me."

So he told me.

Down in the southwest of Vallia, the land I had made my home on Kregen and which empire had fetched me to be their emperor, down there in the southwest in the kovnate of Kaldi a pretty little revolution had broken out. I knew about that. My son Drak had taken his army down there to sort them out, for Kov Vodun Alloran had proclaimed himself as king. During my most recent adventurings I had been somewhat out of touch with the latest developments.

Insur said: "Alloran sought help from Pandahem. He got it. Armies were landed and Prince Drak has fought many hard battles—"

He saw my face and stopped speaking abruptly. Drak! Suppose he was killed in one of these petty little battles, for hard battles mean casualties. Insur saw at once.

"The Prince Majister is safe, and leads the army brilliantly."

"Thank Opaz!"

"Aye."

"And so you cruise the sea lanes to prevent the ferrying of more troops to feed this mad King Vodun Alloran?"

"Yes, majister."

"But—Tomboram! They have been friends for many seasons. I would have thought it of Menaham—"

"They were defeated in a great battle, and Alloran desperately sought fresh allies, and found them in Tomboram."

"Well, I suppose it all adds up," I said in a grudging fashion. "Although it stinks worse than the Fish Souk in Helamlad where there is no ice for fifty dwaburs around."

"Where Helamlad might be, majister, I do not know. What I would dearly like to know is where you came from—oh! Unless—"

"From *Tuscurs Maiden*'s ship's company, Insur, that's where. And she's not of Tomboram, being of Tuscursmot in South Pandahem. We flew the colors of Bormark just because we imagined Vallia and Tomboram, Bormark, allies."

He shook his head; but he was no man's fool.

"Your designs are none of my business, majister. You know I will do all in my power to aid you."

"I know, Insur, and I thank you. So that means you can't take the argenter prisoner."

"Quite."

"I spotted Wersting Rogahan at the forrard varters."

"He will know you, for sure. And Ortyg Fondal and Nath Cwophorlin have made your acquaintance in the past. Once made—"

"I know, I know," I grumped. "They say I've a face like a leem at times."

A tiny smile licked around his lips, and his face, all bronzed and sea-beaten, creaked alarmingly. He was no salt-laden old sea-dog but a fiery and consummately professional naval officer. Men had given their lives to save his. I looked hard at him. "And," I said, "that young Hikdar Varathon . . .?"

"My son, majister."

"Congratulations. He looks likely."

"A sight too likely at times. But—the argenter!"

"Aye, well. I am on passage for Port Marsilus. I can tell you that I and my comrades over in *Tuscurs Maiden* have a mission to burn temples of an evil cult. Pray that cult never sets root in Vallia. It has tried and we have rooted it out. This affects all the peoples of Paz."

He spread his hands. "I and all my people here in *Ovvend Opandar* are at your disposal, majister."

I nodded. "It is a temptation. You have a first-class command, and if the lads are anything like Wersting Rogahan, they are a fearsome bunch. But—I think not, Insur. Your duties lie elsewhere."

He looked disappointed, for he, like many a man and woman of Kregen, well knew that if they followed me they'd get into scrapes and adventures enough to last two lifetimes. I managed a farcical kind of smile.

"The Shanks, Insur, the everlasting damned Shanks. There will be fighting enough and to spare when they arrive."

His eyebrows went up.

"Oh, yes, my friend. They are on the way to invade our lands. We have some tidying up to do first before they get here."

"Do you know where and when they expect to make landfall?"

"I wish I did. I know only that a vast fleet is on the way."

A knock rapped discreetly on the paneled door. Insur did not look annoyed, as a lesser man might well have done.

"Yes?"

"A Khibil from the Pandahem argenter demands to see you, captain. Demands, no less."

The voice beyond the door betrayed amusement.

I sighed.

"Time I was gone, Insur. That'll be a vastly intemperate Khibil whose acquaintance I have the honor to claim. Perhaps if you just tell him that Vallia and Tomboram are allies, ask him to convey your respects to Kov Pando Marsilus na Bormark, and then get rid of him, the quicker we can all get on with our jobs."

"If he's been long in your company, majister, he is likely to demand damages, recompense, an apology."

"I'm sure you can accommodate him."

Insur did not smile; but his nod was of the thoughtful variety, betokening a careful estimation of what he could get away with in dealing with an intemperate Khibil who was the friend of the emperor.

Insur opened the door. There was much we had not spoken of; but Pompino had effectively put an end to deliberations. I bid Insur remberee, and slipped quickly up on deck.

The two vessels rode close, their yards almost interlocking. I cocked my head up. Like a monkey up the ratlines I went and so out along a yard and leaped for *Tuscurs Maiden*'s main yard and so down to her deck.

Cap'n Murkizon regarded me as one might regard a ghost.

"Jak! We thought you done for, for sure! You are not broken from the ib?"

"No, Cap'n Murkizon. I am no ghost."

"By the hairy black warts of the Divine Lady of Belschutz! Right heartily glad to see you!" He seized my hand and pumped away as though extinguishing a conflagration. Others came up. Pompino was not among them.

Larghos the Flatch said: "We saw the finny back of a disgusting Styrorynth. Then we saw blood. And yet—you live!"

"The Vallians hauled me out."

Captain Linson, master of *Tuscurs Maiden* and mindful of responsibilities, congratulated me on a miraculous escape, and then added: "Here comes Horter Pompino. He looks pleased."

Pompino leaped onto the deck, hitching his sword out of the way. He brushed up his whiskers in a gesture that told us—or, at least me—that he was feeling very pleased with himself.

"It was all a mistake," he said, strutting up. "The moment I spoke to their captain he understood. We are to proceed at once."

"What, Pompino," I could not forbear from prodding. "And did he offer an apology?"

"I did not ask for one, Jak. Besides, he had his damned varters swung in my direction. Ugly, those artillery pieces of Vallia. Damned ugly."

I did not laugh.

Then he extended his hand, palm uppermost. A single golden coin glittered. It was a zan-talen, worth ten Vallian talen pieces.

"The captain, an unhanged rascal called Insur ti Fotor, requested me to treat the crew to a wet. Of course, he knew better than to attempt to pacify me in that way."

"Naturally."

Inwardly I was laughing—chuckling, really—over Insur's audacity. The likeness on the coin was of a remarkably ugly fellow, all chin and beard and beaked nose. No one, seeing that indifferent portrait, was going to recognize its subject as me, plain Jak. This had been in my mind when old Larghos

Valdwin had carved the original, and I'd told him to make me look as ferocious and unlike myself as possible. He'd made the expected sly remark on that. The other side of the coin, which I regarded as the more important, showed the glory of Delia, beautifully fashioned and, yet, again, a portrait from which it would be difficult to recognize her.

Self-advertisement for your ordinary everyday emperor and empress is no doubt a worthwhile objective. For folk like Delia and myself, adventuring off around Kregen as we did, a trifle of anonymity paid handsome dividends.

Linson gave his orders and Chandarlie the Gut, the Ship-Deldar, bellowed them into action.

Pompino sniffed.

"You were given up for lost, Jak."

I did not reply. The breeze had backed a few more points and now we could sheet home our full spread of canvas. *Tuscurs Maiden* bowled along merrily. An altogether different air now pervaded the ship's company. It was as though we had come through a dire experience far worse than that through which we had really gone. Such is human nature. Men sang about their tasks. The coast lay ahead, and Port Marsilus, and taverns and dopa dens, no doubt, and a golden zan-talen nestled securely in the Owner's strongbox, to find its way down the thirsty throats of the crew.

"I am glad you were not chomped by that Styrorynth. Ugly customers, with jaws like the black gullet of Armipand himself, Pandrite rot him. No doubt he snapped up some other victim, for there was blood."

"No doubt."

"And, Jak, just think. If you'd been killed, would the Everoinye have held me accountable? The thought has often plagued me."

At once I felt contrition.

"Look, Pompino, as I have told you, I do not think the Star Lords hold me in very high esteem. I curse at them and attempt to evade what they order when it conflicts with what I desire. But I serve them more willingly now than I once did. All the same—if you were killed, I think that perhaps they would frown most unkindly upon me."

"Well," he said, brisking up and giving a twirl to his moustaches. "As we are not about to allow ourselves to be sent off to the Ice Floes of Sicce, let us push these doleful thoughts aside. I'm for a wet."

"I am with you. Port Marsilus is not far off, now. There we can start our deviltry. If the Leem Lovers were other than they are, it might be in my mind to feel sorry for them."

"You may begin being maudlin after they are all safely howling in Cottmer's Caverns!"

CHAPTER FIVE

Aye

"Look!" said Pompino as we sailed in for Port Marsilus. He did not point as one might expect a man to point as he indicated the object of his interest. "D'you see him?"

"Aye. I see him."

As *Tuscurs Maiden* ran on with the bluffly blown spume from her round bows breaking and her canvas drawing as full-bellied as a noble after a feast and the coast of Tomboram neared with the pinnacles of Port Marsilus already in sight, I stared up.

Up there circled a giant raptor, a golden-and-scarlet-feathered bird with sharp black talons extended. He was the Gdoinye, the spy and messenger of the Star Lords.

"They keep watch upon us, Jak." Pompino spoke in a low tone, for we leaned on the quarterdeck bulwarks and Captain Linson and his officers and men on watch stood close.

"You can see the Gdoinye, and I can see him. But, of late, I remark that no one else sees him—"

"Of course not! Why, only a kregoinye, one who has been selected by the Everoinye, can ever see—"

"Yes. But I have known a few people in the past who have seen him."

"I find that hard to believe."

The spoken Kregish tongue is modulated by many tonal variations, so that Pompino's simple words, by being given different inflections, could mean that he was calling me a liar, to an amazed agreement with my statement. This latter meaning he now intended.

"True, Pompino. I believe a certain innocence of mind has an influence, for a lad I know saw the bird, and a caravan master from Xuntal, a true child of the Great Plains. Also, this Kov Pando Marsilus, when he was a youngster, saw the Gdoinye."

"So that is behind your remark. But he is no longer a coy, young and fresh and green and innocent."

"Ha," I said in a kind of grunt. "If ever he was, poor lad."

Pompino let that by.

I did not say that the lad I knew who had seen the scarlet and gold raptor was my eldest son Drak. Pompino was under the impression that I was fancy free and unencumbered by a family. Just why I'd allowed that impression to remain might seem petty and obscure; it saved a quantity of explanations.

The bird circled, a menacing silhouette as he passed beneath the Suns of Scorpio, a glittery glory as the streaming radiance touched his feathers.

"He can only report that we are on our way to carry out our duties," said Pompino.

"Aye," I said in an ugly voice. "And we are on our own time in this."

"True. But I think the Everoinye are now completely involved with us, and we can—"

"We can expect no help from them!"

Pompino let his lips compress. That was true, at least for me, and despite Pompino's attachment to the Star Lords, I suspected for him, also.

There was no sign of the white dove sent by the Savanti. Even Pompino couldn't have seen that bird.

It occurred to me to wonder if he'd ever seen or heard of Zena Iztar, who as a superhuman woman exercised mysterious powers. She had assisted me in the past, and although I might suspect she stood over in opposition to both Star Lords and Savanti, I was not certain of that. She it was who had helped us when the Brotherhood of the Kroveres of Iztar fought their early sacrificial battles. Now the Kroveres with Seg Segutorio as their Grand Archbold were dedicated to righting wrongs, uprooting slavery and injustice, and of countering the Shanks. Naive ends for an Order, you may think—all except the last—but of such naïveté are new and fairer worlds formed.

Continuing his train of thought, Pompino went on: "Here in Bormark we will have to go about the business in a rather different fashion from Memis and Pomdermam."

"Oh?"

"Aye! Look you—I burned a temple to Lem here. No doubt others have sprung up to take its place. But now we have the Lady Tilda with us."

He used the general word for lady—shiume—which has so many gradations of rankings Kregans more often than not omit all these subtle shadings, and say simply "The Shiume" and then the lady's name. This applies from Kovneva to Kotera. I know my Delia has trenchant opinions upon this subject of lick-spittling fawning. Pompino and I, when we did not call Tilda the Beautiful, Tilda of the Many Veils, Kovneva, we addressed her as Shiume, my lady.

I agreed. Then, with a note of caution, I said: "We are duty bound to see her safely to her palace. This may lay us open to observation. It is certain sure that Murgon Marsilus will have spies, no less than the Leem Lovers."

"Then we proceed under cover."

Any Kregan knows the nightly tally of Moons. Tonight we were due the Twins, the two second moons eternally orbiting each other, and the largest moon, the Maiden with the Many Smiles. The fourth moon, She of the Veils, would appear wanly toward dawn. As for the three smaller moons, they hurtle past in their headlong courses, casting little enough light, in so much of a hurry Kregans have a whole repertoire of jokes about them and their resemblance to the energetic hyperthyroid types of people to be found everywhere.

We agreed the best time would be a couple of glasses before the hour of dim, just before the Maiden with the Many Smiles put in her appearance.

All details of entering the harbor and of finding a berth could be left to the captain. We roused out the four hefty fellows selected to carry Tilda's sedan chair, the luxurious palankeen in which, besides cushions and pillows and fans and toiletries and other essential requirements she would have a considerable quantity of interesting bottles stashed away. Everyone knew that the Lady Tilda drank, and was usually a fraction on the other side of lushness and yet was never ever drunk—or, at least, never intoxicated to make it noticeable or herself a nuisance. The chair swung up onto the deck and settled on its clawed feet. The curtains were drawn.

"It might," observed Rondas the Bold, his red feathers whiffling in the breeze, "have been easier to have hauled the gherimcal up with the lady seated inside."

One or two of the hands laughed.

As a serious suggestion it was perfectly sensible. To have dropped the gherimcal back down and put Tilda inside and then have hauled the pair up would smack of the undignified now the damned chair was actually on deck. Tilda, despite the drink and her grossness, was, after all, a kovneva and a lady.

Pompino said, "I, for one, am having nothing to do with getting the lady on deck."

Chandarlie the Gut stepped forward. "Leave it to me, horters." His stomach swelled in its magnificent bow shape; he and Tilda would make a likely pair.

"And handsomely, mind," I said.

It is worth mentioning that of the four men selected to act as calsters and carry the chair, two were apims, Homo sapiens like me, one was a Brokelsh and the other a Brukaj. It has often been said that apims make the best sailors on Kregen, and Fristles among the worst. Brokelsh are found in surprising numbers following the nautical profession. A captain usually has a crew consisting of a mixed bunch of races under command and it is up to him to knock them all into shape.

Tuscurs Maiden negotiated the buoyed channel and we tied up alongside a stone quay with long black-painted sheds across the cobbles. The port officials descended like warvols and these were left strictly to the master and to the Relt stylor, Rasnoli. They knew how to handle these fellows.

The declining suns threw long radiances of jade and ruby across the houses and water, casting umber shadows against the terraces and towers, limning in light the opposite cornices. Gulls winged looking for last minute morsels for supper. The air held an evening tang.

The argenter's new first lieutenant, a shambly man with a pebbly skin, one Boris Pordon, went about his tasks with a worried expression. I could fully sympathize with the tribulations of the Ship Hikdar, by Vox. And, as we went down for a final meal, I suddenly realized that I might be leaving the sea for some time. What we faced with such casual ease was likely to be exceedingly fraught and filled with the clangor of swords. This was very much a case of frying pan and fire.

Pompino must have shared much of this foreboding. As we sat to Limki the Lame's latest creation he chewed thoughtfully.

"We had best take a goodly supply of weapons with us."

"Aye."

"And Captain Linson will spare us enough men."

"Aye."

Pompino eyed me. He took a forkful of Limki's roast quindil and paused, opened his mouth to speak, and then stuffed the quindil in instead. I am not overfond of poultry, and the quindil, a kind of turkey, however beautifully roasted and stuffed, scarcely merited comparison with the vosk chops Limki had prepared for me.

When he had swallowed, Pompino said: "Superb! Limki lost no time in buying fresh foodstuffs—yet you stick with those giant chops—and we will need to take provisions with us, also, I think."

"Aye."

He slammed his knife down hard.

"You are infuriating, Jak! Is that all you can say—aye!"

"Anything else would appear superfluous."

"We are likely to have Murgon Marsilus, King Nemo, the Pandrite-forsaken imps of Lem, and who knows who else, all buzzing about our ears and trying to part us from our heads— yet all you can do is chomp down vosk chops and say Aye."

"I forbore to point out the facts you have just related with such fervor out of respect for the delicacy of your stomach during a meal." He might have blown up then; but I went on in what I hoped was an imperturbable tone: "However, if you wish me to add from all we have unearthed and what we can surmise, my own observations, why, then, I will willingly do so."

Then he had me. He said: "Aye."

I almost laughed around a mouthful of vosk chop.

"Well, then: Firstly—and there may not be a secondly— the Kovneva Tilda wishes to return to her palace here in Port Marsilus for a number of reasons. She wishes to consult with this mysterious Mindi the Mad, whoever she may be. She wishes to see the twins Pynsi and Poldo Mytham. Also she feels safer in her own palace." I took up a glass of wine, a full-bodied red—a Jeu O'fremont, I recall—and watched Pompino. He sat munching his bird and watching me. I went on: "The Leem Lovers have committed themselves too deeply in the attempt to kill her and must continue—"

"Ha!" said Pompino. "We've blattered 'em once—lettem try again, Pandrite rot 'em!"

"Quite. As I was saying. She must have friends in her own capital city, and in her palace. . . . Surely?"

"One would judge so, yes."

"Once we can place her safely in their hands we can breathe more freely. And we can get on with burning temples."

"Aye."

"It also strikes me that young Pando got in over his head. He joined up with the Leem Lovers in order to strike at his cousin Murgon. I think that association with Lem the Silver Leem was too strong for his blood. People get to know about these things—people who count, in responsible positions, who run things. The old values wither. The whole of this kingdom of Tomboram is in a mess, and the kovnate of Bormark is in the worst mess. And Pando is at his wits' end."

"With that reading of the matter I concur."

So, inevitably, I said: "Aye."

We drank a little in silence for a space.

Then Pompino said: "This young lady, the Vadni Dafni Harlstam, whose lands adjoin those of Pando. Murgon designs to marry her to aggrandize himself. So does Pando. One is allowed to wonder, I think, if she, too, is an adherent of Lem."

"Ah," I said, wisely.

"What is sure is that she is not the cause of the quarrel between them. That has festered since their respective births. She is the catalyst that has precipitated the latest outburst. And she is likely to be the last."

"That is a bleak enough prophecy. But, if you look on the bright side, it might be a good one."

He reached for more wine, his whiskers very red under the lamps.

"You mean, Jak, that after we have finished with them all, all their problems will be settled? Aye!"

You had to hand it to Pompino the Iarvin. Confidence was his middle name in these matters. Once he stepped ashore he became a different man.

Nath the Apron came in with the dessert. Limki had prepared looshas pudding, a soldiers' favorite, and both Pompino and I tucked in. There was a cream and fruit trifle to follow that, and Nath the Apron, a quiet and unobtrusive cabin steward, brought in the bowls of fruit and the palines. The wine passed, and we sat, thinking of what lay ahead.

Thankfully, on Kregen, no one was foolish enough to light up and smoke. Although, and sometimes I admit this with a quiver of guilt, a fine after-dinner cigar would not have gone amiss . . .

Presently, Pompino stretched and thumped his glass down. "Time?"

I stood up. Preparations had all been made. So there was but the one rejoinder to make. I said it.

"Aye."

CHAPTER SIX

The Lady Nalfi hides in the Chunkrah's Eye

"Where in the name of Suzi the Bowgirl have you been, Nalfi?" Larghos the Flatch sounded both distraught and relieved.

The Lady Nalfi laughed lightly.

"Why, you silly man, I went ashore to buy certain things a girl must have, with the money you gave me. And I became lost—"

"Think what could have happened to you! Why didn't you ask me—?"

"You were all so busy. Anyway, it is of no moment."

We were crowding down onto the jetty, the four calsters were manipulating Tilda's chair down, we were trying to keep quiet and stop our weapons from clinking. Murkizon was breathing like a whale.

"Once Larghos rescued you, my lady, you placed yourself under his protection. I have done so, and joy in it."

"As you stand by me, Cap'n," burst out Larghos. He looked wild. He'd had a fright.

The Twins shed light enough, too much for nefarious purposes, I fancied with an uncomfortable hitch to my shoulders. Somehow or other, and even allowing for my act with Pompino, the whole business of this night looked awry to me, not quite handled in a logical and successful fashion. But Pompino was trying to shout in a whisper, and his Chulik, Nath Kemchug, dropped a spear, which clattered, and Rondas the Bold, still not abandoning his mail, let it clash slightly as he negotiated the gangplank. Pompino looked to the Moons and stars above, and clutched at my arm.

"A pack of famblys, the lot of them, by Horato the Potent, famblys all."

I did not reply but looked about into the moon-shot darkness of the jetty. The black sheds glistened with runnels of moonshine. The cobbles swam in glisten. I could see no shadows moving out there.

Tilda's chair had been draped with canvas to make it appear less grand, and the fake chair done up out of packing crate wood and painted canvas had been sent off earlier with most of the escort. That should have drawn off any unwelcome attentions; now we simply ran straight for the palace.

That, as I say, was the plan. . . .

We were to follow in a slightly different path from the decoy party. The walls and towers of the palace provided a clear target, and I was perfectly prepared to wake Tilda up and shake information out of her if we could not find an easy road through.

As the Owner, Pompino had selected the composition of the parties, and he had undeniably put more weight into the genuine escort. The Ship Hikdar, Boris Pordon, commanded the fake escort with more men in numbers but not, Pompino judged, in fighting ability.

Also, the fake escort with its wood and canvas dummy chair carried torches to light the way. We, with Tilda in the real gherimcal in our midst, hurried along with only the light of the Twins to guide us. And, as I have indicated, that light was of a sufficiency enough.

Past shuttered houses we sped, the gherimcal swaying as the bearers moved in rhythmic steps. Nath Kemchug had his spear firmly grasped, and Rondas the Bold's mail—as befitted a proud Rapa paktun—no longer chittered, link against link. As was his right and duty, Pompino led. Because of that old itchy feeling betwixt my shoulder blades—usually an infallible sign, not always, of approaching danger and action—I prowled along at the tail end. My head kept on trying to twist itself off my shoulders as I turned this way and that watching our backtrack. Every window could conceal a marksman, every shadow a shrieking swordsman, every archway a charging axeman. . . .

The Brown and Silvers hit us from up front.

They were waiting for us.

They simply rushed out into the mouth of an avenue leading to the palace, fronting a square, and charged.

At the first yell, the first clatter of iron-shod sandals on stone, I was raging up, quivering—and remaining in the rear. Pompino and the others would have to handle the frontal attack. I still suspected a treacherous stab in the back.

"Hit 'em, knock 'em down, tromple all over 'em!" bellowed a fruity voice.

The wicked tinker-hammer of steel against steel racketed up, echoing against the walls.

Anybody who tried to break a way through that powerful human hedge of steel was in for trouble. In the time I'd known them, the comrades I'd made in *Tuscurs Maiden* had proved themselves. Now, once again, they were fighting and earning their hire. I closed up to the chair, setting my back against the curtains, and staring forward and aft. Mainly, I looked to the rear. This ambush was just right for the attack from the rear that would smash into the unprotected backs of the fighters defending in front. Grasping my thraxter, I watched.

The two apims, Nath the Clis and Indur the Rope, and the Brokelsh, Ridzi the Rangora, and the Brukaj, Bendil Fribtix, remained grasping the handles of the chair. They were ready to run like stink to smash a way through surrounded by the fighting men. They had a tough task, and one not to my liking, I can tell you, by Krun!

Something kicked my ankle.

I looked down, the thraxter snouting.

A shapely foot and ankle with a silver bangle kicked and then withdrew. I bent and lifted a flap of canvas, and the sword in my fist nuzzled forward.

"Oh!" gasped Nalfi, twisting around, her pallid face staring up in shock.

"It's all right, my lady. But I do not think you are particularly wise. It is not safe under there if—"

The dagger in her fist glimmered as she crawled out.

"Larghos told me to seek shelter and this seemed the best place. I am frightened—"

We had fixed up boards and bronze in the gherimcal against arrows. Nalfi knew this. All the same, the chair was the target and she had chosen to shelter in the chunkrah's eye, as it were.

The fight up ahead swayed back and forth as we spoke in snatched whispers. Dark shadows moved in convulsive gyrations, and men screamed and died. The noise would bring other men and women, soon, that was sure.

Nath the Clis holding the front near side handle looked back and called: "Larghos was right, Jak. But the lady is still in danger here."

Even if Nalfi could have somehow squeezed into the chair with Tilda and all her belongings, the additional weight, together with the bronze and wood, would slow us too much.

"Crouch down small, Nalfi. Here." I handed her across the shield I'd taken from Nath Kemchug's armory aboard ship. "Hold this over you. We'll see off this rabble up ahead. It won't be long."

"I do hope so!"

Larghos the Flatch ran back to the gherimcal, his bow over his shoulder and his thraxter stained dark.

"You are safe, Nalfi?"

"Yes, yes—"

"They're giving way up there. We can move on now—"

And at that moment the back stab I had anticipated and thought to be a mere overwrought fever of my brain erupted in a yelling mob of Brown and Silvers, hurtling down upon us.

Instantly we were embroiled in a vicious fight to stay alive and to protect Tilda. The four bearers had to thwunk the gherimcal down, draw their weapons and hurl themselves into the fray. We struggled in a mass of contorting bodies across the cobbles, smashing back at the attack, striking and defending, roaring in a mind-wrenching phantasmagoria of action under the light of the Moons.

Having given the shield to Nalfi I was in no mood to foin with this mob of would-be assassins. The left-hand dagger whipped free of its scabbard. With the stout cut and thrust thraxter in my right fist and the main gauche in my left I felt that the combination would prove an interesting variation. The things one dwells on in the fractions of a heartbeat!

The swirl of action revolved away to my left as, with Larghos at my side, we swathed a way through on the right. The Brown and Silvers wore their colored favors openly. Their faces were not masked as assassins' faces are commonly concealed. We hit them hard, and they hit us hard.

Ridzi the Rangora catapulted backwards. A thick spear transfixed his belly. Larghos, with a cunning sideways belt of his sword, despatched the fellow, all eyes and teeth, who had thrust his spear through Ridzi.

The Brokelsh sank down. For a tiny moment his voice reached me through the hubbub.

"By Bridzikelsh the Resplendent! I am done for!"

Blackness gushed from his mouth.

"Hold up, dom," I said. "We'll carry you—"

But the Brokelsh, Ridzi the Rangora, keeled over onto his side, the spear haft drawing up his knees in a rictus of agony. In the next heartbeat he was dead.

In a heavy rush of bodies more of our fellows joined in from the fight up front. Quendur the Ripper cut down his man, swirled at another, called across in a high, bright voice: "They run in front, Jak! Now we have them here!"

I did not reply, catching a heavy blow in a slanting glide on the dagger and thrusting with the thraxter. Recovering, I ducked and belted a blow sideways to take the knees from a Rapa who gobbled and, before he could fall over, had his beak removed by Murkizon's enormous axe.

"Tromple all over 'em!"

"Hai!" roared Pompino, catching a Brown and Silver trying to get at the gherimcal. The man sank down in a puddle. My comrade glared about. Quendur was in the act of swiping at a Fristle who now clearly wished to backpedal. The fight was all but over. The remaining Brown and Silvers drew off.

"Hurry!" I said in that penetrating whisper that cuts like splintered glass. "They'll be shafting us now."

Quendur saw where Ridzi lay, doubled up over the spear, the black stain on the cobbles. He stepped forward, took up the handle of the gherimcal, the other three calsters took their handles. Tilda gave no sign of life. The chair lifted. In a bunch, weapons naked and stained, we ran for the palace.

Unwilling to leave a comrade, I hoisted up Ridzi, breaking the disgusting spear off. I hurled the broken haft into the radiance of the Moons, cursing stupid waste. With the hairy bloody body of the Brokelsh over my shoulder I ran after the others.

The avenue leading from that kyro where we had been ambushed led on for a couple of hundred paces and then opened out into the plaza fronting the palace. The building of itself appeared to be no great size under the moons. Some of its towers lofted to a goodly height, and one dome gleamed silky-sheened in the radiance.

There was no moat or drawbridge. Instead a double gate flanked by watchtowers protected the entrance. I did not give that fortification a long life against an expert siege-master.

Two apim guards in little sentry boxes, their spears slanted, watched us running up.

As we approached in a rushing wheeze of panting breaths and staccato cracks of studded sandals, the gates creaked open. They creaked. Through the noise of our progress the wood and iron creaked loudly and distinctly.

We did not stop but rushed straight through into a walled courtyard where torches flared.

The gates creaked and closed at our backs.

"Safe," said Pompino. He looked wrought up. "We've done it!"

"Aye," I said, as they put the gherimcal down. "And here is some of the cost." Over my shoulder, Ridzi lolled.

There was no decent answer Pompino could find to that.

Tuscurs Maiden's Ship Hikdar, Boris Pordon, appeared. He looked worried sick.

"Thank Pandrite you are safe, horter!" He spoke to Pompino directly. "We were about to run out to your assistance—"

Pompino brushed that aside. "The whole affair was over before you could have reached us. It was a hindrance only."

The decoy party and the fake chair had made a simple, safe journey here, unmolested. The canvas and wood construction stood to one side and I looked at it critically. Well. . . . Seen like this it might have fooled the Leem Lovers. It had not done so, and that luck played against us.

The torches streamed a ruddy light upon the folk clustered

in the courtyard. Their faces wore apprehensive looks, they fidgeted and fingered their weapons. They hardly looked the people to defend a palace against determined onslaughts.

In the light an Ift stepped forward, approaching the carrying chair.

"I bid you welcome, horters, horteras," he said. "Is the Kovneva safe?" He bent to the curtains.

Pompino bristled up.

"Just who are you, horter?"

The Ift straightened. He was under man height, although some Ifts can grow to overtop a full-grown apim, so it is said. He was clad in clothes of varying shades and tones of green, and here in a palace he was out of his usual habitat, for Ifts are folk of the forest. They are accounted fine bowshots. Wayward folk, Ifts, with tall pointed ears reaching almost to the crown of their head, and with slanted, devious eyes. Now this Ift stared challengingly at Pompino.

"Were it not for Hikdar Pordon, I would demand of you the same question, Horter Pompino. But he mentioned that we were to expect a Khibil."

Here Pordon gave a little jump, so I guessed he'd told this Ift a little more about Pompino than he'd care to have the Owner hear.

"I am waiting," said Pompino in his menacing voice.

The Ift reached a thin brown hand to his sword hilt. Then he nodded. "I am Twayne Gullik, the castellan here. My word rules while the kov and the dowager kovneva are absent."

My foxy Khibil comrade wouldn't be foxed by that.

"As the kovneva is now within her palace, you no longer rule. Make sure the lady Tilda is cared for. Summon her handmaidens. She has had a trying journey. She will, no doubt, in her own time, acquaint you with your future duties concerning me and my people."

Twayne Gullik opened his mouth. Even in the radiance of the Twins, slanting into the courtyard, the color in his face darkened ominously. I was not going to step forward. This, now, had become a matter of will-power and of honor between these two. Of course, if they started the nonsense of a ritual fight in the ages-old duelling system of the Hyr Jikordur, I'd have to try to prevent that.

Then Cap'n Murkizon's genial bull-bellow broke into the strained silence.

"By the infested armpit of the Divine Lady of Belschutz! My throat is as dry as Golingar Desert dust! A wet, for the sweet sake of Pandrite!"

That broke the tension. Larghos bustled forward, servants took the poor limp form of Ridzi the Rangora from me, Quendur the Ripper and the others yelped for wine, and so we were able to hustle along. The chair was carried off after Pompino took a look inside. The moment he withdrew, Twayne Gullik looked, also. As they both appeared satisfied, although saying nothing, I surmised Tilda was safe and asleep.

We all trooped into a side corridor and thence to a hall where we sat at tables and the servants poured wine. We were thirsty, at that; but wine would never solve any serious problem.

"That superior Ift," said Pompino.

"They are a haughty and fractious people," said Quendur.

"Twayne Gullik," I said. "By Chusto! Whoever gave him that name marked him from birth."

"Let him go back to his forests," quoth Murkizon, lifting his goblet. "And take out his spite on the tumps, who, being shorter than he is, if broader, and just as mean, stand no nonsense from the Ifts." A few smiles broke out, for the notorious antipathy between Ifts and tumps has been the basis of many a play and many a buffoonery-filled farce in Kregen's playhouses over the seasons. The tumps are, indeed, a race of diffs short of stature; but they are immensely broad and stoutly built, and the men folk grow beards down past their protuberant waists. They are a mining people, delving deep underground, and there is little they value above red gold. "The point is, my friends," went on Murkizon, we have brought the lady Tilda safely home. So—now what lies in store?"

"A few fires?" I suggested.

Pompino clicked his compression tube. "Always ready...."

They laughed.

It would not be as easy as that.

Mind you, nothing in this life is easy, by Zair, unless it be going astray—or shuffling out of life altogether. The itch between my shoulderblades I'd wanted to scratch when we'd hurried through the nighted streets of Port Marsilus persisted. It did not go away. They called this place the Zhantil Palace, for the kov's predilection for the zhantil. I knew why Pando favored that marvelous wild animal of the untamed ways, the golden mane and the superb air of dignified lethality. Something more within this palace caused that itch between my shoulderblades.

And that was not caused by a mere irritating little Ift called Twayne Gullik.

CHAPTER SEVEN

Twayne Gullik

Despite being quartered in a corner of the garrison's barracks within the Zhantil Palace, Pompino and I set watches for the night.

The barracks was practically empty, the long rooms echoing to our voices and footfalls. The rows of bunks, each piled with bedding, lay dustily under the dusty beams. Of men at arms to serve the palace there were but twenty-four. Two dozen fighting men to guard the kovneva, and of these some were not fit to be called paktuns.

The cadade, the captain of the guard, turned out to be a Fristle with patches of fur missing from both cheeks. At least, he saw to a proper burial for Ridzi the Rangora.

For this I thanked him, and gave him a donation in thanks.

"Kov Pando took most of the guards with him when he went to Pomdermam," said Framco the Tranzer, pulling his whiskers, a little unsure at this arrival of a bunch of harumscarum sea dogs. He took his duties as cadade seriously. "He could not know how things were going to turn out."

"And," said Pompino, "how have things turned out?"

We spoke on the steps outside the mess hall, with the archway to the next courtyard and the more splendid buildings of the palace beyond. The night had passed uneventfully and I for one was anxious to speak to Tilda. We had to make a start somewhere within the city, and she ought to know the most likely places.

"Things have not turned out well," said Framco the Franzer.

Pompino just brushed up his whiskers with a gesture which said, more or less, that, oh, yes, he was used to things not turning out well and that, by Horato the Potent, when he was around he soon had the things sorted out, or they'd know what's what.

"The kov's cousin, the Strom Murgon, bears the kov a grudge. He has stirred up the city against him. It is very black." Framco the Tranzer pulled his whiskers unhappily, frowning. "I have a few good men; but the rest are—"

"Little better than masichieri," stuck in Pompino, unarguably.

"Yes."

"But," I said, feeling alarmed. "Surely the citizens would not make an open attack on their kovneva within her own palace in her own capital city? Surely that is not to be believed?"

"You were attacked last night, Horter Jak."

"Yes, but—" And then I stopped. We who knew of Lem the Silver Leem knew the way his followers organized their secrecy and their ways of wielding power. Would the cadade know this? I doubted it, but it was possible.

So, I went on: "They seemed to us a bunch of brigands, drikingers who kill and rob wayfarers and who mistook our mettle."

"That they did, thanks be to Numi-Hyrjiv the Golden Splendor. But I am mindful of my duty to the kovneva. I am from the kov's estates, and no hired mercenary."

"Do you or do you not think the people of Port Marsilus will attempt to storm the palace and harm the kovneva?

He jumped.

"I cannot tell, horter. There is a cult abroad of which I know little, merely rumors and fearful whispers. I fear that the kov is mired in this evil, and I pray Odifor he is not. But it is certain sure that the Strom Murgon Marsilus will take every opportunity to strike against the kov through his mother the kovneva."

It seemed to me, and I am sure to Pompino, that the cadade, Framco the Tranzer, probably knew a great deal more that he was not telling us. And fear of reprisals from an unknown hand held him. The sound of footsteps took our attention to the castellan, the green-clad Twayne Gullik, marching up with a group of his Iftkin about him. Gullik looked savage, and yet contained, as though biding his time.

Now I have mentioned that the color green is splendid for certain purposes, and I would add to that list regimental colors and facings. At this moment on the steps of the mess hall in Tilda's palace I tried to remember that the green connotations here were of Robin Hood and Sherwood and not of the Grodnims of the Eye of the World. With Twayne Gullik's attitude thrust, as it were, under our noses, the effort required was considerable.

He did not beat about the bush.

"I thank you for your efforts on behalf of the kovneva." He stood straight, one hand on his hip. This morning he wore a bow over his shoulder, a short compound-reflex weapon, and a quiver of arrows across his back. Each arrow was fletched green, glistening in the growing power of the Suns. "Now that you have delivered the kovneva safely home, your task is done. You may leave at once. I shall provide an escort for you to the jetty."

Pompino started to let rip, and I said—sharply!— "Escort, Gullik? In daylight? Why do we need an escort in broad daylight in peaceful Port Marsilus?"

He didn't like the way I'd called him Gullik. But he liked the question even less.

"A mere precaution. You will recall you were attacked last night."

Pompino burst out: "How did they know which way we were coming? And why did they not attack the Ship Hikdar and the chair he was protecting? Someone told them, Gullik. Perhaps you told them, hey?"

Twayne Gullik's sword was out. His pallid face, sharp with those slanted eyebrows and those pointed ears, darkened with passion. A man of temper, this.

"If you were not under my protection, Horter Pompino, you would answer for that. Any fool could see that contraption was not the kovneva's chair."

Truth to tell, the thing did look ridiculous in the suns light. But it had been hurried along through moons lighted streets. The puzzle would remain.

"There is no need to quarrel over this," said the Fristle

guard captain, hissing more than usual. His cat face reflected his own puzzlement and uncertainty. "We have enemies enough outside without making more within."

Whatever relationship existed between the castellan and the cadade, these words did have the effect of making Twayne Gullik rein up a trifle, and of Pompino's immediate half-apology.

"I meant no harm, Gullik. We are all on edge."

I notched up one for Pompino. Not like a haughty Khibil to acknowledge anything to an Ift, just down from the trees, all green and dewy. Pompino felt the same unease over this situation as did I. We had a gross half-drunken woman to care for, and her enemies could strike as and when they liked. The responsibility sawed at our nerves.

"Your apology is accepted," said Gullik, and I stepped a little sideways and trod on Pompino's foot.

He glared in hurt surprise.

"The question is," I said, in a voice louder than necessary, "why it is needful for us to leave so soon. I must speak with the kovneva—"

Gullik broke in.

"That is out of the question. The kovneva is—indisposed—and is being cared for by her handmaidens. And as for your leaving, we cannot feed you all comfortably. As it is—"

"As it is," bellowed Pompino, "a mere matter of gold, then we will pay for the kovneva's hospitality!" He lifted up his foot and rubbed it, half-bending down, kneading the soft leather boot. "Pandrite help the poor traveler in this land!"

I said: "It is just after breakfast and I am thirsty, having drunk a mere six cups of tea. I'm for more. Are you with me, Pompino? You have, I recall, a golden zan-talen to spend."

Before Pompino could answer, Twayne Gullik said with a snap: "You may swill your tea, and then you will all immediately leave the palace and return to your ship."

Pompino just said: "Or?"

"Or I shall have to ask the cadade to assist you."

Framco the Tranzer looked decidedly unhappy at this, rolling his eyes at us and fair pulling his whiskers clean out of his furry cat face, it would seem. He, it was clear, wanted no part of any attempt to eject us.

Pompino laughed. "Listen, Twayne Gullik. We are not leaving here until we choose to, until we are ready. Do you understand that?"

"I understand," said the green-clad Ift, "that if that is what you choose you will sorely repent your choice."

With his Iftkin about him he stomped off. Pompino watched him go, laughed, and twirled up his reddish moustaches.

CHAPTER EIGHT

Concerning the traitress Ros the Claw

The Zhantil Palace proved to be an odd sort of residence. Stately halls, winding staircases, cubbyholes, corridors lined with door after door leading to a maze of apartments beyond, lavishly ornamented windows, arrow slits, dovecots—oh, yes, Pando's palace boasted them all. And yet, the place seemed odd. There was a quantity of good porphyry from Molynux, carpets of Walfarg weave, ceramics—naturally—of Pandahem ware. And yet, it was scarcely a place in which to live comfortably or happily.

If there had been no doubts about Tilda's safety, I'd have been overjoyed to get out of Pando's Zhantil Palace.

"That pipsqueak Ift," growled Pompino as we went along the north corridor toward the barracks. "If he thinks he can throw me out just like that he is vastly mistaken."

"It did occur to me to wonder why they had not given us rooms in the main part of the palace. There are guest rooms there which, if mean and unwholesome looking, would perhaps be preferable to the barracks."

"Perhaps, and perhaps not."

"Aye, Pompino. You are probably right."

He twitched that new rapier of his up and down in the scabbard.

"We have yet to meet this person Mindi the Mad. And we must speak with the kovneva. Then we burn temples."

"As I pointed out earlier, I devoutly hope we do not burn down too much of Pando's property. Or that of honest folk."

"From what little we've seen, I doubt there are any in the whole of Port Marsilus, by Horato the Potent!"

From which it was perfectly clear my comrade itched to get his fingers around a tinderbox or compression tube, with a sizable pile of kindling to hand.

Despite the estrangement between him and his wife, the Lady Pompina, I judged he was deeply worried over the threat to her from the Leem Lovers. And if his pair of twins, four beautiful children, were harmed, he might lose his reason. Such an event, for a proud Khibil of passionate convictions, would not be impossible. He had hired swords to protect his loved ones while he went about to root out the evil at its source.

I gave Twayne Gullik few odds if he tried to stand in the way of Scauro Pompino the Iarvin. The Ifts might scorn and play tricks where tumps were concerned, the two races of diffs detesting each other to the point of obsession; a Khibil's feelings of superiority stood in quite another league.

A couple of Fristles marched past, trailing their spears, their armor reasonably bright and cared for. They were hurrying, leaving the barracks, and we guessed they were late for guard duty. They gave us a quick nod of recognition as we passed.

"Humph," said Pompino, staring after them. "A right couple. Like 'em all here, slack, damned slack."

"You going to blame Gullik for that? Or for the state of the people in the city?"

"If I've a mind to, I will. I expect the citizens of Port Marsilus are a spineless lot, undermined by the war and the absence of a strong authority. Oh, yes, I know." He went on speaking quickly. "I know this Kov Pando is a friend from your past. And so is the Lady Tilda. But, all the same—"

"All the same, Pompino, I think you are right."

"As I said. And this Twayne Gullik is no better than a damned masichier, a confounded bandit masquerading as a mercenary. I own I have itchy fingers when he's about."

"Don't forget, my friend, that he will have itchy fingers, too."

"Ha!"

The north corridor contained a long row of tall windows, not quite slit windows affording cover for archers; but windows that were not particularly good at admitting light. They overlooked the north courtyard and the battlemented gate which, as the palace faced west, opened onto a side road. The noise of hooves and the clash of iron-rimmed wheels on cobbles attracted our attention, and we hauled ourselves up on the narrow windowsills to peer over and down. Green slate roofs spread beneath us and, far below, the hint of the north courtyard.

The polished roof of a carriage, partially concealed by a brass-bound traveling trunk, was just disappearing under the archway, the rear of the vehicle and its wheels concealed by a mounted escort whose lances slanted in ungainly fashion. From this angle we could make out few details. The escort, a dozen trotrix men in mail, clattered out and the courtyard lay empty.

Pompino said: "The jutmen carried no colors on their lances."

"By their flags shall ye know them," I quoted. "And, so, we do not know them."

"When," said a mocking voice at our backs and below us, "you are quite finished, the kovneva will see you."

We let go the windowsills and dropped to the floor. The fellow who spoke held a golden-bound balass stick, ivory-topped. He wore long blue robes with a plentiful supply of silver, and his hat—flat, wide, puffed— supported a bunch of cut feathers of so inordinate a height one felt he would take off in a breeze.

"Who the devil are you?" demanded Pompino.

The fellow's puffy face, all pouched eyes and purple nose and sagging jowls, quivered in outrage.

"I am the kovneva's grand chamberlain, Constanchoin the Rod. She has graciously condescended to see you now, and you had best not keep her waiting."

"And," Pompino said, in a brittle voice, "not a horter in all this farrago."

I'd been thinking that a chamberlain, grand or not, would use the simple polite term of horter to a couple of gentlemen, here in his mistress's palace. Mind you, by Krun, most of the time it is difficult to take me for a gentleman, and I do not pretend to be a member of that ilk. I am content to be a plain sailorman, a fighting man or, when it comes to it, an emperor.

All the same, folk called Pompino and me horter out of simple politeness.

The grand chamberlain banged his black staff on the stone floor.

"There is no time to waste. Follow me."

I put a hand on Pompino's arm.

"It would be a sensible idea if we are to see Tilda to take Lisa the Empoin or the Lady Nalfi—"

Pompino's forearm bunched under my fingers, quivered, and then relaxed.

"Agreed." He spoke with some stiffness. "But, if they go, it is certain sure Quendur and Larghos will wish to accompany them, and if Larghos goes, Cap'n Murkizon will—"

"Quite. And, why not? After all," I said to this Constanchion the Rod, "the kovneva will be glad to see all of them, seeing they risked their lives to bring her to safety."

Three flunkeys in a sillier version of the grand chamberlain's attire stood at his back. Constanchoin flicked the pomander on the end of a stick he carried in his left hand. If the gesture was a mere command, or signified what he thought of us, I neither knew nor cared.

"Planath," he said to one of the flunkeys. "Go to the barracks and summon these people. Tell them to hurry in our footsteps."

The flunkey mumbled a reply—not the military quidang— and trotted off, banging his balass staff—bound with silver— against the shins of a slave who almost fell over getting out of the way. A number of slaves passed and repassed, most of them carrying water, for that is a never-ending task in Kregan palaces. Other people had stopped to allow the grand chamberlain to go about his official duties and, also, to watch and enjoy whoever might be discomfited.

Followed by Pompino and me, Constanchoin the Rod started off back the way we had come. Four slaves with a carved lenken box strapped with bronze pressed against the wall to allow us to pass. Just beyond them a girl with a fluted vase of flowers—where she might be going was anybody's guess— waited. She wore a decent gray slave breechclout, and her hair was bound with a grass fillet. Apart from that she wore nothing else, and her feet, besides being dusty, showed a trace of blood. I had to walk on. But, by Zair, the maggots festered, believe you me.

Then I stopped dead.

The fellow who stood like an ale barrel against the wall wore a pale blue tunic, and dark blue trousers, with black boots. He did not wear a hat and his brown hair was cut short. He stood short, stout and robust, on thick legs that waddled when he walked. He wore a pallixter, the Pandahem form of thraxter, belted to his waist—and the word waist was merely a euphemism for his girth. His nose was a mere chunk of gristle, and the redness of his cheeks vied with the sunset of Zim, the red sun of Scorpio.

Pompino swung to look at me in surprise.

I walked on a few paces, as though in thought, and then said: "Do you go on, Pompino. I'll catch you up in a moment."

"But—"

"Hurry!" called the grand chamberlain. His flunkeys pressed close.

"Go on, Pompino. Tilda is, after all, a kovneva."

"What's going on? By Horato the Potent, Jak—you—"

"Something I must do—I'll be along with the others in no time."

Now Pompino is no man's fool. His frown did not lift; but he nodded and swung back to follow Constanchoin and the flunkeys. I breathed out.

There was no danger, I estimated, that the barrel-shaped fellow by the wall would throw himself into the full incline and start majistering me. He was too sly for that.

He started to walk off and turned into the first cross-corridor. I followed. Not too fast, not too slow, walking as though needing to go on an errand of purpose, I followed Naghan Raerdu along the cross-corridor and so into a small room stuffed with dusty barrels and boxes. He closed the door after me and stood back, looking at me.

Then he said: "Jak, is it, majister?"

"Aye, Naghan. And well met. I am glad to see you."

"As I am surprised to see you here. The Prince Majister's latest intelligence is only that you left Ruathytu in the devil of a hurry. But, of course, I have had little news myself in the past few sennights."

I answered in order. "I am not surprised to see you, Naghan, but I am pleased that my son chose you to spy for us here in Pandahem. I've been some way since leaving Ruathytu, and am now engaged in rooting out temples of Lem the Silver Leem. And, although any secret agent must be kept informed, it is his job to gather intelligence."

"Assuredly, Jak, assuredly."

Here Naghan Raerdu shut his eyes and the tears squeezed out from under the lids. He quivered. His red face became even more startlingly colored. Naghan Raerdu laughed in his own special rib-crushing way, spraying tears. When he laughed no one took much notice of what else he was doing.

This, of course, made him a very dangerous man and a first-class wormer out of secrets.

Presently he told me that his cover was a simple ale tradesman—and this fitted, for Naghan Raerdu seldom passed a bur or two without a glass tilted to his lips. Drak wanted to find out all there was to know of the people organizing the opposition to the warmongering factions here in Bormark. Armies were being sent across to the southwest of Vallia to support Kov Vodun Alloran—as I had learned aboard Insur ti Fotor's galleon—and my lad Drak felt we should assist those here in Bormark who stood against this plan.

"And there are such people, people who do not wish to fight against Vallia? You have contacted them?"

"Tsleetha—tseleethi," quoth Raerdu. "Softly-softly. There was a group I had just contacted when half of their number turned up in the River Liximus with slit throats and the other half vanished."

I looked sternly at him.

"If you turn up in the river with your throat slit, Naghan, I shall be extraordinarily annoyed. Not as much as you, perhaps. But remember! If you take stupid risks and such a fate should befall you, the ale would never reach your stomach."

He glared back.

"Few men call me stupid, majister."

"Sink me! If you were stupid you'd be dead twenty times by now."

I was not prepared to go into a long, involved and probably incoherent explanation of my feelings over sending men and women into danger and the risks of nasty deaths. They fought for Vallia, as did I. I'd had my share of risks, and, by Vox, a hell of a lot more lay ahead, as you shall hear. But, as always, I fretted at the unwholesome necessity of sending men and women into dangers I could not share.

"I'm still alive, Jak. That must prove something."

Although in the end we're all going shuffling off to the Ice Floes of Sicce and, if we are fortunate and of stout hearts and hew to the right path, make our way to the sunny uplands beyond, we all feel we wish to push that time off for as long as possible. I've been around Kregen under many assumed names, as you know; I believe I have only once been called Davy Prescott. Amusing as an indication of scholarship though this is, for me it is merely another prod in the direction of staying away from any Alamo, unless something stupid like honor gets in the way. It was in my mind that Naghan Raerdu would never let the stupidity of honor betray him, for all that he was loyal and courageous. He gave me further news—which does not concern my narrative at this time—and he reassured me that those people for whom I had a particular care were still in one piece.

Then he said: "The Princess Dayra was down in the southwest. I was not assigned there, until later, and so cannot vouch for the rumors—"

I congratulated myself on my iron control.

I did not leap forward and seize Naghan Raerdu around his neck and choke him, screaming: "Rumors? Princess Dayra? What rumors? Spit 'em out or you are a dead man!"

No. My self-control was admirable.

Naghan Raerdu jumped, staring at me in that dusty room. His color patched into white and pink.

"Majister. . . ." He stammered, and licked his lips, and said quickly—very quickly—"A colleague said that the Princess Dayra was actively assisting Vodun Alloran. . . ."

I put a hand on a barrel. The dust lay thick.

"And?"

He swallowed.

"As I said, majister, I cannot vouch—"

"Tell me what the rumors are concerning my daughter Dayra."

He straightened, for he saw the crisis had passed. A large number of people knew how much of a trial Dayra was to her family. She was known as Ros the Claw, having been through Lancival where she had been taught the secret Disciplines of the Whip and the Claw. The Sisters of the Rose had taught her and her mother had loved and counselled her; but during the time of her growing up there had been no father in her life. That great rogue had been banished to Earth, distant four hundred light-years, by the Star Lords. For that I had, I thought, forgiven them, for they and I had reached a tatty kind of argreement in these later years. But, as now, the

hideous results of that parting from my family came home to
me with deadly remorse.

The truth was, of course, that even had I been around like
any normal father, Dayra would still have gone off the rails,
although perhaps not to quite the extent she had. She had
been lured off course by bad companions. Some of them were
due a hempen knecktie—when they were caught.

Dayra's mother, the incomparable Delia of Delphond, had
herself been constrained by duty to the Sisters of the Rose. It
was perfectly reasonable to suggest that the SOR themselves,
as much as any other factor, had contributed heavily to
Dayra's wildness.

Naghan's rubicund composure returned. Sweat glimmered
on his red forehead.

"The usual things, Jak. Smashing up wine shops, wrecking
restaurants. But she was seen riding with Alloran when he led
an armored host to war—"

"But he was fighting the Prince Majister! Do you think I
am to believe that my daughter Dayra would go out to fight
her brother?"

"There were no reports of her presence on the battlefield."

"Thank Opaz for that. Is there more?"

"This fellow Zankov was also seen in her company."

"Him," I said, and drew a breath. "I tell you this, Naghan,
for your information. Zankov is a young devil, spurned by his
family and out to make himself master of whatever he can lay
his hands on. He is the man who slew the emperor, the
Princess Dayra's grandfather. I do not think she can know this."

Naghan's brown Vallian eyes widened. "I did not know
this. By Vox! What a coil!"

"Oh, the coil is tighter than that. For the Princess Dayra
hates and detests her father, Dray Prescot, Emperor of Vallia."

All Naghan said was: "That I knew."

An emotion, and I hardly care to call it pride, for it was
more a kind of affronted despair, a desperate call for a
fraction of self-esteem, made me say: "Although when she
thought she could slay me, dubious though the chance was,
she did not strike, and held back the blow. It is in my mind
that, perhaps, her hatred and detestation are not the powerful
forces in her life she thinks they are."

Naghan Raerdu said: "I pray Opaz you are right."

I shook myself. The dust was getting up my nose.

"We have spoken long enough for now. We shall meet

again. Now I'm on my way to see the Kovneva Tilda, for there are temples to be burned."

"The kovneva?" Naghan looked puzzled. "She left the Zhantil Palace very early this morning, Jak. She took a large escort, and no one knew where she had gone."

CHAPTER NINE

How a blood-stained switch changed hands

The problems of my family and particularly of Dayra had to be pushed aside—yet again. The Star Lords overlooked my actions here in Bormark, even if they had not directly commissioned Pompino and me. Because I had defied them in the past they had banished me to Earth for twenty-one years. In those years Dayra and her twin brother Jaidur had grown to maturity. Useless to harp on what might have been. . . .

I found Constanchoin the Rod in a small, black-hung chamber, superintending the chastisement of a slave girl. The under-flunkey I dragged along by an ear had let me know that I was sealing my doom by my actions. But he led me where I wanted to go, even if he dragged along after, his ear stretching.

The slave girl, naked, hung suspended by her ankles from a cross beam. She was past the shrieking stage, and blood ran down to drip from her forehead into her hair and so onto the iron floor. The Rapa who, stripped to the waist, wielded the switch, halted his blow as I bundled in.

Two Rapa guards immediately rushed across, their spears ready to degut me. I threw the junior flunkey at them and took time to take the switch away from the Rapa and hit him a belt across the head. His beak bent. I kicked him as he went down, thus proving the grand chamberlain at least half-right when he'd omitted to address me as horter.

The two guards disentangled themselves from the flunkey

and heaved up. The grand chamberlain was shrieking out something about kill him, you fools, kill him. They charged with their spears low. They'd have killed me, too, I believe, even before anything had been sorted out. As it was I whipped the thraxter out, swished left, cut right, ducked away, got inside the second spear and thrust.

Two Rapa guards lay on the iron floor, bleeding messily.

Three naked and chained girls at the side did not scream. But their eyes were as wide as the Sunset Sea.

No doubt they were next in line for punishment. There had been enough time since the grand chamberlain had summoned us to the kovneva for just the one girl to be chastised.

The tendril-like antennae growing from her forehead and shrouded by her soft dark hair looked limp and woeful. Her small pinched face with the bruised eyes and the full yet small mouth made me kick the Rapa switch-wielder again, hard, and say to him: "Be thankful you are still alive, dom."

The only other person in the chamber, a little six-armed Och in a brown tunic, crouched beside the chained slave girls. Mutely, he handed me the keyring. I did not take it.

"Unchain them," I growled, and then dived for the grand chamberlain who was attempting to scuttle out.

"C'mere, grand chamberlain," I said, and lifted him up by his fancy silver-worked blue robe so that he squeaked. I stuck my ugly old beakhead of a face into his and said: "Where's the kovneva?"

"I don't know!" He chittered it out, swinging with his toes scraping the floor. I shook him.

"You summoned me to see the Kovneva Tilda. She has left the Zhantil Palace. She had left long before you spoke to me. So, dom, where is she?"

His eyes were popping. There was foam on his lips.

"I don't know!"

I did not hit him, for that would have solved nothing. I looked at him sorrowfully. I cocked my head at the beam and dragged him across. Holding him with my left fist I used the thraxter in my right to slash the girl's bonds. She fell into the arms of her three companions who, unchained, were ready to help in this impossible and undreamed of situation. They were girls of spirit, then, and not broken slave grakvushis.

The girls were all trembling, as was natural, yet with that quick summation of their characters I surmised they had not been slave long. One was a Sybli, one a Sylvie and the other apim. They were all pretty, and I sighed.

Constanchoin went upside down with some ease and I looked at the girls.

"Two of you tie his ankles to the beam."

The Sybli with her childish face just smiled and went on bathing the girl who had been beaten. The Sylvie and the apim girl leaped up, eagerly sorted out fresh bonds and fastened Constanchoin upside down. I half bent to stare into his engorged face.

"You know what is going to happen, grand chamberlain. But, of course, you won't let it happen. You'll tell me where the kovneva is."

He was hysterical now, shattered by shock and fright.

But he still chittered out: "I do not know! A great crowd of Twayne Gullik's Iftkin came and took the kovneva away. I was not told—"

I frowned.

This had the ring of truth. That Twayne Gullik . . . Maybe Pompino was right and the Ift was an out and out rogue.

The Sylvie picked up the bloodstained switch.

With the feeling a man gets when he realizes the bottom of his ship has been ripped out on a coral reef I saw that the situation had now overtaken me. What I had begun in so febrile a manner would be continued and probably finished by others with their own interests to slake. I bent again to Constanchoin the Rod.

"If you know, tell me. These girls will not be easy on you."

"I do not know!"

"Well, where would Gullik most likely take her?"

"His kin have a castle at Igbolo, deep in the forest—"

The Sylvie whistled the switch around with a hiss and the grand chamberlain yelped although not touched. His blue robes hung around his head, but I felt sure the girls would remove the rest of his clothes before they started.

"Igbolo," I said. "That is not much help." Igbolo was like saying Greentree. "You'll have to do better than that."

"I can take you there—I think." He spoke with a rush, seeing a way out of his predicament. I wasn't at all sure I could stop these poor girls once they'd started.

"What do you mean, you think?"

"The way is guarded by traps. It is lost in the forest. I have never been there—'' He regretted saying that instantly. He tried to cover. "But I have been told."

By this time I felt reasonably confident that he didn't know where the kovneva was. She might be at Gullik's Iftkin's castle of Igbolo. But she might not be. Gullik would know for sure that the search would be prosecuted there.

"Anywhere else?"

"No! I don't know—save me, save me, Horter Jak!"

I did not smile.

"If you insist on tying up girls and having them beaten painfully with a switch, you surely cannot complain if girls tie you up and reciprocate? Is there not justice in that?"

"As you love Pandrite, save me!"

"Horter," said the Sylvie. "I do not know who you are; but I am growing tired of waiting."

"We take turns," said the apim girl.

"Of course, Natalini, we take turns. Only I go first."

"You always do get first go at the men, Sharmin."

"And this time it will be different, by Shiusas the Insatiable, vastly different."

As all Kregans know, if anyone is cognizant of insatiability, it has to be the Sylvies, of whom most men are strangely ignorant—or, perhaps not strangely, seeing that they wish to remain on speaking terms with their own womenfolk. Or, so it is said.

Constanchoin fell into an incoherent mumble, interlarded with prayers and pleadings. The broken-beaked Rapa slumbered. The two guards lay in their own blood. The Och had vanished. There seemed to me nothing left here for me, except a difficult decision. Why did I have to become embroiled? I'd told this damned grand chamberlain that, hoisted with his own petard as he was, he could expect no other punishment than that which he had meted out. But was this a civilized action? It was not, certainly in many areas of Kregen. Just as I had decided—and, I might add, with some reluctance—to halt the girls in their revengeful beating after each had had a whack or two, the whole problem was terminated in an unsurprising and typical way.

The black-hung chamber echoed to the clash of iron-soled sandals on the iron floor and a mob of guards burst in.

Since I stood in front of the upside-down grand chamberlain hanging from the beam all the newcomers would see of him would be his ankles bound up. They took as little interest in those as they did in the wounded and unconscious Rapas. Most of the guards were Fristles. They looked at the Sylvie.

I said in a hard voice: "Have you seen the kovneva, Framco the Tranzer?"

The cadade hauled up and looked at me. He recognized me.

"The kovneva? No, of course not. We had report of a disturbance, of a wild man—what's going on, Horter Jak?"

"Why, only that that rogue of a Twayne Gullik has kidnapped the kovneva. As for the business here, your grand chamberlain was about to taste his own switch. But I think that may not be necessary now."

The Fristle cadade peered around. He saw what had been going on. I readied myself for a bout of handstrokes; but what I'd said worried him far more than the plight of the grand chamberlain. It was not difficult to guess that Constanchoin had given Framco a hard time in the past.

"Gullik's kidnapped the kovneva! You are sure? It is a most serious allegation." Framco did not pull his whiskers. He looked competent, on a sudden, in his mail. "Forgon—cut down the grand chamberlain. Catch him before he falls." To the Och, who ran in grimacing and ducking his head: "You, Nathamcar, see these girls back to their quarters." To an ob-Deldar whose whiskers were dyed blue: "Anfer, take two men and guard them. I'll question them, if ever I get around to it . . . Now, Horter Jak, perhaps you'd best tell me all about it from the beginning."

"Gladly, if I knew what the hell was going on."

Constanchoin, cut down, was carried past, moaning.

Framco said: "You'll have to answer as to what has happened to the grand chamberlain. Although if he's in the plot I'll be the first to string him up again."

At the time I found nothing unusual in the cadade's immediate acceptance of my story. That there was strong animosity between him and Twayne Gullik was obvious, and that antipathy extended to the grand chamberlain. Also, Framco the Tranzer was no hired paktun. He came from Pando's estates, and would be expected in the normal way to be loyal, given fair dealings. That he had been chosen to be the captain of the guard indicated something of his mettle.

The girls walked past, the antennae of the fanpi drooping as she was carried by two men.

The Sylvie, bold, stopped by me and looked up.

"You deprived me of my revenge, horter."

I said: "You will be thankful, one day, that you did not take your revenge. When I see the kovneva I will buy you and your friends—"

She showed her teeth.

"I would not willingly be slave to you—"

"I do not keep slaves. I will manumit you all. That is a promise."

Her face changed color.

"What is the name of the fanpi who was beaten?"

"Tinli, horter."

"I shall remember the four of you, and see you are freed, for you can face nothing but pain here now. Tinli, Suli, Natalini—and Sharmin. I shall remember."

"If you do, horter, then Shiusas the Insatiable will surely reward you."

Framco said: "We have to find the kovneva first."

"Aye. But where has Gullik taken her? And," I said, for I was still unsure, "It could be he has merely taken her to another place of refuge. . . ."

"That is a possibility, of course. But I know that rogue Gullik."

"Suppose he mistrusted us?"

"Had you wished to kill the kovneva, I am sure you would have done so long ago, and run no further risks in bringing her into the Zhantil Palace. By Odifor! I may be wrong in this, but my whiskers tell me I am right!"

The smiling Sybli girl with her childish face turned as she passed. They are simple folk, the Syblians, but not as simple as they look.

"The mistress wanted to take me to the estate at Plaxing, if that helps, horter. She told me so last night."

I looked at her, said thank you and she smiled, her babyish face rosy and now free from worry, for she, like any truly sensible person, might look into the future but refused to worry over it, unlike most of us.

"Tilda spoke to her last night, when she was supposed to be unwell." I could hear the edge in my voice. "There has been a plot at work here."

"Yes," said Framco, agreeing. "But I do not think Gullik would take the kovneva to her estate at Plaxing."

"You agree there is a plot. Tell me what you think has been going on." For my money the cadade knew nothing, and Twayne Gullik had, following his name, gulled him. "You'd better send some of your men to make inquiries. A party of Iftkin with a chair or a coach may have attracted attention."

The carriage Pompino and I had seen leaving might belong to the plot. When I mentioned it, Framco sent to make inquiries. Then we went off to find Pompino.

On the way through the corridors with scared slaves keeping out of the way, Framco told me that if there was a plot, as he now believed, he knew nothing of it. He'd always mistrusted the Ift from the day Pando took him on as castellan. No doubt Pando had his motives in the appointment; I could not guess what they were. Some of Pando's estates consisted of entire stretches of forest. Maybe that was the answer.

We found Pompino and the rest of the people from *Tuscurs Maiden* fuming.

"Kept me waiting like some cur dog!" Pompino started off. "No formality, no courtesy—"

He quieted down when I cut in to explain what had happened. Then he broke out afresh.

"We'll scour every street, every tavern, every hole and corner! Someone, somewhere, will know where the kovneva has been taken."

"That," I said, "will take time."

"If only Mindi the Mad were here," said Framco. I noticed that he'd started pulling his whiskers again. "She has the power. I am confident she would be able to spy out the kovneva's whereabouts."

"A witch?" demanded Pompino.

"A good witch, a female wizard, a sorceress, a seer, yes."

"You trust her?"

"Oh," said Framco the Tranzer, "no."

Towards the hour of mid when we thought of taking a little light refreshment one of Framco's men reported back that a party of Ifts with three wagons had been observed leaving the Inward Gate, which led out into the hinterland.

"After them!" he cried. "Mount up, all. We'll overtake them and demand a reckoning, by Odifor!"

A bunch of hersanys were brought from the stables and saddled up. Big ugly brutes, hersanys, with coats of thick chalk-white hair, and their six legs are as ungainly as any totrix's. But they have stamina, and do well in the bruising jolt of a cavalry charge. Framco's guards mounted up, and Pompino called down to me from his saddle.

"Mount up, Jak! This is nip and tuck."

"Listen, Pompino." I walked across and put my hand on his bridle. "Do you go on after the Ifts. You may find the Lady Tilda with them—"

He looked alarmed.

"You think not?"

"I don't know, by Pandrite! But I do not think it wise to expend all our energy in one direction."

He nodded. "Then I'll follow this clue. If you root out anything, send a messenger—these locals will know the direction we've taken."

"I'll do that."

"Maybe I should stay with you and let Framco go—"

"That is your decision. But I want to poke about myself. I want to use my nose."

"A damned great beakhead it is, to be sure. Very well. I'll give this chase a day, then I'll be back."

"Agreed."

They clattered off, like a hunt after leems, and I went back into the palace, free to go about my own nefarious activities.

CHAPTER TEN

Of the power of the Lemmites

Looked at dispassionately, the perfectly logical deduction from what had happened was that Twayne Gullik, a conscientious castellan, concerned for the safety of his mistress and much distrusting us rough new arrivals, had taken her off to a place of greater sanctuary. This was perfectly possible.

His attempt to get us out of the palace had failed. But—we

knew that the kovneva had left the palace before Gullik spoke to us. Copper-bottoming his bet? Maybe.

One way or the other, we had covered the options. If Tilda was safe with Gullik, no harm would have been done. If she was being abducted—and one could hardly say against her will because she was probably in a state of happy befuddlement—Pompino and the crew from *Tuscurs Maiden* and Framco and his guards would take the necessary measures to secure her from the rascally Ift. If he was a rascal.

Framco had left a handful of men under an ord-Deldar to hold the palace. They'd be occupied if anything untoward happened. My judgment was that some of the peril we had anticipated, directed as it was against persons and not property, might have been exaggerated. It might not have been. If a howling mob broke in to loot the palace the guards would see them off; if assassins sneaked in they'd find no quarry, their kitchews all flown, and if any of the other folk who wanted Tilda dead attacked they'd have dust and ashes to show for their pains.

So, feeling discontented but aware that in that direction nothing further remained to be done, I set about the next task.

If I burned a temple before Pompino got back to join in he'd feel cheated of his amusement. But, I could see about finding the locations of the temples. As I did this I'd make inquiries after the Ifts and the kovneva.

A change of costume being desirable I went along to see the grand chamberlain.

He was still in a distressed state, lying shivering in his bed in his apartments. A couple of flunkeys wanted to cut up; but I looked at them, and went across the carpets to look down on Constanchoin.

He glared up, feverishly, black rings under his eyes.

"I refuse to feel sorry for you," I told him. "If you order girls to be beaten then you must expect to be beaten yourself. As it was, you came off lightly."

He moaned. This was all shock, indignity, fright; he hadn't been physically harmed.

"I need a change of clothes. I came to see if you were all right and to tell you that I am plundering the kov's wardrobe. He will be pleased to let me have whatever clothes I wish to take, believe me. As for you; when you are recovered you will take great care of the people, both men and women, in your charge. Otherwise—well, in the Blue Distance of Pandrite, anything may happen. *Dernun?*"

That rather fierce way of demanding understanding jolted him. He managed a feeble nod. A slave girl wiped spittle from his lips. I looked at her, a Fristle girl with silvery fur and a tail adorned with a blue and green bow.

"If he hits you, fifi, tell me. He will not hit you again."

With that foolish statement echoing in my ears I went off. As you will observe, I was a trifle warm about the domestic arrangements young Pando kept up in his palace.

In the lavishly furnished apartments given over to the kov's personal use I found he did himself proud in the wardrobe department. His tunics wouldn't stretch to fit my shoulders, of course; but I needed a Pandahem hat, and a loose cape-like upper garment known in Pandahem as a puttah. I chose one with a blue ground and not too much black and silver embroidery, for they are foppish in these things. With this slung over my shoulders, the wide hat pulled down, and a fresh pair of gray trousers, I was perfectly decently dressed.

The Fristle ord-Deldar, who reported himself in as Naghan the Pellendur, offered me a hersany. I told him I'd prefer to walk, thanked him, and sauntered out of the gate. I felt a tickle of amusement as the two guards in their little sentry boxes slapped up their spears in salute. I touched the brim of the hat to them, shoved the puttah over my left shoulder in the style of a pelisse, and took myself off to explore Pando's Port Marsilus.

His hat, I should mention, was of a fine pearl-gray color, most elegant, with a black velvet band. In that band a jaunty tuft of green feathers gave, I now admit, life to the combination. With a gesture I admit, I admit! was entirely petty, I ripped the green feathers out and scattered them on the roadway. Of such things are a fellow's life made. Meaningless gestures, irrational loyalties, a childish approach to the serious things of life. . . .

The way to handle children. . . . Well, I knew that, didn't I? Of course I did—or thought I did like any fond parent. But children do not grow up in the same mold as their parents. I couldn't honestly say that a single one of my children took after me—except in a twisted sense that Dayra would like to take after me with her Whip and her Claw. Although she hadn't struck that final blow. . . .

So, thinking dark and unpleasant thoughts, all occasioned

by a bunch of green feathers, I tried to brisk up my steps. The first port of call would be a tavern, by Krun!

At the sign of the Hersany and Queng I downed a tankard of ale and devoured two cheese sandwiches with a great deal of pickle, and all the time I sized up the clientele—middling tradesmen, a fellow who was clearly an artist from the paint on his fingers and the well-worn portfolio leaning against his chair leg, a farmer into the big city over important affairs and dressed up in a hideous melange of color and style, a mercenary—a little out of his milieu—who was tazll and being unemployed had a lean and hungry look. To this last customer I insinuated myself with the usual tricks of intro-duction, and bought him a tankard, and so sat down easily at his side.

The suns light struck across the settle so that he stood out in fine detail, whereas I leaned back in the shadows.

"And they say they're taking anybody. Masichieri, most likely, so a paktun like me can expect a good position."

"Hikdar?" I said, lazily.

He blinked.

"Well—perhaps not at first. But shebov-Deldar, at the least."

Shebov-Deldar—seven steps up the ladder of promotions within the Deldar ranking—would be handsome, I judged. He was apim, like me, well-built, and with a crop of dark hair tied into a knot with a blue ribbon at the back of his head. He wore a leather brass-studded jerkin, and carried a pallixter. He had no helmet I could see.

He said his name was Apgarl Apring, called the Strigicaw; but I did not believe him.

His business on that score was his own; what he could tell me of the recruiting going on was going to be mine also.

"You looked a fine handy fellow when I saw you come in," he said, quaffing the ale I'd bought him. "Why don't you come along o' me, and we'll sign up together?"

"Why not?"

He looked pleased. If he'd run off from some scrape he'd welcome a friend. He wore neither golden zhantil-head nor silver mortil-head at his throat; but in these latter days on Kregen he called himself a paktun, which is really a name reserved for mercenaries who have acquired renown.

He knew nothing of any party of Ifts, and allowing my voice to rise when the question was posed, I received no response for my pains from anyone else.

This Apgarl Apring possessed no saddle-animal, no helmet, no spear, no shield. The obvious conclusion was that association with him would bring accumulated suspicion down on my head. This might work both ways, of course. . . .

We went along to the Street of the Jiktars where, at an imposing structure stuccoed white, we went in to see about signing up. The courtyard was busy with comings and goings of military men and women, and the place hummed with activity.

In many of the countries in this part of the world in the days following the great war against Hamal, employment for mercenaries had thinned. Men and women to be hired for guard duty and to protect caravans or ships were always in demand; now the markets were overflowing. In the normal course, then, one would expect Apgarl to find some difficulty in securing employment.

No such thing. Oh, no! The moment we sized up the layout, saw the different regimental tables with their recruiting Deldars, the heaps of gold coins, the busy bustle, saw the speed with which any new arrival was snapped up, we saw there would be no difficulty. Apgarl looked at the different tables.

He smiled and then he frowned.

"I shall, of course, choose a first-class regiment."

"Of course."

I'd seen enough—already. If they wanted men so desperately as to take on Apgarl Apring—who was in all probability a decent enough fellow except for his unfortunate circumstances—then an expedition of some size was planned. Given the information I was already possessed of, it seemed to me that the destination of the expedition had to be southwestern Vallia.

"Where are you off to, then, Nath?" Apgarl looked surprised. I'd told him I was Nath the Bludgeon.

"A previous appointment, Apgarl. Don't wait for me."

"I won't, by Acker of the Brass Tail! But if you're in the Hersany and Queng I'll treat you out of my first pay."

"Done, Apgarl. Remberee."

He trotted off to sign up and I wandered in the other direction where a bulbous-nosed fellow wearing a gorgeous uniform that had been stitched together to close the rents, and chalked over the white and painted over the colors, stood at a table and bellowed fruitlessly. A standard of blue and white with yellow slashes hung at his back. Its edges were shredded. His own uniform of similar colors looked as though he'd been ridden over by the same charge of armored cavalry.

"Come along, dom," he called to me. "You look a fine upstanding fellow." His spiel followed the usual line of desperate recruiting Deldars. Things were hot, then!

"Tell me, Deldar," I said in an easy voice. "Just where are you expecting to fight? For, I can tell you, I have a weak stomach. If there're ships involved—"

"Weak stomach!" He managed a laugh, although his cheeks, bearded and pitted with tiny blackheads, for he was apim, changed not at all and his eyes remained dull. "Why, we can soon cure that for you! We'll see to it that you get a first-class berth, with all the trimmings. Come along, lad, sign up and take the silver in your hand." He tossed a silver dhem up and down on his palm.

This time of day the recruiting Deldars might wait at their tables here in Headquarters in the Street of the Jiktars, their serious work took place later in the various taverns about the city. They expected eager volunteers now.

"So it is over the sea," I said, looking downcast.

"It don't matter to a fighting man where he fights! When you take up the profession of arms, you look no further than the next meal and the purse o' gold, the next jovial company and the next battle."

"Who, Deldar, are you fighting?"

Still his expression remained in that pathetic joviality overlaying deadness.

"That's for the orffizers to say, dom. Here, take the silver and we'll make two men of you—"

"You look, Deldar, as though you've just staggered off a battlefield. You're not a good advertisement for your regiment."

He goggled at me now, taken aback. Then he banged the ornate brass badge set in the front of his leather helmet. Half the blue and white feathers were missing from the socket.

"See that, lad! That's the badge o' the Corrundum Rig'ment, known as the Korfs. Proud, we are, and don't you—"

"Archers, then. . . . You don't know I can pull a bow."

He laughed now, and there was some amusement there. "I seen your shoulders, dom. I know a bowman when I see one."

A Deldar at the adjoining table shouted across.

"Corrundum Krasnys! Step over here, dom, and join a *real* rig'ment!"

He wore a splendid uniform of blue and yellow with much gold ornament and a veritable peacock's tail in his helmet. Giving him a casual glance, I was held by the small silver brooch at his left shoulder, fastening the flamboyant sash. A small tuft of brown feathers surmounted the silver image of a leem.

About to saunter across, ignoring the pleas of the Deldar of the Corrundum Korfs, I had to step aside as a great wash of men surged in, shouting and laughing, stamping their boots and swishing their capes.

"They'll pick and choose," said the Corrundum Deldar. He clearly regarded me as a lost cause. "Proud we are, right enough; but we've had hard times lately."

If a pang touched me I had to thrust it aside.

"Been in it, lately?"

"Aye, dom. Down in Hamal, I was. Paktun." He was a true paktun, for he wore the silver mortilhead at his throat. "Fought them Pandrite-forsaken Schtarkins, the Shanks. Beat 'em, too—"

Jolted, I said, "You were at the Battle of the Incendiary Vosks?"

His eyes opened. "Aye, I was. You, too?"

"Aye."

He looked alive, suddenly. I could not afford to get involved in old-soldier campaigning talk, much as I might have enjoyed it over a wet. He was a mercenary, last season fighting with me against a common foe, this season fighting for my enemies against my own country. All the time, if he were your true paktun of Kregen, he would remain loyal to the employer to whom he had sworn his allegiance. I edged a little away, not because of any ill-feeling against paktuns, but out of the pressing necessity of getting on with the task in hand. I looked at the sumptuously-clad Deldar in the blue and yellow with the badge of the Silver Leem.

A fellow, a moltingur, all proboscis and carapace, was speaking to the Deldar. He wore brass-studded leathers and carried a formidable armory. He leaned over and I heard him say: "Yes, indeed, Deldar, I am choosy; but, as you can see from this I am not your ordinary paktun." And he touched his own silver and brown badge pinned to his shoulder.

The Deldar simply asked a question, couched in the ritual—

and rigmarole—of the secret passwords of the Leem Lovers. I was privy to these secrets, having been inducted into the vile cult to save my life down in Ruathytu. The moltingur had no idea what was being said, and gave a noncommittal answer that branded him as one who knew nothing of Lem the Silver Leem.

Fascinated, I listened and watched.

The Deldar of the Corrundum Korfs sniffed at my back and said in a growly bass: "That lot get promoted, right enough."

I faced him.

"You know about that badge—the leem and the brown feathers?"

"I know nothing and I want to know nothing. But you see it more and more every day. That moltingur will get made up to ord-Deldar on the strength of it, you mark my words."

I thought not; I did not say so.

Loath though I was to give any credit to anyone belonging to the Leem Lovers, in what next occurred I saw that, perhaps, some men and women—and particularly the military—might sign up with the cult out of other reasons than religious fervor, misguided ambition and love of orgies. I fancied that this Deldar might be absent when it came to torturing and sacrificing children.

He spoke swiftly to the Moltingur, in a low voice, and then called across to the Deldar of the Corrundum Korfs.

"Hai, Deldar Poll! Here is a fellow for you—"

The Moltingur's proboscis shoved forward and he grabbed the rich uniform before him, starting to protest. That, as anyone could see, was a great mistake.

The Deldar did not hit him, made no move to withdraw. He simply called: "Glemshos! Autmoil!* *Bratch!*"

The next few moments witnessed a boil of fellows in bright uniforms descending on the unfortunate moltingur and beating anywhere they could reach with stout and heavy cudgels. They knocked him down and kicked him, and then they dragged him up by his ears and threw him into the center of the courtyard.

One of them, a pinch-faced fellow whose brown and silver badge was of an ornateness surpassing the others, spat down: "If you attempt to deceive or impersonate us again, you will try to swim with a slit throat, by Flem!"

*Autmoil: stranger

The moltingur lay on the flagstones, shattered.

The pinchfaced fellow swaggered back. "That's the way to deal with that trash, Deldar Loparn. We are not people to be fooled or trifled with."

The word used by this Deldar Loparn—Glemshos—intrigued me. Clearly the shos part came from the common word fanshos, being a band of companions, a gang of likely lads, all pals together. The Glem was merely one of the ways the Leem Lovers disguised their adherence. But the use of the word in just this way meant that here in Bormark the cult of Lem the Silver Leem operated much more in the open. The words spoken and the acts performed testified eloquently to this. I'd seen Lem the Silver Leem worshipped openly in Canopdrin, seasons ago, and we'd settled up that question. Now the Canops lived on the island of Canopjik and kept watch and ward for the Shanks who raided up into Havilfar. Deldar Poll at my back coughed and said: "Bad cess to 'em."

"You don't fear them?"

"Of course I do, dom!"

He wiped a sleeve across his mouth.

I said: "There's little enough doing here. Come along for a wet."

He hesitated; but agreed when I took one of Pompino's golden deldys out and twinkled it between my fingers. He called a shiv-Deldar out to take over, not that there would be much doing, for this fellow's uniform was in almost as sorry a state as Poll's. We went off toward the wing of the Head-quarters turned into an ale house for the recruiting period.

Our conversation followed along traditional lines. As Nath the Bludgeon I contrived to put on a half-vacant look, not quite imbecilic, although my friends claim that this is a natural expression. He said he was Tom Poll called the Nose. That organ was not as colorful or as plentiful as many nourished in the taverns of Kregen, but it was of a certain quivering splendor.

A vague idea that I could join up with a Brown and Silver regiment and thus worm my way into the heart of things had been dashed. Tom the Nose said his commander, Jiktar Naghan Lappartom, was a fair man, but short of the readies, both of cash and equipment.

"We've been in Vallia, and we had a tough time." He was into the confidence stage now, past trying to recruit me.

"This new army they're putting together will probably beat the Vallians; but you never can tell. They fight hard."

"So I believe."

"You must have heard of them at the Incendiary Vosks. By Pandrite—they and those devilish Djangs! I was with a regiment contracted to old King Hot and Cold. I can tell you, I'm glad we did not have to thwack it out with the Vallians."

I hoisted my stein and gave him a quizzical look.

"You sound as though the Vallians you saw then and the ones you fought over in Vallia recently are not the same."

"Too right, dom! The best Vallian regiments are still in Hamal, or are up in the north of Vallia. It won't be easy; but this time we can do it. Their King Alloran will sweep most of his section of the country clean. There'll be rich pickings. I wasn't at the sack of Rahartdrin—"

"Sack of Rahartdrin?"

He slopped ale.

"What's wrong?"

"Nothing. I knew someone from there. That's all."

He leered, his nose wobbling. "A girl, hey?"

"Yes."

"Don't we all."

"By the way," I said, trying to sound casual and making a pretty poor fist of it, "d'you hear anything of what happened to the kovneva there: Katrin Rashumin, I think her name was. My girl slaved for her."

He cocked an eye at me.

"She ran off, was all I heard. And the Vallians don't keep slaves anymore—"

"Figure of speech, dom, figure of speech."

I drank ale, to hide the fury in my face. Being caught up in my own wishes and orders! Ironical—and infuriating with it. The fact that Vallians had done away with slavery in almost all their provinces was now a well-known item of news even though it remained a marvel.

"So this King Vodun Alloran has conquered Rahartdrin." That kovnate consisted of a large island off the southwest coast. Katrin Rashumin was a loyal friend to Delia. And this maniacal king was on the move, clearly taking other islands and also making his way up to the northeast. Soon he might reach Delphond—what the hell was Drak doing?

This Tom Poll the Nose, with whom I sat companionably drinking ale, was a zan-Deldar. He wore the silver mortilhead.

Now he quaffed ale, and said: "Oh, yes, right enough. As soon as we get there we'll be off, you mark my words. We'll be off into Vallia and bring their capital city, Vondium, down about their ears. King Vodun Alloran has vowed to cut off the emperor's head." He drank again, a paktun discussing his trade. "It's certain sure. This Dray Prescot emperor is for the chop this time." He eyed me. "What's stopping you from coming along and helping us fight this Dray Prescot?"

CHAPTER ELEVEN

How the Great Lie spread

"What's stopping me from going and fighting Dray Prescot, Emperor of Vallia?" I said. "Why, Tom, I told you. I'd get seasick."

He looked over the rim of his stein at me, quite clearly nonplussed.

"You were down in Hamal—"

"Certainly. Never again."

The large hall in this wing of the grandiose building given over as a tavern for the military resounded with the clink of bottles, the surf-foaming-roar of voices, the occasional quick snap of argument. Most of the men were recruiters, conscious of their dignity; the arguments did not degenerate into fights. They'd come later, out at the taverns, when the competition grew fiercer.

I leaned closer.

"Did you see this Emperor of Vallia at the Incendiary Vosks?"

"No. He kept out of it. That's his style."

"Oh?"

"Surely. Why, dom, it's no secret. He was built up as the Prince Majister of Vallia, before the old emperor died, given false credentials, a fake glamour, made out to be a fighting man, when in truth he's nothing more than a ninny.''

"I'd heard that. But I thought those old stories had been disbelieved by now.''

"Some folk were gulled. But we've been told the truth. We know what kind of a devil Dray Prescot is. Cunning, cowardly, scheming, as soon murder a friend and run from an enemy as stand and take decent handstrokes like a warrior.''

"You've been told?''

He let a satisfied smile twist his lips. I'd summed him up as a decent sort of fellow, one who followed his profession with devotion, probably pushed into it when he'd been so young and wet behind the ears he knew no better. But, at that, a real paktun on Kregen, a man of honor, has no need in those terms to feel shame. I'd known mercenaries one would put down as a blight upon civilization; others helped to ensure that that civilization endured.

"Oh, yes, dom, we've been told. We know the truth. Prescot is no good. Even if he was as brave as two zhantils, which he isn't, he'd still be evil and crooked and ripe only for the chop.''

Patiently, I said: "It is difficult to believe—''

"Would you believe it if it came from his own family?''

So, then, of course, I knew.

To delay, now, the moment, I said: "He has a son Drak, the Prince Majister. He is fighting you now. He has a daughter, the Princess Majestrix—''

"And who knows where she is? No, dom, this Prescot's daughter, Princess Dayra. She knows her father only too well. She's had trouble with him before. She's the one who knows the truth.''

My fist closed on the jug, and clenched, and I could not speak.

Tom the Nose drank ale, flushed with this imparting of high affairs. I felt sick. I managed to get the jug to my lips, and drank, and wiped the back of my hand across my mouth and did not say: "By Mother Zinzu the Blessed, I needed that!'' although it was true, by Zair!

"She must hate her father.''

"Hate? No. She told us, just before the Battle of Corvamsmot. Contempt, that's what she feels.''

"Did she—did she ride out to the battle? Did she fight?''

"A princess? Not likely!''

Little he knew of the princesses I knew, then. . . .

I had to go on, although Tom the Nose would start to wonder pretty soon at my insistence on matters so far removed from our station. "But you mean she urged you to go and fight her brother?"

He put his stein down. It was empty, and I signaled the Fristle fifi nearest with a replacement. As the ale was poured Tom the Nose picked his teeth, reflecting. He looked just a little puzzled.

"Well—she was there, on the high platform when we formed ranks. Most of the talking was done by King Vodun Alloran and his Kapt-Crebent, a great noble who had been cheated of his estates and inheritance by this Prescot."

Patiently, now, stalking the meanings like a leem, I said: "Oh? Who was that, then?"

"A great noble called Zankov."

So it all began to fit into place . . .

"Zankov? Just that? Nobles usually have a long string of names—"

"Of course! But he called himself that until he'd won back his rightful titles from this Dray Prescot."

No true paktun was going to get fuddled on three or four steins of ale in the mid afternoon. Tom the Nose was prepared to talk on while I bought the drinks. There was little more he had to say on these scores that burned so painfully in my brain. I decided that I'd better go and see Naghan Raerdu, Drak's spy, and sort something out of this mess.

As I say, Tom Poll the Nose had little more to say until, as I was rising to leave, he looked up.

"You ought to change your mind. There will be good pickings in Vallia, although we of the Corrundum Korfs always respect the proprieties in these matters. We do not go in for wholesale rapine and slaughter against the ordinary folk. It's these nobles and emperors who cause the trouble—"

"You are indisputably right there, dom."

"Well, come with us. Anyway, whether what the great Zankov says is right or wrong, and whether or not the Princess Dayra told him or not is all beside the point." He suddenly looked fierce, his bountiful nose quivering with a new menace, quite without mirth. "I lost my mother and father when I was a youngster, and I never knew my grandparents. But I wish I had. Any person ought to respect their parents and grandparents."

"Agreed—"

"This Dray Prescot, Emperor of Vallia—d'you know how he got to be emperor? Why, dom, I'll tell you. He murdered the old emperor. He killed the Princess Dayra's grandfather. D'you wonder she wants to be revenged?"

I tottered out.

This was so new, so shattering, so—

I came to my senses wandering along the Street of a Thousand Clepsydras. People looked at me and then walked on swiftly. I'd been very fortunate not to have been taken up.

The Suns of Scorpio were very low, streaming their mingled radiance along the street and turning everything into a golden-tinged glory of amber, jade and ruby.

The taste in my mouth was of ashes, and dungheaps.

By the time I reached the Zhantil Palace the Suns were gone. I did not feel hungry, just empty.

Then I said to myself: By Zair! So I am Dray Prescot, Emperor of Vallia, for my sins. I was fetched to be the confounded emperor and I've tried to do a decent job and have the place in a reasonable state for Drak. All right! It's this bastard Zankov—the man who really murdered the old emperor—who's poisoned Dayra's mind against me. Quite apart from my absence on Earth which she blames on me—rightly enough, given her understanding. That, I thought, was settled when she refused to strike when she might have done. I marched up toward the gate with the little sentry boxes, and the two guards stiffened up into columns of iron. What my face must have been like, Zair alone knows. Right, I said to myself as I marched on through, Right. That does it. I'll settle Zankov's hash and tell Dayra the truth—when I can find the girl—and she'll believe me. Oh, yes, she'll believe me.

With that high-sounding and exceedingly hollow promise to myself, I went in to seek Naghan Raerdu.

"Sink me!" I said to myself as I marched along the palace corridors. "When Pompino gets back what am I to say to him when he asks me what I've been doing all day?"

I had the nastiest of suspicions that Pompino and Framco would return without Tilda. This was just a hunch, of course, and depended on no cerebral deductive efforts on my part. They might catch up with Twayne Gullik; they might not. Tilda might be with the Ift; she might not. All I could do was repair my fences by questioning Naghan Raerdu.

I found him superintending the broaching of barrels for the evening. He was fussy, for where ale was concerned Naghan was a connoisseur. The ripe smells in the cellars, the tang of dust, the gonging notes as the slaves worked, the lively feeling of the slaves all served to rouse me. Naghan Raerdu was of Vallia, a good man, and he had abjured slavery. Forced to conform to the customs of another country, he did what I hoped any modern Vallian would do. The slaves were well treated and they knew that this job, broaching ale barrels and bringing supplies up to the mess halls and dining rooms of the palace, would hold plenty of perks. They'd get a skinful tonight, or they weren't smart know-it-all slaves!

"Jak."

"Naghan."

"You look—if you will pardon my saying so—mind that spigot, Olan the Fumble-Fingered!—as though you have had bad news. I trust I am mistaken—hammer it in soundly, you great fambly, Nodgen Nog-Ears!—for your new comrades and the cadade have not returned nor sent a message."

"It does not concern them, Naghan. I must talk to you—"

"Assuredly, assuredly, Jak—tilt the bucket, you enormous heap of famblys!—catch the ale, the wonderful ale!"

Froth spilled across the stone floor. Naghan did not go down on his knees and lap up the spilled beer; he might well have done and no one feel surprise. He had proved loyal and wise during the affair at the Headless Zorcaman. I felt he could be trusted; that was not the reason I wished to talk to him.

Presently, the barrel chuckling itself empty into the procession of carrying buckets, Naghan could devote all his attention to me.

I gave it to him straight.

"Says you murdered the old emperor, does she? H'mm . . ." Here Naghan pulled a face. "One can well see why she hates you."

"I intend to take this Zankov by the neck and choke the truth out of him, so that the Princess Dayra makes no further mistake."

"A highly desirable ambition, Jak, if uncomfortable for Zankov."

"You never saw him?"

"No."

"A pity. Still, you'll recognize him—"

Naghan Raerdu had kept half an eye on his slaves as they carried the ale away. Now he turned to face me.

"He's here, in Port Marsilus?"

"Probably. That is what I want you to find out."

"That, of course, I can do."

I told him what I'd been doing and he nodded, and the tears squeezed out from under his closed lids. "They'll take their fine fancy new army across and the Prince Majister will whip 'em, like he did last time."

"This fellow, Tom the Nose, and he seemed your decent paktun, was mighty confident."

"Name me a recruiting Deldar who isn't."

"You were Relianchun of the Phalanx, Naghan. We don't employ mercenaries in Vallia. I am confident that Drak will whip 'em; but it's up to us to do what we can to help him before this damned army even steps ashore in Vallia. It would be a beautiful thing if they never did so."

"Your son, Prince Drak, saw them off at the Battle of Corvamsmot. He will do so again, if we can't prevent the army sailing." He looked around; we were not overheard, all the same, he leaned closer. "Majister! Brace up, brassud! You give me a queasy in the inward parts."

Naghan Raerdu and I were old campaigners; I took no offense. Rather, I felt a quick spurt of gratitude to this short chunky barrel of a fellow with his red face and his blob of gristle for a nose. By Zair! I was not acting like your high and mighty emperor—which I was not, anyway—and I had to get the future into perspective. My own personal problems had, as always, to be pushed aside to serve greater ends.

"You're right, Naghan, by Vox. You find Zankov for me and I'll try to put things right with the Princess Dayra. Also, there is the kovneva Tilda to worry me—"

"Us."

"Yes, Naghan. If we Vallians can't stick together, then the whole wide world of Kregen will tumble down."

"My people," said Naghan, and I did not inquire what he meant. Any good spy will set up an apparat as soon as he can, and it was clear that Nagan had recruited people to go about spying for him. In all probability many of them just didn't realize what they were doing for this happy laughing merry fellow who was so lavish with ale and gold. "They report the city has seen more Ifts than usual recently. I do not wish to sound negative or pessimistic; but I fear the party of

Ifts and the three wagons your friends chased after do not carry the kovneva Tilda with them.''

"You do not surprise me. I felt that in my bones.''

"I am having inquiries prosecuted.''

You had to laugh when Naghan Raerdu said that. He was so unlike the chief spymaster of Vallia, Naghan.Vanki. I'd set up my own inner circle of espionage, independently of Naghan Vanki, not because I mistrusted the spychief but because I wished to have my own sources of information. The thought made me say: ''What are Naghan Vanki's people up to here?''

His laugh was a wonderful phenomenon of nature; his cheeks glistened, red as Zim, his closed lids sprayed tears. He spluttered. At last he said: ''They poke and pry. One of 'em—Nath the Long—signed up with the army and they put him to peeling momolams, the great fambly. Another of 'em—Ortyg the Sko-handed—broke into the Headquarters building at night and only got away with half his trousers missing. I tell you, Jak, Naghan Vanki, for all he is a clever spymaster, needs better folk to serve him. At least, by Vox, here!''

From this it was perfectly apparent that Naghan Raerdu had a source of information within the official Vallian spy network in Bormark. This seemed to me eminently satisfactory. I just hoped Naghan Vanki never got to find out. Loyal to Vallia, he was a dry master at his craft with whom I'd had a few run-ins before now. . . .

An under-chamberlain clad in his fussy flunkey robes came in looking all hot and bothered.

"Naghan Raerdu!'' he called. ''You are to be blamed! You must keep a tighter control on the slaves, who are fit only to be beaten.''

"Now what?''

"Two of them are rolling down the half-stairs, drunk as kovs. And they spilled the buckets—''

"Pandrite rot all!'' yelped Naghan. ''There's no harm in a few slaves getting a bellyful of ale like any honest fellow. But when it comes to spilling the precious fluid—'' He scuttled off on his waddling legs, scarlet and snorting, and I took myself off, mightily cheered despite all.

Naghan did not work for the palace, he supplied ale and superintended its initial distribution. The under-chamberlain would no doubt get the rough edge of Constanchoin's tongue when the grand chamberlain recovered. Who would have to pay for the spilled ale would most certainly prove an enjoyable exercise in argument and legal debate.

Suddenly discovering I had an appetite I headed for the mess hall. The place would be practically empty; that would not worry me.

At the end of a cross corridor a woman stood looking down as I approached.

My way lay off to the right. At the time, just why I looked at her with such sudden interest did not register. I just looked. She stood completely still and composed. She wore a long pale blue gown that reached to a circle around her feet. Her hair shone a glimmering auburn. Her hands were folded before her, half-hidden in the full sleeves of the pale blue robe. Her head was bent down, shielding her face, so that I had only a suggestion of a small nose and high cheekbones. I walked on and a hurrying slave passed, getting out of the way, in the natural reflex of his daily life, and when I looked back the woman in blue had vanished.

Thinking no more, my thoughts on a choice vosk pie, or perhaps a prime cut of ordel steak, I hurried on toward the mess hall.

Just before I entered I saw the woman in the blue robe again. She stood in exactly the same posture, fixed and unmoving, her auburn hair a bronze shimmer in the lanternlight. As I looked she shimmered, wavered, vanished. I blinked.

One of Framco's guards, hurrying to get to his evening meal, almost collided with me as I hauled up.

He started to swear, saw who I was, and apologized.

I said, "Did you see that woman? In the blue robe?"

"Yes," he said. "She went into the mess hall. I wouldn't mind making her acquaintance."

He went on and I followed. The woman had vanished, it seemed to me, far too quickly to admit of a normal method of going into the hall. Maybe I'd missed something, maybe I'd blinked at the wrong time. All the same, as I went in to find a seat I reflected that the woman in the pale blue robe had taken herself off mightily fast. Mighty fast!

Also—she was nowhere in the messhall I could see . . .

The meal turned out to be Leavings Pie, and none too savory leavings at that. Raerdu's ale was on the table, fine and frothing, and after a single jugful I pushed the plate of

Leavings Pie away and stood up. It would be a tavern and a lash-up meal for me, this night.

The clothes I'd worn all day could do with a change, and once more I plundered Pando's wardrobe. This time my outfit was of the refined yet adventurous sort a young blood might wear when he went on the town. If they had anywhere here in Port Marsilus to compare with Ruathytu's Sacred Quarter, then I was dressed for the part.

The color combinations of gray and green and blue were entirely conventional. The puttah over my left shoulder in a base of apple green reeked of gold wire and embroidery. Gold and silver embellishments smothered the rest of the outfit. The low boots were soft-leather engraved and encrusted with gold, almost as fine as the leatherwork of Magdag. My hat, very dark gray, sported a dark blue feather in its jeweled clasp. Knowing Pando's fortunes I wondered if the jewels were superior fakes; they looked genuine but I did not test them. I felt this would demean Pando and me—foolish fellow!

With this fandango of clothing draping me I ambled off to the city. If you wonder that I thus fabulated myself in phantasmagorical clothes—well, I'd done it before and was to do it again. I looked your true fop, me, who was far more used to swinging along in a scarlet breechclout wielding a two-handed Krozair longsword!

Finding a slap-up meal—that cost the better part of a golden deldy—in the Paline and Brunestaff, I washed it down with a miserly allowance of ale. When I shifted onto wine I needed to remain crystal clear. The Paline and Brunestaff was a superior establishment. Most of the patrons were senior officers of the military services. That was why I had chosen it. I tended to stick out like a coy in the arena's kaidur pairs.

Striking up conversations was easy enough, particularly when the wine went around; discovering anything of moment was quite another venture. I found out nothing. No veiled hints, no cautious questions, elicited what I wanted to know. They started singing when the Twins rose in the night sky to shed gold and rosy light upon the cobbled street outside. The lanterns inside the tavern swamped that moonshine outside. They began singing with a Pandahem ditty: "The Song of Patoc Punji the Neemu."

I didn't mind that. It starts: "When I was a lad in jolly old Panj, my life it was a bore-o. Then I went for a paktun to be, and made my name in the war-o." This is, as you will readily perceive, a poor translation; but it conveys something of the original. Patoc Punji went on his expeditions, performing incredible feats, rising from the rank of Patoc to that of Deldar, and thence to Hikdar, and—in some versions—to Jiktar before—horror!—he got himself into trouble with the lord's lady, and found himself busted back down to Patoc again.

So, as I say, I sang along with the rest, trying to think I was accomplishing something, anything, of help to my quest. Then they started up on "The Swingeon of Drak the Devil."

The tune was a famous old tune of Vallia. The words were, apart from being obscene, grossly contemptuous of Vallia. So, I went out, fuming, helpless, and ready to go back to bed.

You could in all honesty say that the Emperor of Vallia had been bested by a song. The way I felt. . . .

The troubling factor was that Pandahem ought to have been in alliance with Vallia, since Vallia had been instrumental in flinging out the hated Hamalese conquerors. I'd had some of this stupid nationalistic intolerance in Hamal. By Vox, I said to myself, I'll have a few sharp questions for Pando when he gets here.

So, feeling I'd accomplished nothing and found out unwelcome facts, a day not so much wasted as unwanted, I crawled back to the Zhantil Palace.

CHAPTER TWELVE

Of the Pied Piper of Port Marsilus

The next morning I awoke and rolled over and groaned. One of the fancy tooled leather boots lay in a corner of the barracks and the other halfway along the side wall where I'd hurled them the night before. I went along to Pando's apartments and routed out a somber kit of grays and blues, and then trundled into the mess hall where the morning porridge was not laced with red honey, and the bread was stale, the palines wilting and the tea weak. Disgruntled, I ambled along to see Naghan Raerdu.

Here was I wasting my time on bad commons, doing nothing, only finding out unwelcome facts, when my comrades were out no doubt having exciting adventures chasing rogues through the forests.

As I walked along the corridor toward Naghan's cellar entrance a slave girl undulated up to me. She wore a gray slave breechclout and her feet were bare; but she had a flower in her hair, which was combed, and a string of beads around her neck. She pouted up most artfully, and—I swear it!—fluttered her eyelashes.

"Horter Jak—"

"Well?"

"My master requests you see him at once."

"He does, does he," I said, most weakly. "And who may your master be?"

"Why, the Alemaster, of course, master."

"Lead on, for that is where I am going."

She led me past the cellar door and through a curtained archway into a narrow room where on shelves along one wall row after row of crystal bottles caught the morning sunlight through a high window. Apple green and palely pink, that morning light of the twin suns, Zim and Genodras. They were called that quite often in North Pandahem, for the culture of the island is split between north and south. Down in South Pandahem Zim and Genodras were often called Far and Havil. One pair of the most common Pandahem names for the Suns is Panronium and Panigium; one heard them sometimes from the older folk.

Naghan Raerdu was carefully siphoning a deep orange liquid from one crystal flask into a retort. He looked up, nodded a cheerful good morning, and finished off his task.

Then he said: "Thank you, Saffi. Now run along and find me a nice loaf of bread and a piece of Loguetter. I am famished."

The slavegirl, Saffi, nodded and ran off instantly. She was an impish thing, with smoothly rounded shoulders, and a swing to her hips. I fancied Naghan would manumit her in Pandahem terms the moment this assignment was through.

He looked out of the door, closed it almost shut and stood so that he could see through the slit if anyone should come by. Over his shoulder, he said: "I have certain news that Strom Murgon Marsilus will reach the city today."

I felt disappointment.

Then I said: "I was hoping Kov Pando would be here first."

"My source was imprecise. She seemed to think the young kov was on his way. She said that the king was much displeased with him."

"Now that is a disappointment. I had cherished a thought the king was dead, burned up in his palace."

"That is why he bears so heavily on Kov Pando. He blames him for the fire."

"As I said, Naghan, my comrades set that fire in the temple of Lem the Silver Leem that was underneath the king's palace. When I find the temples here, we will burn those also."

"Praise be to Opaz. There is no word on the Ifts."

"If Pando is in trouble with the king," I said, fretfully, I admit, "that will heap more problems on his shoulders. I just hope his mother Tilda is found before he arrives."

"That ninny Trandor the Broad, who claims to have been an archer before his fingers were chopped off, is headed this way. He will gossip, mark me. Can you meet me in the Awkward Swod at the hour of mid? It is in the Kyro of the Sword. I have ale to deliver there."

"Yes. Any reason?"

"I hope to have intelligence of Zankov by then—hai, Trandor, you old soak! Come to cadge a few mouthfuls, have you?"

Trandor the Broad smiled and grimaced, a lowly servitor in the palace and not a slave. He possessed only the thumb and little finger of his right hand. A barbarous practice, that, reminiscent of the Hundred Years War on this Earth. Some nations fear bowmen above all else.

I walked off with a polite word to Trandor and a mock thankyou to Naghan for wares I had not sampled, and so trundled off to find a decent breakfast. This accomplished at a little stall in one of the side streets off the main Avenue of Triumph, I thought that I had a few burs to go before meeting Naghan. In that time I might redeem myself in my own eyes.

Depressingly enough, there were plenty and to spare of folk walking about sporting the brown and silver favors.

With so many Leem Lovers openly flaunting their allegiance, even if only the cognoscenti—in their estimation—would recognize and understand, there shouldn't be too much difficulty in finding one of their Opaz-forsaken temples. I followed a few Brown and Silvers, and the more I went about Pando's Port Marsilus the more I was dismayed. The place seemed alive with the evil cult. At last I selected a place that had once been a theater of some kind and was now in ruins. The door looked solid enough and the loungers outside lounged with a purpose. All were armed. There were at least a dozen. I wondered if news that their temples were being burned had reached the cultists here.

Down a side street and around the back I went, and found three fellows talking on the corner. The back of the theater had been propped up at some time; but the walls looked perilous. These were just the sort of premises the cult might choose. I sauntered up to the three. All wore the little silver leem and the tuft of brown feathers.

They didn't waste time.

"Shove off, dom. Move along!"

"But," I said, in a high falsetto. "I only wanted—"

"You'll get a smashed skull. *Schtump!*"

So, I, instead of schtumping, leaped for them.

I drew two-handed and used the hilts on them. They went to sleep peaceably enough, one, two, three, ob, dwa, so.

Their limp forms had to be dragged into the rubble out of sight. This I did. I confess I was drawn on. I'd intended merely to scout this place; but one thing led to another, and, well, I penetrated past the outer ruined wall and so came across a fine new wall, built of baked brick, with a new door of lenk, bronze bound. This opened to a touch. All beyond lay swathed in darkness but for a distant ruby wink of light. So, in I went. There was no excuse. I chafed for something to do after the days of relative inaction. What Pompino would say I didn't care to dwell on.

The ruby light from a lantern illuminated a turn in the corridor. At the far end another door tempted me. I tried to tell myself to turn around. Quite clearly, this *was* a temple to the Silver Leem. Ergo, return, fetch up Pompino and a gang of our lads, and deal with the foul place. But, on I went, like any onker.

The door led into a maze of alleyways and storerooms, mostly disused, at the back of the building. As I cautiously worked my way forward I was sorting out the combustibles in my mind, seeing what would burn easily and what might need a little encouragement.

The sound of crying drew me to a small door with a single opening, iron-barred. Very quietly, I looked in.

The room was jam-packed with little girls. Children, not above six years old, I'd guess, most of them naked but a few with dingy scraps of cloth around their waists, they lay supine or huddled in foetal positions, they ran about screaming, they fought each other, they added to the filth of the room. They were all gargoyles of mud and dirt, as though just dragged in from the gutters. You could carve a slice of the smell and serve it out on a plate.

Down at the far end of the room an opening door made me duck down until only my eyes showed above the iron-barred grille. A woman wearing a yellow smock and gloves walked in. She just hoicked up the nearest child, swung her over her hip in a most professional fashion, and walked out.

The door was solid, iron-studded, and I wasn't going to break it down in a month of the Maiden with the Many Smiles. That child had been taken off—for sacrifice, for torture, perhaps just for experiments, training in how to chop up a baby girl. There had to be a way around to the back through the maze of corridors. I started off, hurrying. . . .

For the sake of the person concerned, it was fortunate that I bumped into no one on that crazy rushing progress through the dusty ill-smelling rooms and corridors.

Evidently, the front of the abandoned theater had been turned into the temple, and all these backstage areas used only occasionally or never. Keeping my bearings and twisting through the twisting corridors I hurried on and so came into a small foyer-like place with double-doors to my right. These were bolted on the inside. Faintly—very faintly—from outside came the sound of animals' hooves and the grinding rattle of wheels. Ahead a door with a glass panel gave ingress to a chamber I felt reasonably confident must lie at the opposite end of the room of children. Only a fellow in a yellow apron tried to stop me and I put him to sleep, with some care, and looked around.

An opening to the side glowed with orange light. From there came the sound of cries, and splashings, and the tinkle of running water. I stuck my head around the edge of bricks framing the opening.

The woman I'd seen take the child out was bending over a bathtub. The child in the tub, yelling blue murder, was being given a thorough, a rough, a very hard bath. There was soap in the girl's eyes; that was for sure.

Rows of white dresses hung from a line of pegs. On a side table stood an open box bulging with candies.

I knew this set-up of old.

There was even a cabinet full of pretty satin ribbons.

I took the woman by her yellow clad shoulder and turned her around. She did not hesitate. She tried to hit me with the soaped scrubbing brush.

That powerful instrument went flying. I looked at her.

"You are a dead woman if you make a commotion."

She stared back, flushed, her brown hair in rat-tails over her sweaty forehead, her forearms hot-water pink. She had that hard, institutional look about her, perennially harrassed, suspicious, always on the lookout for number one and ways to beat the system.

The child was rubbing her eyes and bawling.

Soap flew. I shook the woman. "You have stolen these children from their mothers. Is that any work for a woman?"

She spat back at me. "They are not stolen! Each one has been paid for—"

"Aye," I said. "Aye, paid for by a silken dress and gold coin."

"The bargain was just. The guards will cut you into very small pieces—"

"As small as you would cut these girls into?"

"You do not understand." She wasn't afraid. She was just impatient that some boorish buffoon had happened along to interfere with her work. No doubt she had to get a certain number of the children ready in time.

Now I faced a quandary of some magnitude. Just how many girl children there were I could only guess; certainly no less than twenty-five and probably as many as forty. By Krun! What a mess!

"What do you want?" The lines around her mouth showed a pinched look. "I must bathe ten girls—"

"You will not be bathing anymore, I think, for what you intend. They will be bathed, in love and care; but not by you or any of your harridan crew."

She sneered, and—despite all—you had to acknowledge her courage. "What can you do? Let them all go into the street? Don't you think the guards will be here soon?"

So, feeling the idiocy of the bravado, I had to say: "Let them come. They can all die if they choose."

Tired of this fruitless wrangling I hoisted her upside down and shook, and among a cascade of oddments out fell the keys. I upended her and dumped her down, hoicked the child out of the bath, not without a soapy chubby finger whistling perilously close to my eye, and heaved the woman in.

Her knees stuck up past her nose.

"Stay there. If you cry out, or try to run off, you are most certainly a dead woman."

"There is no need to call or run for the guards."

With those ominous words floating behind me I ran to the door, opened it and then surveyed the appalling sight within. If you imagine an ant's nest, disturbed . . . Well . . .

Not having a pipe handy I'd not be able to play the Pied Piper. But some device had to be discovered to organize the girls, just for the time it would take to get them out—of course! I scuttled back, ripped out the box of candies and nipped back to the door. I held up a sweet and threw it to the nearest girl. The one I'd taken from the bath hung onto my legs, and bellowed: "Banje! Banje!"

"Here," I said, and gave her a sweet.

The others caught on quickly. I backed off. By Zair! What an unnerving sight! A host of unwashed naked girl children, all screaming and howling and rushing down on me demanding candies! I just fled.

I did not drop a single sweet until we were at the bolted double doors leading outside. Here I gulped a breath, said a prayer to Zair, and unbolted.

In those few seconds the girls reached me and were all over me, clawing at the candy box. I put my foot against the door, closing it. I seized up the girl from the bath, who was chewing her sweet with dedication and demanding more.

"What is your name?"

At last, she mumbled out something that sounded like: Lobbi."

"Look, Lobbi—over there. Wouldn't you like a nice new dress? And a pretty ribbon?"

She was off like a woflo after cheese.

The other girls saw, and between grabbing candies from

the spilled box and plundering the dresses, they resembled the ladies—and gents—on opening day of the January sales.

By the time each girl, grubby as she was, had struggled into a dress—and, by Krun, half of them didn't fit—I felt it was past time for the guards to appear.

The double-doors opened easily enough. The Suns said it was almost to the hour of mid. Naghan Raerdu would have to wait. We trooped outside, and I went last, and then, late but deadly with their swords and spears, the guards rushed after us.

The woman bath attendant led them, the soap suds still glistening on her yellow smock.

"There he is!" she screeched. "The vile Lem defiler! Kill him!"

CHAPTER THIRTEEN

The Little Sisters of Impurity

There were only six guards, and I felt I could handle them, allowing always for my caveat that one day, apart from Mefto the Kazzur, I'll meet a better swordsman. There was no time for fancy work. The children were out on the street, gawping, some still crying and huddling, but enough of them wandering off. Those loungers on the corner, who lounged with purpose, should not be allowed to see their sacrifices wandering off. . . .

So it was a case of skip and jump, of duck and bash.

"Take that, you tapo!" screeched the first, a fine big Rapa with bright yellow feathers around his beak. I took the flung spear from the air and almost in the instant he cast it it returned embedded in his chest. The woman screamed and urged them on, getting in the way. The next two, Rapas both, seeing what had happened to the first bore in with their spears at the port and a few quick and meaty thwunks had to be dealt to see them off. One fell awkwardly, breaking his spear which jammed in alongside his body, point up.

The next three, the final three, came on together. They wielded swords. Two foined—a waste of time in a bashing match of this description—and went down and the last faced me, his thraxter held in a professional fighting man's grip.

The woman pushed him on, shrieking: "Get on, Nodgen, get on and spit him!"

He gave her an impatient thrust of his free hand, clearing her out of his way.

"Stand back, Mitli, stand back—"

She tripped on a body and fell helplessly. The point of the upright spear pierced her through. Even as this fellow Nodgen, who was a bit of a swordsman, yelled and charged again, I saw the bright blood leap from the woman Mitli's mouth.

"Stand and fight, you tapo! By the Blade of Kurin, you are for the chop now!"

He was very good for a mercenary, not a paktun, hired out as your ordinary kreutzin, a light infantryman. He wanted to fight as he had always fought, sword against sword, and to him the victory.

There was no time for that.

I took him with a nasty little trick that left his thraxter twirled up with my main gauche while my rapier went stick-plink through his throat above the brass rim of his leathers. He choked and dropped.

Instantly, the bloodstained blades naked in my fists, I had to hare off to round up the wandering children.

Controlling their direction, I found, could best be accomplished by shouting: "Naje! Candies!" to them, and shooing them along. Only when we'd crossed that street and were well down the next could I afford to relax a little. A couple of folk hurried past, avoiding us. They were gauffrers, with flat hats pulled well down over their rodentlike faces, minding their own business. City folk, gauffrers, suspicious of trees and grasslands, making their varied livings out of city customs.

The half-imbecilic face I'd put on to assuage any fears my ugly old beakhead might inspire in the children did little to reassure the gauffrers. The bloodstained weapons in my hands. . . . Well, on Kregen that sight is not as infrequent as it ought to be. Carefully wiping the blades on an inside flap of the little cape I wore, I thrust them back into their scabbards.

A matched pair I'd received as a gift from Captain Nath Periklain aboard *Schydan Imperial*, they ought not to be maltreated. Then we set off on the next stage of this Hamelin-like progress.

This crocodile of girl children could be taken down to the docks to join the other children we had rescued aboard *Tuscurs Maiden*. What Captain Linson would say almost made me decide to do just that. They could be taken back to the palace. Wherever they went, they and I would attract attention and the spies from the Leem Lovers would smell us out. Wherever we went we'd bring grief with us. . . .

That meant *Tuscurs Maiden* was out of the reckoning. The girls would have to go along to the Zhantil Palace. It was high time that young rip Pando took the running of his kovnate seriously. If he faced grief from the adherents of Lem the Silver Leem, that might make him shake himself up. If he still pretended to be a member, maybe he could get away with that. Either way, I wanted to unload this pathetic collection of human and juvenile detritus—for that is what the girls would be in the eyes of most folk in Port Marsilus—and get on with the job. For a start—Pompino would gape at me when I told him of this damned adventure, and say: "By Horato the Potent, Jak! And you didn't burn the temple down!"

Huh, I said to myself, he should've been there!

The chances remain problematical whether or not I might have shepherded the girls all the way safely to the palace. We passed along the street before the low-doorwayed entrance of a building of slate roofs and many small windows. Few people walked the streets this close to the hour of mid. Over the doorway which crouched bowered in Moonblooms a sign showed up in weathered gold leaf. The gold leaf was a reminder of past glories.

The sign said, simply: "If you are of impure heart you are welcome, stranger, for purity exists only with the Dahemin."

Without pulling the bell cord I pushed the low door open and we all trooped through into a flower-bowered courtyard. The Dahemin, the twins, the god Dahemo and the goddess Dahema, had fallen out of favor when the green religion of Havil was new. The pious women here, the Sisters of Impurity, kept up the old mysteries and beliefs. I felt I could appeal to them for help. If I could not, there was nowhere else as far as I knew in all the city.

The Sisters oohed and aahed over the children and, fluffing

clear yellow kerchiefs around their noses, led the girls off to be bathed. This bathing would be of an entirely different order from that in the Silver Leem's temple. The Mother Superior—to give a bowdlerized form of her title—made me sit down to a glass of parclear and a plate of miscils. As the tiny cakes melted on my tongue she asked me and I told her. I told her that the adherents of Lem the Silver Leem would seek out the whereabouts of the girls to take them back for sacrifice. I did not expect her to keep them here in her house of seclusion. I did not tell her where I intended to take them.

She said her name was Mistress Mire. She was not old, clad in a severe gray gown with a rope girdle and bare feet, a flap of gray cloth over her hair, which shone most beautifully. The Little Sisters of Impurity ministered to any who sought their services, and the small charges they made sustained them in their frugal way of life. I refused to pass any judgments.

Pompino's gold spilled out of the purse onto the table between us. I'd take up a loan from Pando next, if necessary. Sister Mire smiled her sweet smile.

"We can offer you a refreshing personal service—"

"I am in need of keeping an appointment, sister. I hope I do not offend by this refusal?"

"When you feel the imperfections of the spirit and the flesh, you will call on us. We are here to minister to your needs in the supernal name of the Dahemin, man and woman both."

"Quite. I give you thanks. I will make arrangements to collect the children later when the Suns have gone."

There was clear disappointment on her face. No doubt she was hoping I'd just leave the girls and clear off. They'd make a capital addition to her house of seclusion when they were a few seasons older.

When I left I started to make the rote farewell along with the remberees—"May Pandrite have you in his keeping." I halted myself. These women followed a religion old before the religion of Havil, which here in Pandahem had been materially supplanted by that of Pandrite. She might have considered that I blasphemed her. In impurity are all hearts as one.

As they say in the inner sea, the Eye of the World: "Only Zair knows the cleanliness of a human heart."

Bidding Mistress Mire remberee I hurried off to the Awkward Swod, keeping a sharp lookout. Naghan was still waiting.

He'd secured a side table under a wide black beam, and ale stood upon that table, and a meal which, covered, was still edible.

"Trouble, Jak?"

Eating, I told him. "I'll have to arrange tonight to——"

He lifted a hand. "Leave all that to me."

"My thanks."

"It is now certain that Kov Pando follows Strom Murgon as fast as he can. It is said that when they meet one will die."

Naghan would have messages carried by relays of merfluts, or possibly some other form of Kregan homing pigeon. Merfluts are exceptionally fast and reliable.

"And Pompino is not back yet, I'll warrant."

"He is not."

"And no message from him?"

"None I'm privy to."

I didn't say that if Naghan Raerdu knew of no message it was certain sure no message existed. But that was so near the truth as to convince me Pompino had sent no message. Or, rather, no message had been received at the Zhantil Palace.

He drank and then said: "I must tell you that this morning someone unknown burned down the Vallian embassy here."

Quelling my annoyance was not difficult; after all, with the temper of this place it was a wonder they hadn't burned our embassy before this. I said: "Was anyone hurt?"

"No, thankfully enough. The ambassador sought refuge in the palace. It adds another complication."

"Too right it does, by Chusto! I don't want him catching sight of me up there."

"Strazab Larghos ti Therminsax knows you well enough, I'd think, seeing he received the title of Strazab at your hands."

One of the Vallian diplomatic corps, Larghos ti Therminsax was an earnest, serious man who, loyal in the Times of Troubles, had made a career in the diplomatic. As a strazab, an imperial creation on a level with a strom in the regular nobility, he was of the right rank to be ambassador to Bormark. In fact, ambassadorial status was high for a mere kovnate within a kingdom, and that was because of my personal feelings regarding Pando. I frowned. I'd been using the Zhantil palace as a base; I didn't really fancy poking around to find a new.

With a squeezing shut of his eyes and a copious flow of

merry tears, Naghan said: "It may be that Strazab Larghos will happily return to Vallia. If it is suggested."

In rather too sour a voice, I said: "Well, you can't suggest it to him, and neither can I."

Naghan Raerdu was not discomfitted.

"I will go down to see Captain Linson and have a messenger return with word from Vallia. It can be arranged. Strazab Larghos can be recalled."

"H'm. It might work. Although Linson's a stickler, and you'll have to cross his palm with gold, not silver. And that reminds me. I paid all the gold I had to the Little Sisters of Impurity—"

Naghan Raerdu laughed so much he almost choked.

"—so, my friend, I shall crop your ears for a loan."

"Done, Jak, done!"

If Strazab Larghos believed a Pandahem argenter brought the signal for his recall from Vallia, it would be a wonder. But honest and loyal though he was, he'd be in the frame of mind for a recall. Then I expounded my scheme to Naghan, and he listened, growing grave, although every now and then whetting the throstle with a glug or two.

At one point he said: "I refrained from setting anyone on to keeping an observation on you. I surmised you would object."

"I'd have been glad of some help when those poor girl children were running about all over the street, I can tell you!"

"Just so. The riding animal is easily obtained—a trotrix, or hersany—?"

"No. A freymul, I think, the poor man's zorca. That will suit the style."

"You'll see to providing the robes and badge yourself?"

"Oh, aye," I said. "I'll see to that."

"Until you spoke so freely to me I had taken little interest in this Lem thing. There has been little time. But I fancy, with some help from Opaz, that I can insinuate a fellow into—"

I looked sternly at this unlikely-looking secret agent.

"I caution you most strongly, Naghan. The Leem Lovers have their rigmaroles of secret signs and passwords. If you try to put any poor fellow in without sure knowledge, he's done for."

He rubbed a finger around his blobby gristle nose.

"I believe I have paid good red gold to just such a one. A little questioning more, a little suggestion—and the fellow has a girl, too. She might be the more useful."

"Just don't get good people killed on my behalf."

We were sitting comfortably in a tavern, the Awkward Swod, and drinking and eating and taking our ease, and we plotted dark doings and nefarious expeditions. What we decided could cause many deaths, could cause riots and conflagrations, and not always to the evil ones of the world. We had to step with great caution.

Naghan said: "Just in case, then. Tipp the Kaktu. Monsi the Bosom."

"I'll remember."

As I may have remarked before, a number of times, if you want to stay alive and in one piece on Kregen you have to remember names.

"My information contains nothing on Zankov, Jak."

"Confound it! By Chusto! I was hoping—still, no matter. He'll turn up like a hole in your sandal."

"Strom Murgon will be coming in through the west gate. The Inward Gate is not grand enough for him, it seems."

"As they say in a place I know—when the chavnik's away the woflo will play."

"I'll meet you there in three burs."

"Capital."

Naghan rose on his stumpy legs, puffing, finishing the last of his ale. He plunked the jug down, lifted his purse and unlatched it and thunked it down on the table. I picked it up. It weighed.

"My thanks, Naghan."

His laugh was a marvel of compression and of explosion. The one of his eyelids, the other his tears.

"You paid it to me, Jak, you paid it to me."

"Aye. And you'll have it all returned, with interest. I'll see you at the west gate in three burs."

On that, with the remberees, we parted.

Going out of the Awkward Swod into the streaming mingled radiance of the Suns of Scorpio, two thoughts made me reflect that, one, it was a grand comfort to a fellow to have loyal helpmates, and, two, it was just as well that Pompino the Iarvin was still not with me. By Krun! I'd have had one hell of a job keeping his itchy fingers off a tinderbox!

CHAPTER FOURTEEN

Strom Murgon puts on a show

Pando's chief city of Port Marsilus was set into a cup-shaped indentation of the coastline on the western edge of the Bay of Panderk. Consequently, the north and eastern sides were washed by the sea, and the southern flank, being walled off by a ridge of ground the locals called the Spine of Lhorcas, the road wound in and around this ridge and so fetched up with the main gate of the city, the west gate.

There were other gates; I fancied, along with the judgment of Naghan Raerdu, that Strom Murgon would choose to ride in through the chief gate of the city.

Murgon Marsilus, Strom of Ribenor, cousin to the Kov of Bormark, stood no nonsense from anyone. A powerful man, dark of temper, an adherent of Lem the Silver Leem, he was not content to lord it over his little stromnate within the kovnate; he lusted after greater power.

If Pando was in trouble with King Nemo—and why hadn't he burned up with his damned palace?—Murgon would step forth more openly in his ambitious designs.

They both craved this Dafni girl to increase their domains and power. When two men want the same girl, and the girl has a mind of her own, empires may totter and fall. I did not know how much credence to put in Tilda's words when she'd told me that Dafni Harlstam had settled on Murgon and then Pando had happened along to upset the arrangements. If he had, it could mean that Dafni Harlstam herself had wanted that. Otherwise Pando's suit would have fallen.

But, then, he was a kov. Dafni was a vadni, and her vadvarate of Tenpanam marched border for border with Pando's lands. It was a coil. Maybe I'd have to wring the answers

from each of them in turn. As to why it concerned me, that
was obvious. One, Pando was a friend. Two, I was the
Emperor of Vallia. And, if you cared to admit it, Three, we
hadn't much liked Murgon Marsilus, even though he had put
himself in jeopardy to rescue us from a scrape.

He'd done that because he thought Pompino and I were
adherents of Lem the Silver Leem.

Three burs exactly saw Naghan Raerdu trot gently up in the
shadows of the west wall. He rode a freymul and he led
another on a headrope. Both animals were fine examples of
their breed. He saw me and halted and dismounted. His face,
in the shadows short still in mid afternoon, looked a mere
splodge. I guessed he was laughing. He tied the second
freymul to a hitching ring stapled into the wall. Plenty of
people were about, going about their business, with the gray
slink of slaves gliding unnoticed through the throngs. Then
Naghan mounted up and trotted off. I ambled over.

The freymul had a scrap of paper tucked into his harness.
One word—FRUPP.

"Hai, Frupp," I said, knuckling in behind his ears.

He bowed his head and twisted it around. Freymuls do not
have the single spiral horn of the zorca, and they are, although willing in their fashion, limited in performance. This
Frupp had curly amber streaks below and a chocolate-colored
coat. His eyes were bright. I liked him instantly.

Along the wall beside the gate sat a line of beggars,
cripples, folk in buckets, folk on crutches, folk hideously
disfigured, women exposing themselves to show deformities
and scars and the tied ends of amputations. By this time in
my life upon Kregen, that wonderful if horrific world four
hundred light years from Earth, I had become, if not inured to
sights like these, at least understanding of them. This was one
unpleasant facet of life. Some of these people were in the
begging profession. As small children they would have been
mutilated by their parents, all in the name of earning a living.
As usual, I distributed a few coins; but too great generosity,
harsh as this may sound, was a mistake.

Among those pitable morsels of near-humanity, I wouldn't
mind taking a wager, squatted one of Naghan's people.

The noise burst all about me, chaffering people, the beggars whining, saddle animals jingling, the discordant music
from the juggling troupe. Outside the gate lay the main
Wayfarer's Drinnik, the wide space where caravans formed up

or disbanded. Although this scene was wildly familiar in
many aspects, and even although the Star Lords—as I thought—
had for their own purposes imposed some uniformity upon
peoples and customs, there was no doubt I was in a foreign
land. This scene before me was not one that would be enacted
in Vallia, or even in Havilfar. The elements might appear to
be the same; the underlying structures might appear to share
the same rules; but the effects were totally different. Kregen
is a world of violent contrasts, and of uniformity, and of a
never-ending wonder.

An armored man astride a hersany clip-clopped in through
the gate, followed by a string of calsanys, all laden with straw
baskets, two each side, lolling along held by the guide ropes.
Guards prowled. This was a caravan destined for some spe-
cific destination and pleased to be within the walls before
sundown. The juggling troupe carried on, and now they were
rivaled by a group performing some kind of primitive play,
full of bladders and false tails. A musician with all his
instruments lashed about him jigged up and down and, I
found with pleased surprise, producing a not unattractive
melody—punctuated, of course, by many bangings of the
drums and the cymbals between his knees.

I mounted up on Frupp and gently guided him out through
the gate when space permitted. I wished to attract no attention.
Outside and past Wayfarer's Drinnik the land opened out.
Here all the trees had long since been cut down. Any lord
with any sense does not allow cover for hostile archers within
bowshot of his walls. The track stretched away, rounding the
curve of the Spine of Lhorcas. I ambled along astride Frupp.
Presently the forests began, closing up to the road. This made
me fret over Pompino and that rascally Ift, Twayne Gullik,
and the fate of the Kovneva Tilda. What I was doing riding out
like this had seemed to me to be a sensible idea. I'd catch
sight of Strom Murgon early on.

That wouldn't help. Not really. I was riding to still the
quiver in my nerves. So, incontinently, I turned Frupp's head
and rode back. He did not complain.

I needed to find my turkey; that would be more fruitful.

Riding easily about the streets might not prove to be the
best plan. But it was no use leaving it too late.

I needed somebody not too unlike me. The obvious problem would be that the fellow would be well-known. How to
legislate against that concerned me; apart from asking him,

there was no way I'd find out. Eventually, I found a likely recruit to my nefarious plans just leaving a tavern, the Boiwink and Clooke, reeling just enough to betray him to my grasping fists. . . .

This happened down the side alley into which he'd reeled to relieve himself. He made not a sound. I didn't particularly want his clothes, which were not greatly different from my own—or, rather, Pando's—or his money or weapons. I took his waist-length cloak, which, gray on the outside, was brown on the inside, edged with silver lace. His badge—that I had. The silver leem was finely chased, the tuft of brown feathers rampant. I trusted this fellow was not too high up. His pouch yielded what was perhaps the most important necessity of all—his silver leem mask. I'd worn these things before. It fitted up on leather straps, a snarling vicious countenance all whiskers and fangs. Once a Leem Lover wore his or her silver leem mask, all restraints vanished.

The mask went back into the velvet-lined pouch and was hooked onto my belt. His purse was one of those vainglorious items you could buy in the flash zouks, a thing of stringed netting so that the gold within could glint through and proclaim your wealth. It fastened with a jeweled clasp. Vainglorious, yes, and foolish, too. . . .

As I straightened up from the fellow's unconscious body the first shafting ray of ruby radiance of Zim shone down the alley as the great red sun of Antares dropped beyond the corner building. A party of tumps trudged past the end of the side alley. No doubt they'd come into the city to spend their gold for new tools to dig more, and for ale and provisions. They lived in their mines and caves in the countryside, and quarreled with the Ifts and anyone else. They saw the bright wink of gold, they saw me crouched over the body on the ground. Instantly, on their stumpy legs, their heavy-headed hammers raised and their beards flying, they charged.

Without any self-consciousness I jumped up and ran.

Bashing a posse of pint-sized tumps over the head was not on the agenda this evening. . . .

Also, and this I freely concede, short and stout though they are, and massively bearded, if a tump hits you over the head with his hammer you're likely never to hear the famous old Bells of Beng Kishi. Those hammers are reputed to stove in vosk skulls, although this I doubt.

Mounting up on Frupp I nudged him and obediently he

trotted off and out onto the main street. I turned toward the
west gate. There could not be much time left now. . . .

You had to say this for Strom Murgon Marsilus. He knew
how to put on a show.

First of all trotted a posse of trumpeters mounted on gray
zorcas. They tootled away, the golden notes blasting into the
warm evening air and proclaiming the imminent arrival of a
great lord. A strom is not ordinarily a great lord, just a lord of
the upper middle rankings. But Murgon had great plans.

There followed a troupe of dancing girls, scantily clad,
who scattered flower petals. Unquestionably they had been
brought along in wagons from Pomdermam, and would have
alighted and begun their flower-strewing dance just before
they entered the west gate. Onlookers crowded up, forming a
lane along which the procession wended its colorful way.

A half-pastang of hersany lancers rode next, and then the
first of the infantry, kreutzin in light equipment and little
decoration. A yell broke from the crowd at the next sight to
lumber through the gate. Murgon had brought a pair of
thumping great dermiflons, lurching, idiot-headed, ten-legged,
their blue skin glistening like olive oil under the Suns. They
were often a favorite with the ordinary folk; some nations
could not abide them. There was no doubt the people of Port
Marsilus considered them a rare treat.

More cavalry and infantry followed, the sword and shield
men, the churgurs, and—which interested me more than a
trifle—a whole regiment of swarthmen. These cavalrymen
rode their two-legged reptilian mounts with almost, almost,
the confidence of well-trained jutmen. I fancied the swarths
were new to their riders. Certain sure it was, the riders were
new to swarths.

Music of a tin-banging, rattling kind was provided by
splendidly attired bands which marched along at ear-splitting
distance. Murgon would have positioned his baggage wagons
at the tail of the procession, with a rough-rider band to look
after them. Folk might still hang about admiring the number
of wagons in a rich lord's entourage. If Murgon was as rich
as this show attested, he would have a sizable train. If he was
as rich as Pando had implied, he could never in a thousand
seasons afford all this.

The strom himself rode a black zorca, whose spiral horn,
adorned with silver, nodded up and down in a fretful way, for

Murgon held him on too tight a rein. The animal was superb. Murgon, too, clad sumptuously, looked superb.

His black beard, cut short, his sharp and haughty features, the level arrogant unseeing stare in his dark eyes, all stamped him as a notor of Tomboram. I did think that there was about him more than a hint, a definable impression, of defiance. Pinned to the front of his tunic, partially concealed by the massed gilt-lacing to the edge of his cape, he wore a device. From this distance what it might be was problematical to all save those who would know.

He wore the imago of the silver leem, with its brown and silver ribbons. Openly, the strom wore the badge of Lem the Silver Leem. Many a man and many a woman in the crowd wore their own silver leem badge, with the tuft of brown feathers or the brown and silver ribbons. They would know, and, knowing approve. . . .

The cheers that greeted Strom Murgon bellowed to the evening sky. They depressed me, by Vox, they depressed me.

I remembered how, in the cabin of *Tuscurs Maiden*, I'd discussed with Pompino the chances of Murgon or of Pando reaching Bormark first. It seemed that Murgon had won. He clearly had the people with him. He did not harm his chances or his popularity by the lavish handfuls of silver men dressed in fantastic costumes scattered from wicker baskets. Murgon was displaying his wealth, his largesse, and thereby his power. Again, I pondered—where was all this hard cash coming from?

Pando, in the nature of a kov, would be rich. The king was displeased with him, his cousin was buying his people—Pando was getting the cold shoulder, the Big E.

This, I believed, must tie in with the enterprise against southwest Vallia. I'd be hitting two birds with one shaft this night, I fancied.

Discreetly, after the great man had passed, I guided Frupp through the throngs, following on. Jollity broke out, Murgon's silver being immediately put to useful purposes.

Now I knew just how many stromnates and eltenates and other of the lesser nobilities existed in Pando's Bormark, for I had made it my business to know. I knew, also, who did and who did not keep up villas in the kovnate's capital city. Murgon maintained a modest villa along the Avenue of Miscils. . . . The procession did not make for the villa of

Ribenor. Oh, no, they headed for a certain tumbledown old theater.

Gradually, the bands ceased playing, the soldiers parceled themselves off to seek billets, the dancing girls disappeared, the men had emptied their baskets of silver.

With only a small escort and retinue, Murgon reined up before the old theater. People still followed him, and I was not at all conspicuous.

The twin Suns were almost gone. In the flaring light of torches his face showed, dark and brooding. I caught the fierce impression he dearly loved to order his men: "Clear me this rabble away!" Instead, he called a courteous remberee and then headed into the side street. One of his aides, a Gon whose bald head shone butter-bright in the torchlight, shouted: "The strom bids you all a restful night and he wishes you well and your wonderful families and now he wishes to be alone and will quarter in the Speckled Gyp and remberee one and all." All on a breath.

The high-class tavern and hotel called The Speckled Gyp did lie in the next avenue across. I did not think Murgon would reach there. He'd be in that side door like a leem after a ponsho, going through the dusty corridors, making his way to the chambers reserved for him. He'd be attending the rites of Lem after he'd eaten and freshened up.

Now that I knew his location I could see about my own inward hollowness. As Kregans are fond of telling you, there is nothing like six or eight square meals a day.

Trotting gently back to The Awkward Swod, I attempted to put the pieces of this puzzle together.

On the face of it, a kovnate like Bormark, or even a kingdom like Tomboram, would stand little chance of invading a still-powerful empire like Vallia. Oh, yes, Vallia was still rent by factions. The empire remained partitioned. There was a king in Evir in the far north, there was a king of Womox Island to the west, and now there was this King Vodun Alloran in what he called Thothclef Vallia. Also there were dissidents still resisting unification in the northwest of the island of Vallia. But with our capital at Vondium, and our armies and air cavalry and vollers, we were no pushover.

If Alloran made an alliance of convenience with this King of Womox, for instance. . . . He'd taken Katrin's kovnate of Rahartdrin. He was attempting to march to the northeast, which would bring him into immediate conflict with loyal provinces. My lad Drak resisted; but that blob-nosed Deldar, Tom the Nose, had merely confirmed what I suspected, that Drak did not have the best regiments with him. We'd all have to rally around: Delia could get regiments from Valka, Seg could send men up from Hamal—although, confound it! Seg was off somewhere lost in the jungles of Pandahem south of the central mountains. I'd call on Inch in the Black Mountains, and Korf Aighos and Filbarrka, and anyone else. We could not afford to allow a fresh collapse of our hard-won hegemony.

But none of the thoughts in my old vosk-skull of a head as I dismounted and hitched up Frupp revealed to me who might be financing this latest enterprise against Vallia.

Once the first bites were taken in the southwest, once the swarms of tazll mercenaries learned what was afoot, we'd be swamped with the rogues, reivers, flutsmen, aragorn, all the vile batteners on human misery that had before tried to ruin our land and whom we had thrown out. We'd be right back to the Times of Troubles again. . . .

So, troubled myself, I went into the tavern and ordered up whatever first struck my appetite, and ate almost without tasting. I went sparingly with the wine.

Vallia had been invaded before. No doubt Vallia would be invaded again in the future. However much a part of life that might be on a turbulent maelstrom of a planet, it remained damned unsettling, by Vox, highly unwanted.

However important my mission here was to destroy the evil cult of the Silver Wonder and not destroy but attempt to convert back to decency its adherents, maybe my responsibility to Vallia should come first. Once the island empire was whole and healed again, once the old empire had been re-established and the people lived together in harmony, these constant invasions would no longer take place. The reivers and flutsmen and aragorn of the world would think more than twice before they set out on an enterprise against Vallia.

Into the equation I must add the promise I'd made that I'd hand over everything to Drak, let him be the poor bewildered emperor, as soon as the empire was whole. Well, Deb-Lu-Quienyin, a famous and mystically powerful Wizard of Loh and a good comrade, had advised me to let Drak handle affairs down in the southwest. Drak was the intense, serious, level-headed one of my sons. He'd make a splendid emperor. But maybe, just maybe, I ought to have gone back home and sorted things out myself, first. . . .

I quaffed the last of the wine—I've no idea what it might have been—and tossed down two silver dhems, and then added a third to pay the reckoning. A Fristle fifi with a yellow apron and a green bow to her tail had been attentive and had put up with my absent-mindedness. She deserved recompense for my ill humor and reward for her smiling service. I stood up and she handed me my cloak and I found some sort of skull-faced smile for her.

The hostler had seen to Frupp, and I tipped him a few coins, and so mounted up and turned the willing and well-fed freymul in the direction of that infamous theater.

Under the archway at the end of the deserted yard, the hostler having taken himself off with his hand clenched on the coins, a lamp burned in a crooked holder. The iron bars shed bars of shadow across the yard. The scent of moonblooms hung heavily in the air. Under that crumbling archway a woman appeared.

She stood with her head bowed; but not bowed enough that I did not realize she studied me. Her auburn hair caught some of the lamplight; it did not shine in quite the way it should have; the angles and the shadows threw projections in the wrong places. Her long pale blue gown draped in a circle about her feet, and her hands were folded into the sleeves of the gown.

She stood, silent, unmoving, her head just that tiny bit bowed, her nose and her high cheekbones washed with a light I swore did not come from the lamp above her head.

Abruptly, she moved.

Her figure wavered, as objects swim beyond heated air.

I started forward on Frupp, anxious to question her.

She looked up, and then she looked around. I saw a face that, piquant and dainty as it was, yet held a darker and more profound power than any elfin face might hold. She looked at me, and her eyes took in my senses, and she lifted a hand as though to ward off a blow.

Then she vanished.

She vanished.

I was not discomposed—well, not overly so.

Apparitions and ghosts, these are not unknown upon Kregen.

Only a moment ago I'd been thinking of Deb-Lu-Quienyin. I would not have been surprised, I'd have been overjoyed, if he had appeared under the archway. Wherever he was, in Vallia or Valka, or down in Hamal, he could put himself into

the trance state of lupu and using his kharrna send out a
ghostly image of himself to survey what might be of interest
in distant places. Good old Deb-Lu! But he did not appear, and
the lamp under the archway shone on stone and cobble.

Frupp's ears pricked up. He reacted uneasily to these weird
comings and goings. I patted his neck, bending forward,
soothing him.

Now if, I said to myself as we trotted out under that
haunted archway onto the street beyond, now if I knew whose
side you supported, mysterious witch-lady in the pale blue
gown, that might be more than useful.

One fact was absolutely certain and without doubt.

On Kregen it is a far far better state of affairs to have a
witch or a wizard on your side than opposing you.

By Vox, yes!

CHAPTER FIFTEEN

Dafni

When I contemplated what might lie ahead I had half a mind
to go along and torch the temple of Lem the Silver Leem. The
temptation was very great. Mind you, as I may have remarked on previous occasions, many of my blade comrades
would agree with vast enthusiasm that, yes indeed, I did have
only half a mind.

If I wanted to find out the truth behind the enterprise
against Vallia, it behooved me to proceed with far more
caution than I would have done if it had been a mere case of
burn, hack and run, or if Pompino were here with free advice.

The excitement engendered by the strom's arrival lingered
on in the streets and squares of Port Marsilus. Folk would be
up late this night, roistering. Everyone bore an eager look, as
though they all knew exactly what was going on, had a hand

in it, and couldn't wait for the off. That this was a totally
misleading impression was beside the point. They were merely
caught up in the atmosphere. But, with the problems I had,
that impression was galling, I can tell you, damned galling.

Going along gently on a slack rein I neared the abandoned
theater that was now a hidden temple. The sound of hoofbeats
astern and a chorus of shouts warned me, and I nudged Frupp
into the side, out of the roadway. I reined in and sat, hunched,
my face down under the hat, watching.

A party of zorca riders rattled past. They conveyed the
impression of flaring cloaks, feathered hats, the dark glimmer
of weapons, a bunched group of riders on an errand of
importance.

They clustered about the figure of a girl, for as she passed
me the light of a torch fell across her face under the hat. A
girl, then, surrounded by armed men. Escorts are of two
kinds—those that protect you and those that imprison you.

The impression I'd taken, fleeting and as swiftly gone as a
snowflake falling into flames, was of a fine pallid face with
wide dark eyes. The look, and I could easily have been
mistaken, on that face was of absorption, a kind of rapt inner
awareness that denied exterior objects. I shook Frupp's reins
and walked him on toward the temple.

The party of zorca riders turned into the side alley.

By the time I'd reached the mouth of the alley they had
vanished.

People who had moved aside to let the cavalcade pass now
resumed their apparently casual evening strolls. About half of
them were mounted, so I attracted no attention as I allowed
Frupp to go easily with the drift. We circled the building, and
on the farther side the people moved into the shadows under
an overhang where an arch, much weathered, supported a
flying wing of the place. I went along.

A row of stalls to the side accommodated the riding animals,
and hostlers in brown tunics took charge as the people alighted
and entered the building. Without a word I dismounted,
handed the reins to a villainous-looking fellow and followed
on. Casually, I turned the waist-length cloak inside out so that
the brown side showed, the silver bullion thick along the
edges. Around me the flowering of brown and silver glinted
menacingly under the light of torches.

In the random and erratic shafts of light we all went
through into the foyer where debris and splintered beams told

anyone looking in that this was a deserted and abandoned place. As we went along, the silver masks came out of the pouches. The light flicked from silver eye-holes, silver whiskers, snarling silver masks of primeval savagery.

I put the silver leem mask on, thankfully, over my face. At least, I would not have to suffer the bee-sting agony of holding a different face for too long a time.

Beyond the portal in the far wall where guards stood ready to deal with any unwanted intruders, the congregation turned left and right to enter the auditorium. Lights spattered the curtains concealing the stage. The floor was swept. People stood in clumps, talking in low tones, waiting. I eased along to the side, taking as my aiming point any one of the small exists under the side balconies. What struck me most forcibly was the casual lack of real secrecy. Despite the guards, despite the obvious attempts to make the old theater appear as merely an abandoned building, the Leem Lovers were arrogant in their use of the place. They congregated here, and if any outsider observed them then he knew what he could do—keep silent or suffer the consequences.

Voices suddenly lifted in what was a coarse way over by the other side of the auditorium. People moved in an agitated way. I stopped under a balcony and looked back.

Presently the cause of the disturbance reached the group of men and women nearest and they turned to one another, gesticulating, obviously annoyed, and yet, even so, subdued.

"It is so disappointing," a woman protested.

"Tomorrow, my dear. We shall come back tomorrow."

People were now leaving the hall.

Walking quietly up to the group I had no need to ask what had happened, for the woman's husband turned to me and said: "The strom has canceled the ceremony for this evening. He gives no reason; but quite clearly he is tired and we hear important developments have taken place."

"Quite," I said, and went back into the shadows under the balcony as though mightily disappointed. Well, by Krun, I was and I wasn't. The auditorium cleared of people; before the last of them went I slid through the side exit and found myself in a long dusty corridor. Down this I went, padding lightfooted.

The first door, half-open, showed a room full of dancing girls. They were taking off their jeweled bangles and beads, unpinning their feathers, and putting their clothes on. Among

the apim girls and Sylvies and Fristles were three lieshas and
a couple of numims. I was surprised to see the lion-girls, for
numims are generally above that sort of occupation.

Two doors along I found a room full of guards, also standing down from duty, coughing and spitting and stacking their
spears and looking forward to a night off drinking. I scuttled
past there rapidly and went on.

More rooms lay empty, dusty and cobwebbed. Here I was
on the other side of the building from where I'd found the girl
sacrifices and their bathing establishment. I prowled on.

The fellow who'd turned and told me the ceremony was
canceled for this evening had referred to Murgon as the
strom. This, alone, was intriguing. Normally the Leem Lovers concealed their identities under a farrago of nonsense
names, all high-flown and pompous. This, surely, must be
just another example of the power and eminence the cult had
reached here in Bormark.

Toward the corner of the building I came across a stairway
leading up. Just a simple wooden affair, it led through an
opening onto a higher corridor. At the foot stood a man in
half-armor, carrying a sword, who stared at me in my leem
mask and said: "They have all gone, no one—"

He said no more as he sank down, mightily surprised, I
feel sure, that the world had gone black. I dragged him into a
doorway and left him breathing heavily, out to the wide, and
padded quietly up the wooden stairs.

These old buildings are often warrens of tiny rooms. The
sound of voices led me to a narrow window at the side of a
closed door. There were two voices, and one of them was
Murgon's. Without a doubt. I remembered that harsh, over-
powering and yet resigned voice. The other voice was that of
a woman.

I put my eyeball around the edge of the narrow window,
looked in, and listened.

"You will marry and that's an end of it!" Murgon's voice
pulsed with menace.

The woman was the one I'd seen ride up here closely
surrounded by her escort. Her pallid face, still half hidden by
the flap of her hat, looked distraught.

"I cannot, Murgon! It is against nature to ask me!"

"You will!" He reached out both hands and shook her by
the shoulders. He put his face close to hers, shouting. "You
will!"

"No—please—"

He had his two cronies with him, the giant malevolent Chulik, Chekumte the Fist, and the sly and slinky Dopitka the Deft. They stood to one side, watching, ready instantly to do whatever Strom Murgon commanded them.

The woman crumpled. She slid to her knees, her arms trailing down Murgon's body. She stared up under that silly hat.

"Dafni," said Murgon in that grating voice. "There is no sense arguing. This you must do—this you will do!"

As though unable to argue longer, her head lowered, and she lay, trembling, grasping his knees. It was not an edifying scene.

Murgon gestured to his henchmen.

"Take the vadni away." Then he added, almost as an afterthought: "Treat her gently."

The two plug uglies started forward.

Now, as I may have mentioned before, on Kregen it seems to me rescuing ladies from villains is a perfectly normal occupation. You usually have to be quick. There is no sense in hanging about. Unlike other normal occupations on Earth, it's a job at which you can get yourself very messily killed.

Still wearing the snarling silver leem mask I kicked the door in and leaped.

Chekumte the Fist simply hauled out his sword and rushed at me. His tusks, gilded and polished, caught the light from the samphron-oil lamp. His dangling pigtail flew out like a bolt of blue rope. I did to him what Pompino had already done once and he flew up and over and fell, to lie snorting. Then I did to Dopitka the Deft what Quendur the Ripper had done to him and he fell to lie beside his fellow.

Murgon's rapier was out.

As he flew at me he tangled up with the lady Dafni. I eluded that first attack, gripped his wrist, ready to pull, twist or break, and Dafni, shrieking, fell all over us. Murgon caught me a nasty whack alongside the head. For a moment dizzied, I stumbled back. The rast nearly had me and I just managed to evade his savage thrust. Dafni fell all asprawl against him, I jumped up, head ringing, to hit him and he toppled back over the girl. His head hit the floor. He sprawled, rapier tinkling away. I shook myself.

The blow had struck shrewder than I'd realized. Maybe there was not the full campanological chorus of Beng Kishi's famous Bells—but my head clanged like an old bucket kicked over down an alley on a moonless night.

A hand to my head I staggered up. The four of them slumbered. What a mess! Vadni Dafni came up in my fists and I slung her over my shoulder. She flopped like a sack of meal.

"By Krun!" I said to myself. "The things a fellow does!"

Out the doorway and with a swift look up and down—no one in sight—and a careful pad down the stairs—still no one about—and a cautious quiet prowl along the dusty corridor—and still no one to challenge me. I could taste the dust on my tongue. The smells were laced by the after-scents of the dancing girls' perfumes.

There seemed to me to be few chances of getting away scot free. Someone was going to be about still, that is the nature of the beast. Instead of re-entering the temple area I turned in the other direction and wended on, looking for the first doorway out. That the door I found was bolted had little to do with it. I put the lady Dafni down, propped against the wall—where she immediately flopped over like a baby—and gave the door a thumping kick. The bolt snapped.

The night breeze blew in, scented with the fragrance of moonblooms. Moons shine glistered on cobblestones. A corner of the building jutted here in an angle where the roof dropped low, and a couple of the loungers who did not lounge were just strolling back. Watching them, I waited until they turned in their apparently casual amble. Then I leaped.

The luck that was with me in that they had been at the far end of their patrol when I'd kicked the door open persisted. Both men went down without a sound. I straightened. For all I could see in the Moons shine, no one had seen me.

I ran around to the front of the building. A couple of the hostlers in their brown tunics hung about, and the stalls contained perhaps a dozen or so riding animals. My freymul was brought out and I mounted up. Over this matter of tipping, a little dash, I could betray myself if they didn't go in for it between the members of the cult here in Port Marsilus; and although it went against the grain to hand out money to the people in brown tunics, I handed down a couple of silver coins.

"Our thanks," said the fellow with the most silver spattered over the brown. He took the money all right.

I trotted off, letting Frupp flick his head up and down as though pleased to see me again.

By the time I'd ridden around to where the door I'd broken open flapped more than I liked, I was reassured that the hostlers suspected nothing. Also the pain in my head, still throbbing, was beginning to lose some of the scarlet claws that dug into my brain.

The lady Dafni lay half on her side, half on her front, sprawled, and she made snoring sounds that, I felt convinced, would have offended her had she known she was making them. I hefted her up, went outside and arranged her across Frupp. Freymuls, like zorcas, are close-coupled animals with room enough for two people if they squeeze up tighter than peas in a pod. I decided to walk alongside. The silver leem mask would have to come off now. It had served well, the damned thing, and I stowed it away in the velvet pouch.

Frupp and I with our limp burden walked sedately through the nighted streets of Port Marsilus.

There was going to be a pursuit, as surely as Zim and Genodras would rise in the morning sky.

No sense in rushing along in a galloping lather, attracting the attention of everybody on the streets this late. Just a nice careful walk along in the shadows, with the girl over the saddle held gently, and Frupp acting as though well aware that he carried a burden somewhat different from that to which he was accustomed.

In the kyro where we had first been ambushed I wended around on the shadowed side. The memory of that first attack made me screw my head around, watching every opening and doorway. A couple of passersby gave me a look; but I'd put on a nondescript face, one of the sort that Deb-Lu-Quienyin called a gyp-face, quite unremarkable. Deb-Lu's powers as a Wizard of Loh had enabled him to overcome ferocious sorceries, and give me sage advice, and they had taught me through his own charisma how to alter my own harsh physiognomy.

She of the Veils rode the night sky, flirting with skirts of cloud, gilding the night with beauty, casting roseate shadows through which I walked with Frupp at my side. The lady Dafni was showing signs of returning consciousness, and I wanted to be along the avenue and into the palace before she awoke.

The guards in their little sentry boxes were a couple of Fristles I recognized, men serving under ord-Deldar Naghan

the Pellendur who, I trusted, was keeping the palace function-
ing and intact. I say I recognized these two cat-men; they did
not recognize me.

They stepped out and the two spears slapped across forming a saltire to bar onward progress. I halted and Frupp let a
little ripple of breath escape his nostrils. I patted his neck,
and said: "All right, all right, old lad. The stables and a bale
of hay are coming right up." Then, to the Fristles: "Lahal,
doms. Naghan the Pellendur, ord-Deldar. He'll want to see
me at once, or before that if it were humanly possible. I'll
wait inside, if I may, while you summon him or a patoc—
patoc Lurgan Crooknose might be on duty now, might he
not?"

Lurgan Crooknose happened to be a Fristle whose name I
recalled from hearing Naghan the Pellendur bellowing at him.

The cat-men took no offense at my easy way; they carried
out their duties punctiliously, bidding me stand fast, not
letting me through the gate—whereat although not faulting
them I waxed a trifle warm, and looked back over my
shoulder—waiting until patoc Froindarf the Clis arrived.

I said: "Patoc. Kov Pando sends me with this lady to his
palace. You—"

He interrupted. "You seem to know a deal about us. You
ask for Naghan the Pellendur, so you must know he com-
mands here while the cadade is away. Yet—how could you
know this if you did not spy on us?"

Mind you, I ought to have got rid of that confounded
gyp-face before this; but I'd been dwelling on other items in
the night's doings. I went on with great patience, realizing the
farcical waste of time this was; but trapped by my own stupid
cleverness.

"You are right to say I spy—but I spy for Kov Pando." He
moved across to the freymul and lifted a hand. One of the
guards hauled a torch from its becket and swung it over
Frupp.

"This lady," said patoc Froindarf the Clis. "This is the
Vadni Dafni! You'd better bring her in." He ran back to the
gate and helped to open it wider, and yelled: "Send for
handmaidens! Hurry! The vadni needs assistance!"

Frupp ambled through. Just as the gate was pushed shut,
and I put my shoulder to it, I can assure you, I saw through
the closing gap a string of torches debouching from the
avenue, and the dark exaggerated forms of zorca riders, and

the wink of steel. The gate slammed solidly. I let out a breath. And—I nearly lost that gyp-face. It did not sting overmuch, and I could hold it for some time.

The courtyard buzzed with activity. Naghan the Pellendur arrived, sorted out the confusion, and came over to Frupp. Dafni was assisted down. She opened her eyes as she stood up, supported by a couple of scantily dressed handmaidens hastily dug out, and she looked about in a bewildered way.

"It is all right, my lady," I said. "There is nothing to fear."

"Where—oh, this is Pando's palace—I recognize—what? How did I . . . ? Murgon!"

"Hush, my lady. Murgon need no longer concern you. You have been rescued from his clutches—"

For a moment I thought she would collapse again. The handmaidens held her, trying to fuss, patting her clothes straight. Then she drew a deep breath and opened her eyes and looked at us surrounding her. She could see the concern on our faces.

"By the agate-winged jutmen of Hodan-Set," she whispered. "It is scarcely to be believed."

"Kov Pando will be here soon. You must rest and recover from your ordeal."

"Ordeal? Yes, you are right. You were the man who burst in wearing the silver mask? Yes, I remember—"

"Then forget that, my lady. Murgon can no longer harm you here. You are now under Kov Pando's protection. All his people will care for you."

"Pando. . . . So I am here, then. It is da'eslam. What I am fated to do I will do. Da'eslam."

The lady Dafni Harlstam, Vadni of Tenpanam, put out a trembling hand to clutch at the handmaid, and she burst into a torrent of tears.

CHAPTER SIXTEEN

Mindi the Mad

The lady Dafni, so Tilda had told us, was a vivacious girl.

Tilda was right.

Too right.

There are a couple of apocryphal squibs, not, I hasten to point out, attributed to San Blarnoi, which go something like: "Why is language called the mother tongue, because father doesn't often get to use it; and when a woman tells a doctor she is exhausted he asks to see her tongue."

Yes, Dafni chattered.

She recovered from what she kept on referring to as her "Ordeal." When, the following morning, I turned up in different clothes and wearing my ordinary face, I was able to ooh and aah along with the rest as she told her story again and again. Vivacious. Yes, she was that, all right. That and a lot, a whole lot, more.

Pompino and Framco the Tranzer arrived back during the day. They brought all the people with whom they had set out, not having lost a soul. They did not return with Tilda or Twayne Gullik.

Pompino was disgusted.

"Not a sight of 'em. Then we got a trail, turned out to be a bunch of idiot Ifts taking supplies back to their forests. Waste of time, complete and utter."

"You did not send a message."

"Not send a message? Of course we sent a—oh!"

I waited.

We were sitting in the mess hall, drinking sazz and parclear, for it was too early for wine. Framco said: "That messenger, then, either betrayed us or was waylaid."

"But you returned with everyone—"

"A numim who said he was going to the Zhantil Palace—he was not a great lord; but he had a retinue of stout fighting men—took the message."

"And you trusted him?"

"He was clearly a man of honor—"

"All numims look like that, for the sake of Pranxco the Gullible!"

"Well—" began Pompino truculently.

"Did he give you a name?"

"Of course. We made the pappattu. He was Mazdo the Splandu."

I said nothing more on that, and changed the subject of conversation immediately, by trying to tell Pompino that my priorities had changed, and not tell him why.

"Leaving me to burn the temples?" he said, outraged. ."Here I've been traipsing up and down those diabolical forests and you've been idling your time away here! By Horato the Potent, Jak! What are you up to?"

I couldn't tell him that these confounded people were hiring on an army to invade my home country. Rather, I could tell him, and after all the marvelings and wonderings, he'd just say something like: "Well, you know, Jak. You have to serve the Star Lords first!"

To hell with that. I had to stop these villains from invading Vallia. That was the priority number one.

"There wasn't time to burn the temple in the old theater because I was rescuing the lady Dafni at the time."

"Yes, yes, a fine handy piece of work. But the temple is still *there!*"

"I," I said with a great show of magnanimity, "left it all for you!"

"In all this," put in Framco the Tranzer. "What of the Kovneva Tilda?"

There was no sensible answer we could give to that heart-felt question.

I did not want to lose my freymul, Frupp, for I had grown attached to him. So I hummed and hawed, and then said: "There was a fellow in a silver leem mask who helped me with the lady Dafni. He brought her back on my freymul. Nath the Bludgeon, he said his name was. Useful. He—"

"Ah!" said Pompino, brushing up his whiskers. "Now we

are getting the truth! This fellow Nath the Bludgeon did all the rescuing while you were admiring the scenery—I see!''

"We-ell," I said, choking up a trifle, and determined not to let Pompino catch on.

"So now perhaps we'll find the real reason you didn't burn the confounded temple!''

I was saved on that one by the arrival of Constanchoin, just about recovered although still inclined to shiver a trifle when he saw me—which was a pity, really. He thumped his black balass wood staff down. He looked put out.

"All these children!" he said, crossly. "Do you know anything about them? They're running everywhere like a flood of tinklehoils who've just lost their tails."

"Ah, now," I said, and leaned back in my chair, and picked up a paline from the pottery dish. "Well, now—"

"Yes, Horter Jak?" Constanchoin had learned one lesson, apparently.

"They are the guests of Kov Pando. He will welcome them when he arrives. Just give them lots of sweets—bring in a Banje shop's stock, if you can."

"But they're getting everywhere! I just managed to stop them swinging on the bellropes—"

Framco the Tranzer started up, aghast.

"By Odifor! If they ring the bells . . . !"

"Quite," said Constanchoin in a kind of moan. "What are we to do?"

"Keep them occupied." I was glad the girl sacrifices were safe; they were the past at the moment, and only in the future would they become part of the present. That damned army recruiting to sail against Vallia. . . . That was the conundrum.

Murgon and the army, they were the present and immediate future. But I could not abandon Pompino. So I said: "They postponed their diabolical ceremony until tonight. No doubt they'll buy some more sacrifices." I rattled through what had happened with the smells and the bathing glossed over. Constanchoin, clearly, wanted to hear nothing of this and took himself off. Framco listened, pulling his whiskers and every now and again saying: "I don't know what we are to do."

Pompino crowed. "So you've been to the place twice, and it still stands! And all these girls—"

Warm, I snapped out: "We'll burn the dump tonight, if you wish. But we'll have to get any more sacrifices out first.

You burned a temple here. I do not see it has lessened the worshippers' zeal in the slightest."

"By Horato the Potent! You speak hard!"

"As I told you; we have to find a more successful method of uprooting the cult than merely burning temples. We have to change the minds and hearts of the worshippers—"

"Part their heads from their shoulders. That'll change their minds, ha!"

The arguing and wrangling went on and then, with an amusement in which I delighted, I remembered the catty remarks about Dafni and her incessant chattering. By Vox! These men had been nattering away fit to rival Dafni in full flow.

On Kregen there are many and various delightful stories concerning Hyrzibar, a shishi who exclusively serves the minor godlings of various mythologies. Her chatter fills many a fat tome and many a guffaw-worthy anecdote. The lady Dafni and Hyrzibar were, in the opinion of those able to make the comparison, well-matched.

From the vantage point of the battlements of the Zhantil Palace the Sea of Opaz glittered under the lights of the Suns. That sea represented a highway between Pandahem and Vallia. In my mind's eye I could see it filled with the sails of argosies, fleets of ships all bearing on toward Vallia, carrying hordes of armed and armored fighting men to invade and, once again, lay waste to the island empire I called home.

The thought of all I and my comrades had striven for once more being destroyed, put to the torch and the sword, hacked down, was not to be borne.

Out I went along the ramparts, ignoring my friends here, letting the breeze cool my fevers. Was I not Dray Prescot, Lord of Strombor and Krozair of Zy? Was I not the Emperor of Vallia? Well, then, I had to prevent that enterprise from sailing against Vallia, or clip its wings—at least, I felt the thankfulness, here in Pandahem they would have to use sailing ships. They did not possess the airboats of other nations, or the flying sailing vessels. They had no vollers to pelt through thin air and descend upon my land of Vallia.

A racket of footsteps on the ramparts at my back did not halt me. I strode on, feeling the breeze, staring at the dancing sea.

"Jak! What the hell . . . ?"

I took no notice.

Ahead along the stone ramparts by an embrasure stood a woman. Her head was downbent, and her pale blue robe descended in straight folds into a circle around her feet.

She lifted her head and the auburn hair blazed in a light that never came from the twin suns overhead.

Her mouth, small, amost black in that odd lighting, circled. She was speaking. I heard nothing, only the screeching of gulls as they chased tails over the battlements. The breeze blew, the Suns shone and a few high clouds parceled off toward the east.

She spoke to me. There was strain on that face. And I could make out nothing.

"By Horato the Potent! A ghost!" Pompino shoved up beside me, and I could hear his breathing, ragged and hoarse. "A witch, broken from the ib!"

"She is trying to say something—but what?"

The phantasmal form beckoned. A slim white hand lifted from an enveloping sleeve. And the lips writhed in panto-mime over words—a word—that I could not grasp.

A high, excited voice at our backs shouted.

"Mindi!"

She spoke now, a torrent of soundless words.

Then, as a feather is consumed in the Furnace Fires of Inshurfrazz, she vanished.

I swiveled.

"Framco—if that was Mindi the Mad, what was she trying to tell us?"

The Fristle cadade pulled his whiskers; but he looked fierce, determined.

"I think, horters, I am sure—she was saying Plaxing—"

"That is where the Sybli, Suli, said Tilda wanted to take her, on the evening we arrived."

"This," said Pompino, "could be some sorcerous trick."

"You said, Framco, that you did not trust Mindi the Mad."

"I do not. But she has been of great use to Kov Pando and his mother the kovneva in the past. I am not sure. . . ."

"It is certain sure we must send to Plaxing. That is the least we can do." Pompino sounded vexed. "I would offer to go. But time has been wasted, and there is a temple to burn. Framco, you will go?"

"It is my duty."

"Good. Then that is settled."

"There is one concern," I pointed out. "If we all go

haring off we leave the palace open to Murgon's attack. He may guess this is where the lady Dafni is held for her safety . . ."

Pompino spoke up with the obvious answer; although it was one I disliked muchly.

"The lady Dafni will have to go with one of the parties. And she cannot go with us, therefore. . . ."

Framco nodded heavily. "I agree. For her own safety she will have to ride with me."

I didn't like it. But it made sense.

So it was arranged. Orders were given. I was interested to see the way in which the Fristle, Framco; the Chulik, Nath Kemchug; and the Rapa, Rondas the Bold, acted, one with the other. I have previously remarked about the Rapas and Chuliks, and even more so this so-called hereditary enmity between Fristles and Chuliks is a matter of particular subdivisions of the races. At the least, these three specimens of their peoples rubbed along.

Rondas the Bold and Nath Kemchug would stay in the Zhantil Palace with the guards Framco would leave. They would deal with any attacks. They promised this in a species of sullen resentment that they were not included in our force to go and blatter the Leem Lovers.

Pompino was all fire and eagerness to start. He just wanted to work for the Everoinye and burn temples to Lem. I wanted to get hold of Murgon and obtain a few answers from him.

As though pointing up that Rapas and Chuliks and Fristles and most of the other splendid array of diffs on Kregen share with apims a divided heritage, Nath Kemchug came in swearing that: "He'd rather spend a sennight in the Cheerless Barracks in Vorcheng." And that, believe you me, by Chozputz, is a legendary location to set the shivers up anyone's spine.

Rondas the Bold said: "By Rhapaporgolam the Reiver of Souls! If any wight tries to break into the palace tonight, his beak will be bent to inspect his backside!" which is, as you will perceive, a mighty oath for a Rapa.

We took what comfort we could from this manifested fighting spirit of those left on guard.

Nath Kemchug had a clever trick some Chuliks are capable of employing. Always fascinated, I watched as he used the sharp blade of his spear, flat on, to polish up his tusks. He had such control of his weapons that the steel blade kissed up and down the tusk, sweetly. So, this time, I said: "If you'd stuck a few diamonds in your tusk, Nath, or banded them with gold, you'd find that trick more difficult.''

"By Likshu the Treacherous, folk who do that are plain mad! I don't hold with the custom, although it is common enough. For one thing, if you don't clean your tusks with extra care you'll get tusk rot for sure."

"I can believe it."

So, we divided our forces into three, and settled down to wait out the hours of daylight, we who were to raid the temple and we who would remain on guard. Framco led his party off to ride for Plaxing. We ate and rested and tried to contain ourselves in patience for the derring-do that lay ahead.

At the least, although we had kept away from most of it, we were now spared the incessant chatter of the lady Dafni.

Pando possessed a fine library and I sought solace there for a bur or so; but was driven out by half a dozen remarkably clean-looking girl children who rolled in with the utmost determination to get themselves as dirty as they could in the shortest possible time. As I scuttled off, one of the under-chamberlains panted in, puffing and sweating, trying to get the girls to come along and behave. It seemed to me that Constanchoin and his underlings were being most severely punished by this juvenile invasion, and I found that of a come-uppance most sweet. Opaz alone knew what we were going to do with the quondam sacrifices; I fancied a good life lay in store for them—if they survived the consequences of their own conduct. On that uncharitable thought I went off to get dressed up for the night's entertainment.

As we gathered in the courtyard I was instructed to learn that the Divine Lady Of Belschutz had, no doubt in some wayward and long-forgotten escapade, contracted a most painful condition affecting certain of her more tender parts. Captain Murkizon was on form, in fine fettle, and his swishing axe was going to be a danger to all his comrades until we got into action.

Larghos the Flatch kept asking people if they'd seen the lady Nalfi. No one had lately. In the general hubbub more jocose remarks were thrown at him than real concern; she had proved a girl of her own mind and spirit and Larghos was not having an easy time with her. Eventually he discovered her, so he told everyone leading her back and fussing over her, bravely doing up her own armor, trying to buckle the straps over her back. He strutted as he paced beside her, and one could not help feeling both sorry and envious—and a little of some emotion no sane man would give a name to—as one looked at him and the lady Nalfi together.

In the end it was decided that Lisa the Empoin and the lady Nalfi would not go with us.

They protested; they were overruled.

All day there had been no sign of Drak's spy, Naghan Raerdu. Carefully casual inquiries about ale in the pantry brought forth the information that Raerdu was expected tomorrow with a fresh consignment of Amber Spirit, a fine ale of which he could supply the finest quality. This was inconvenient; but I took comfort from the thought that had there been any startling intelligence Naghan would have found a way to convey it to me.

We set off in small groups, walking inconspicuously, riding separately. I'd taken pains to discover what there was to know of the ruined theater, and found that it had been badly damaged in a raid by the Bloody Menahem, repaired and then ruined all over again, only worse, during the time the Hyr Notor ruled in Pandahem. Its name was The Playhouse of the Singing Lotus. Fine and fanciful, I thought. A new playhouse had recently been completed two blocks away, called the Golden Zhantil. Pando had contributed heavily to its construction. Grimly, I wondered how long it would be before the adherents of Lem the Silver Leem took it over.

The Bloody Menahem, as the Tomboramin called their neighbors to the west, readied themselves for further raids against Bormark. Pando's province usually took the first brunt of the attacks from Menaham. Defeated they may have been in Vallia; the Bloody Menahem who had been the most vociferous supporters of the infamous wizard called the Hyr Notor would not long delay in having a fresh onslaught started against their neighbors.

As we went along through the dimness with only two of Kregen's smaller moons hurtling low above us in the sky, I reflected that it was a great pity that the Pachaks Pompino had signed on in Tuscursmot were no longer with us. Brave and loyal, devoted to their employers under their honor code of nikobi, they had been among the first to die during the affrays and combats we had endured reaching here. I thought of them and the fights we'd seen, and consigned their ibs to a successful passage beyond the Ice Floes of Sicce to the sunny uplands beyond. As you know, I have tremendous admiration and affection for Pachaks among the splendid diffs of Kregen.

The Twins, eternally orbiting each other and shedding light enough to reveal desperadoes to the eyes of honest men, even if the honest folk were thus illuminated for the drikingers, sailed into the sky. Some of the nearer stars paled; but the sparks of light above scintillated brilliantly. The air tanged with night scents. Ah, a night on Kregen! There can be no other planet in all this wide galaxy, it seems to me, to compare with Kregen—beautiful, terrible Kregen under the Suns of Scorpio.

So through the splendid Moons' glitter we went, and I recalled how I'd begun this adventure with the simple object of burning a temple or two. Then I had been deflected by what seemed to me to be more important objectives. What a single man was going to do against an army I was not as yet perfectly sure. That I must contrive something was the only thought in my head on that score. But, this being Kregen, I began this night's jaunt with one priority ousting another, only to come full tilt against what was in my estimation another and altogether overriding priority. . . .

Pompino's plan was simple, as he had indicated to me earlier on. As to the sorting out of who married whom, that had been materially furthered, I fancied, by the rescuing of the Vadni Dafni from the clutches of Murgon Marsilus. Ha!

"We all take different doors, bash 'em in, and throw in the firepots. That'll smoke 'em out, the rasts!"

So, that was the plan.

I'd demurred on one point.

Pompino's reply, brisk, no nonsense, summed it all up.

"Very well, Jak. We'll arrange a party to go in and get the sacrifices out. We'd better take—"

"No. I'll do it alone. I have the silver leem mask."

"You believe it can be done alone?"

"Yes."

"Then may the brightness of Pandrite shine upon you."

So, here we were, at the temple to Lem the Silver Leem and the firepots were being brought to a fine state of combustion, cloaks were thrown back from sword arms, and we were spreading out to cover every bolthole. I put on the silver mask and marched boldly into the entrance from which I'd brought the freed girl sacrifices. From here I could strike any way. Pompino would not burn here until the last.

In the event, striding out, I met no one who offered to stop me. This, I judged, had something to do with the amount of silver lace on the brown cape, and the embroideries which, as far as I could fathom out, put the owner of this rig around halfway up their devilish hierarchy. He must have been discovered by now. Entering at the back instead of the front, I hoped, would avoid any checks. The corridor matched the one on the other side, and I entered the auditorium under a balcony matching the one I'd sheltered in the previous time I was here. This time the place was full, agog with anticipation and expectant excitement. And the girl sacrifice was there, in her iron cage, to one side of the stage, with all the blasphemous impedimenta of the Lem cult spread out.

The place reeked of unwholesomeness. Incense stank. Candelabra burned, and I eyed these with a view to incendiary activity. No one took any notice of me as I joined the congregation.

The girl in her white dress in the iron cage sucked on her sweets and played with a scrap of satin ribbon. Next to her the slab waited, flanked by ranked instruments. The statue of Lem in a silver glitter hovered above.

Three turns of his pocket glass, Pompino had agreed, would give me time to infiltrate and position myself ready. My own sense of timing told me the three glasses must be almost spent. I eased a little forward. The stage remained empty of all save the girl sacrifice, and I was minded to feel disappointed on this score for I'd marked any of the vile crew who tried to stop me for instant destruction.

The high priests and their acolytes and sycophants did not appear just yet, and the congregation waited, talking, excited, keyed-up.

The crash of splintering wood and shattering tiles jerked everyone's astonished gaze upward.

From the balconies to either hand men leaped down, their weapons flashing in the lights.

These startling newcomers wore armor, and helmets tufted with yellow feathers. But their faces! Each warrior's face was covered by a mask—but not by any ordinary assassin's mask—oh no. As the fighting men leaped down and ripped into the shrieking congregation, their faces snarled with the savage and frightening golden semblances of untamed zhantils.

CHAPTER SEVENTEEN

A Rose between two thorns

Without hesitation I roared up onto the stage, leaping a screaming woman and kicking her companion in the face—quite accidentally—as I whipped up onto the boards. The girl in the cage held the scrap of blue satin ribbon before her face, her eyes wide, staring, not quite ready to start crying at all the hubbub.

Just about then the first firepots sailed in.

This place would burn like dry shavings.

The cage of the sacrifice, which, as I knew, sometimes held leems, was bolted. The bolt clicked back with a snick audible in the hullabaloo. I reached in.

"I have some more sweets for you," I said in what I tried to make a modulated and reasonable voice. "We're going to a special Banje shop—"

"You won't take me back?"

She drew away, the ribbon held like a shield.

I knew what she meant. These Leem Lovers knew where to go to buy their sacrifices.

"No. I promise you. To a Banje shop, that's where."

"There's a fire."

She spoke in her light treble, interested in what was going on, allured by the thought of candies, ready to cry or laugh as the occasion warranted. I flung a quick look back.

Pompino's lads were hard at it. Fire raced up the drapes and smoke roiled from two of the side openings flanking the main doorway. In the auditorium the zhantil-masked warriors were cutting down men and women indifferently and some, who appeared to be in authority, superintended the rounding up of those worshippers who threw down their arms and

141

surrendered. It was frighteningly obvious that whoever the men in zhantil masks were, they were not over-bothered if the Leem Lovers fought or surrendered.

I snatched up the girl and leaped for the drapes at the rear of the stage.

If I cut to the side through any convenient doorway I ought to get back to the clear way out. Thank Zair there were no more girl children imprisoned there.

Others besides me had the same idea. They knew the layout and a bunch of them followed me along the dusty corridor. There was no point in fighting them at this stage, for however much the itch might have trembled my sword arm, fires burst up at our backs, and if we didn't get out we'd all be roasted—the girl sacrifice and me along with the rest.

People who attempted to escape through other exits would be met by walls of fire. Up ahead the corridor stretched empty both of flame and smoke. Pompino's folk would wait until I was out—and they wouldn't wait overlong, by Krun—and then this place would fire up, too. If, that was, the temple hadn't burned down already.

Empty of smoke and flame this exit might have been—it was not empty of golden-masked zhantil men.

As we broke out of the last doorway and made for the double doors leading outside, a line of fighting men in the zhantil masks fronted us, weapons glittering.

Now anyone who resisted Lem the Silver Leem was an ally of mine. Also, I had an idea I knew who had sent these men here, who employed them, who would use the zhantil mask as an emblem in defiance of the leem mask.

It was no part of my plan to fight allies.

To the side lay the other corridor, and there might be a way past there, so that I could circle. . . . Clutching the girl child, who was now, most understandably, crying at all the din and confusion and the roar of the flames, the stink of the smoke, I turned sharply to break a way through. The zhantil-masked fighters crowded up to the rear. The Leem Lovers, yelling, pressed back. Smoke choked down, obscuring much of what was going on, and the evil crackle of the flames beat against the din of combat.

A hand clutched my elbow.

A leem mask glinted as a slender fellow in a short brown cape with little silver adorning its folds tugged at me.

"This way, Jak! Hurry!"

At his side a woman, more bulky than he, urged me on.

At once I realized these two must be Tipp the Kaktu and Monsi the Bosom, Naghan Raerdu's spies.

They guided me through the smoke away from the main mass of struggling people; three or four of the Lem worshippers spotted our movement and followed. Seven or eight of us crowded along, stumbling, coughing as the smoke retched into our mouths. Tipp the Kaktu threw up a trapdoor in the floor, Monsi the Bosom held out her arms to take the girl sacrifice.

"Quick, Jak—we must be quick!"

There was nothing else for it.

Monsi took the girl and bundled through the opening in the floor, I followed, dropping onto a straw-scattered floor with only the dim glow of the fire angling down to provide illumination. A body dropped after me and Tipp's reedy voice husked: "Go on! Go on!"

He smashed into me, and he cursed as more bodies dropped down after. The quick-witted among the Leem-Lovers desperate to escape the zhantil-masked killers had not missed this chance. In a bunch we ran along the murky corridor.

Naghan must have given strict instructions to his two agents. They would have had me under observation all the time, discreetly shadowing my movements. Just how far into the cult were they? They knew their way about what had been the Playhouse of the Singing Lotus. The cellars wound about confusingly and we had to backtrack at one point where the roof had fallen in, a mass of blazing timber. In the lurid orange light I saw the Leem-Lovers with us. Two men and a girl, quick and active figures, swinging around at once and retreating and then waiting for Tipp and Monsi to take up the lead. These were survivors, that was clear.

Gobbets of flaming wood tumbled about our ears as the floor above burned through.

One of the Leem-Lovers gave Monsi a savage thrust, shrieking: "Get on, you cramph, if you know the way out! Hurry!"

This behavior was normal for the Lemmites. Monsi stumbled and the girl cried out in terror. I caught Monsi about her waist—surprisingly slender for so large a woman—and took the Leem-Lover by the arm. I bent a trifle to him.

"Ill-treat this woman again and you go headfirst into the flames."

His silver mask ran with ruddy highlights. He tried to hit me and I threw him away, one-handed, and then hustled on with Monsi. "Shall I carry the girl?"

"I can manage, I thank you."

We did not use names.

As I say, the sequence confused. One moment we were hurrying along the cellar passageway the next the whole roof collapsed. Monsi sprawled forward and the girl, her legs flailing, rolled over and over. Tipp screamed and jumped.

The woman Leem-Lover fell on top of me. The others were mere contorted shadows, writhing in the smoke and turmoil. I struggled to rise, pushing a burning bulk of timber away. I hauled the female Lemmite up and she sprang to her feet, lithe and lissom, swinging instantly to the help of her male companion. The way ahead was blocked. The three of us were cut off, walled in by flames.

"Which way?" shrieked the man.

"Any way so long as it is up," said the girl.

Again the sequence confuses. We tried more than one of the cellar passageways and bolt holes, and we passed gagging through the space where, behind bars of solid iron, the leems were caged. No one thought of releasing them, poor dumb brutes though they were, in the common parlance, for the whole section of roof and wall collapsed into the thunder of an inferno as we shielded ourselves and ran on.

The girl had to drag the man past a tongue of flame that scorched across a narrow alleyway. I jumped through when it was my turn, and the Furnace Fires of Inshurfrazz were no doubt hotter; but not by much, by Krun!

Beyond that point the girl sniffed out a way where fresh air was drawn in. We bundled along, colliding with the old worn projections of walls, barely seeing where we were going, finding steps with their treads hollowed into halfmoons, panting up, pushing desperately at the wooden trapdoor above.

The two halves of the trap flapped back. There was an impression of the night sky speckled with stars, a cool night breeze. Blocky silhouettes moved against the stars. A hoarse voice shouted: "Here are more!"

And the answer, begun: "Hit them gently for—" and a blurred shadow in the corner of my eye and the black cloak of Notor Zan swooped down and engulfed me.

*   *   *

As I must repeat, the sequence blurs.

Looking back at that frightful period I think I must have made an attempt to fight, so they hit me again, perhaps they hit me many times. My memory, which in the normal course of events, because of the immersion in the sacred Pool of Baptism, is well-nigh perfect, fails me in this. When exactly the dark cloak of Notor Zan enfolded me is open to conjecture. I recall nothing with clarity after that brief glimpse of the stars of Kregen, for I remember nothing of any internal stars in my old vosk-skull of a head. A pain in my wrists kept pricking at me, and I couldn't move my feet, and I felt awful, and my head hung down.

They'd hung us up in a row on hooks against the wall.

A hoarse voice croaked out: "By Lem! They'll pay for this."

The girl's voice, next to me and from the same direction, on my right: "Who will make them pay?"

Ungluing my eyes may not have been as painful as the uproar clanging away in my head; it was agony enough. I could see my feet, bound together, and the rough stone of the floor below, with an air gap between. I could see my legs, and the scarlet breechclout which I had, when I'd dressed myself up for the evening's entertainment, donned without a thought that this might be the outcome. Scarlet. Well, I'd chosen the brave old color out of sentiment, and because we struck a blow which might aid Vallia. So they'd stripped us of clothes. Yet they'd left the silver leem masks on, and the reason for this was made at once clear by another voice, harshly dominating, that broke across the girl's pointed question.

"Aye, you rast. The girl is right. It is you who will pay when our master arrives. Your masks are the badges of your shame and I spit on them and you!"

I swivelled my eyeballs and squinted at the fellow who spoke. That I shared his sentiments would not be believed. He wore bulky armor, and the yellow tuft of feathers in his helmet, and his zhantil mask glittered golden in the light of the becketted torches.

Just so we were kept alive until this fellow's master arrived. . . . I was so sure that master had to be Pando I had already fathomed out his whole scheme, and approved, and wished I'd thought of it, and determined to put it to the best use of which I was capable as soon as I could.

There were four or five of the zhantil-masked guards and

they began an argument among themselves whether or not the
leem masks should stay on or come off the captives. I managed to get my eyeballs to swivel to my right and saw the girl
hanging as I was hanging, her arms spread out and hooked to
the wall by leather thongs. Her body, stripped to a breechclout,
as was mine, arched in an instinctive and futile struggle to
free herself. She, like me, wore a red breechclout and this—I
confess—amused me. It seemed odd. As for the fellow beyond,
the glimpse I could catch of him showed a wiry body and a
green breechclout. In other circumstances if it came to a
fight, my natural ally would be the red and my natural foe
would be the green; here they were both Leem Lovers,
Lemmites, as the word was, and they could both go hang.

As, by Vox, would I!

Eventually the zhantilman who wanted to keep the leem
masks on was overruled. One of his companions, a pot-
bellied individual, said: "I'll jump up and down on 'em!"

Another one—and, in the nature of these things he was thin
and quick—said swiftly: "Aye, dom, you do that. And when
you're finished I'll melt 'em down. They'll fetch a fair price
down the Boulevard of Silversmiths."

Thick fingers reached out to unlatch the leem masks, the
thin quick fellow merely slashed my latchings away so that
the mask fell into his clawed hand. He laughed, a hollow
rattle behind his own mask.

I blinked.

With the skills taught me by Deb-Lu I managed to fashion
a gyp-face; but it stung like the devil, and I guessed the
repeated knocks on the head had done me no good at all. I'd
recover fully, thanks to the Sacred Pool of Baptism in far
Aphrasöe, but right now I was still muzzy, not quite in
command of myself, and feeling as though I'd been in a fight
with a leem. . . .

My head hanging, I watched dully as the guards, chuckling
over their booty, left the cell. The door clanged.

There seemed little chance that this dungeon cell was in the
Zhantil Palace. Probably Pando had set up his headquarters
for his zhantil masks in a safe house in Port Marsilus. The
quicker he got here the better, for I surmised his delay had
been caused by the arrangements for this sort of exercise. The
problem from his point of view was that the Vadni Dafni,
whom he had been trying to rescue, was already rescued.

The fellow in the green breechclout started a long complaining monologue, filled with imprecations and obscene curses and threats. He would have his powerful friends carve up the zhantil faces. His sorcerous friend would blast them into black cinders. He would scatter their ashes across the Sea of Opaz, and glee as each cinder fell. He did not sound at all pleasant, and with the Bells of Beng Kishi ringing and clanging away in my head I found him tiresome. Also, muzzy as I was, I thought I knew that voice.

The girl said: "Do leave off! Think of a way to get out of here, by Vox!"

Jolted, I said: "If you're a Vallian they'll kill you twice over here." My head hung down, and I was too shattered to open my eyes against the sparking glitter of the torches.

The man said in his shrill hiss: "Vallia is doomed! The great enterprise will most certainly destroy all that proud and haughty land!"

And the girl, in her hard yet modulated voice, said: "The battle is not yet won, Zankov, and if we're dead before it begins, where is the profit in that?"

Zankov!

The bastard was hanging up helplessly—and so was I.

And this girl. . . .

I opened my eyes against the sting and squinted.

I could remember her only as a grown woman. All the time she had been growing up, as a little child in her white dress with her toys—her dolls and beads and daggers—I'd been on Earth. I'd seen her as Ros the Claw, fighting splendidly for what she believed in. She had tried to slash my eyes out. I'd carpeted her, and carried her out of a pit of evil. She had, when she understood that—at last and so late, like any cretin—I knew who she was, she had withheld her blow. She had not slashed her lethal Claw and taken off half my face.

Confident that Pando would soon be here, light-headed with the blows I'd taken, muzzy, I cast all thoughts of caution aside.

So few words I'd spoken to her, so few, and now the important ones had to be of death. . . .

"Dayra," I said. "That fellow Zankov, hanging next to you, killed your grandfather. He slew your mother's father, not me."

In the silence the torches spat and crackled.

She turned to look at me. The gyp-face was gone, smoke blown with the wind.

Yes—she was my daughter Dayra. That face, passionate, willful, stubborn, beautiful in a way that her mother Delia was beautiful and yet with an added darkness that—to my despair—I knew must come from me, that face that had haunted me now regarded me with a look I could not comprehend.

Then she said, in a whisper: "So you continue to lie and cheat and betray! How typical of you—the man I most loathe in all the world!"

My old head was going up and down like a swifter in a rashoon. I swallowed down the sick. I couldn't shake my head for fear of the consequences.

I said: "You are willful, and also a fool. Zankov betrayed you, more than once, and plotted to take the crown and throne and to kill me—which might not be altogether a bad thing—and to kill all the family. He tricked you at the Sakkora Stones—your mother was chained up, and he would have slain her. Barty Vessler—"

Zankov's thin bitter voice cut in, hatefully.

"Do not believe this kleesh! He lies! It is clear he lies!"

"I do not lie. You have betrayed Dayra too many times—"

"Perjurer!"

"There is no need for me to lie. What I say can be tested by witnesses—"

"Foul cramphs like yourself!"

The whole dungeon spun about me and the heavy blows inside my head beat and reverberated. For a space I could not say any more, only dwell agonizedly upon the bitter memories, while these two hung up beside me spoke in fierce, staccato whispers I barely heard, let alone comprehended.

Odd words spurted out, as they do from vaguely heard conversations. "Great enterprise." "Argenters." "Galleons." "Delphond." "Gold." The word gold spat out, more than once, something about the treasure and its safekeeping in trust.

Why didn't Dayra ask this bastard Zankov? Why was I so useless? Zankov had killed the emperor, slain him before witnesses including the Lord Farris and others, chief among whom was Delia. Delia! Hanging there in my agony I thought of her, and—as always, as always, thanks be to Zair and to Opaz and Djan—her presence in my life, whether beside me or on the other side of the world, uplifted me and strengthened me, gave a spark of courage to go on.

"Ask him!" I bellowed out and my words husked like a dry broom sweeping a gutter in the stews. "Ask him why your mother was hung up as we are hung up now, and he with a dagger in his fist. Ask him how Barty Vessler was slain! Ask him to his face, and let him deny that he killed the emperor your grandfather!"

"Hold your tongue, you stupid old fool!" came that bitter venomous voice. "Dayra knows who her friends are."

Desperately, reaching out with all the willpower I could muster, I said: "Dayra—you know your mother. I plead for myself in a despicable way, now, I admit. But—but, Dayra, do you think she would remain with me if I had killed her father?"

Her face turned to me and I saw that she was far more troubled and disturbed than I had thought, imagining her hard and brittle, and hating me so. "I—have wondered. Mother would not tolerate. . . . No. . . . I have not seen her since—"

"Since that cur-dog there tried to kill her!"

"Do not listen to him, Dayra!"

"Your mother and I miss you sorely—I own to my misdeeds. If you spoke to her, you would learn the truth—"

Zankov spluttered out in his staccato way: "Your mother believes this rogue, of course! She is easily duped. No doubt she lusts after him as a—"

"Zankov!"

But he rattled on, letting all the bile spill out, conscious of his own illegitimate ancestry and the deviltry to which he had resorted to place the crown of Vallia upon his own head. He'd had the help of the arch-Wizard of Loh, Phu-Si-Yantong, the Hyr Notor, who was now—thank Opaz—dead and gone. He had the aid of many enemies of mine.

If it does not sound too bombastically pompous, too egomaniacal, they were the enemies of Vallia, also. . . .

If I reiterate that the blows on my head interfered with my thoughts, turned my brains into a sludgy puddle, I do so, I believe, as much to explain the fogginess of my perceptions as the lacunae in my memories. Head hanging, a thread of blood running down from scalp to ear and so dripping drop by drop upon the stone floor, I persisted in this petulant obsession—why did not Dayra question this bastard? The grayness swirled about my eyes; yet my ears picked up drifts and snatches of their words—and, yes, Dayra did question him, I hoped, and his answers, at first convincing gradually

became more incoherent, more shrill, so that he ended by
simple blasphemies and kept harping on the enterprise against
Vallia and his ambitions and the great treasure. He was
greatly concerned about the treasure.

". . . damned treasure," said Dayra. I strained to hear in a
lucid moment, only to have the sounds in the cell swirl away
as though caught in a silent storm. When I could hear again,
Dayra was saying: ". . . You and everyone said my father
was a ninny, a puffed-up propaganda hero of a prince. Yet I
found out differently, when he fought under the voller and
escaped you all."

"Tricks, Roz, tricks only!"

"Because of you and our friends I tried to kill my own
father! By Opaz—" and here her voice shook with more than
the pulse of blood in my own ears. "—You've never properly
explained why mother was treated so cruelly at the Sakkora
Stones—"

"We had to convince her! You know that!"

"So you told me and so I believed. But chained up—"

Then the grayness returned and when I could take stock of
what was going on again they spoke more harshly, one to the
other, with more bitterness.

"I wish Hyr Brun was with me," and Dayra spoke passion-
ately of the yellow-haired giant who was her faithful bodyguard.

I croaked out: "I hope Hyr Brun is not dead, Dayra, for he
is a good man, and the child, Vaxnik, also, a brave proud
spirit—"

"They live. They are not here. Had they been—"

"Thanks to Opaz they are alive—and I hope the girl sacrifice I sought to rescue is safe, also. . . ."

"Who cares for a slave girl bought for the glory of Lem!"
Zankov spoke as any worshipper of Lem the Silver Leem.

Stung, I said, "Dayra—I am disappointed, I find it hard to
believe—how could you descend to this evil nonsense of Lem
the Silver Leem—?"

"And you! You wore the silver mask! You are a Leem
Lover! That damns you, that causes me to distrust and hate
you—" She did not go on. Banal words, but spoken with a
fire that scorched.

So—I took heart!

"Listen, daughter, and mark me well. I and my friends
oppose Lem. We set fire to the temple tonight. Aye! My
comrades burn the stinking temples to Lem. I wore the silver

mask only so that I would have the chance to rescue the girl sacrifice. . . .''

"How can I believe!"

"He lies, Ros, he lies!"

Then Zankov stopped his shouting, abruptly. Dayra spoke slowly. "If he lies, then . . . And if speaks the truth, then . . .''

Zankov was caught both ways. He blustered and raged, swearing most vilely. I kept silent, head hanging, feeling awful. How I had contemplated this meeting with my daughter, the Princess Dayra, known as Ros the Claw. . . . How often I had imagined its circumstances. How could I have foreseen that it would be like this—with Dayra hanging like a Rose between two thorns!

Their voices blended, one shrill and bitter and loaded with invective, the other hard and growing harder, suspicious, horrified. I'd started this adventure with a simple objective, as Pompino had said, but that had been deflected by a greater urgency, and I was now in a peril so great as to cause me to tremble, me, Dray Prescot, father of this girl who was troubled out of her wits. . . . Bad advice, no advice, bad example and no example. . . . Her life, despite the connotations and her connection with the Sisters of the Rose, had been no bed of roses. . . . She deserved more from me than I could repay.

I do not think any words of mine—the stupid, stumbling, feeble words—tipped the balance. Dayra had been misled, deceived; but she was not a stupid girl—how could she be, how could any daughter of Delia's be stupid? She must have harbored doubts. That she had rationalized the sight of her mother hanging in chains must have caused her intense agony; doubts persisted, engendered despite all the wily and malevolent advice heaped upon her by her friends.

Zankov confirmed my suspicions.

Among the threats, the taunting, the obscenities, he reproached Dayra. "You have proved stubborn in the past, and have grown worse lately." The thin bitter words crackled as the torches spat sparks. "I have lost a great deal of the hope and trust I once had in you. You are an ingrate—and this miserable kleesh, your father—"

"I have tried!" She sounded distraught and yet, and yet, through all her desperate despair, that hard note of reawakening reality heartened me. "I believed you and our friends. The Kataki twins—I believed what they said. All of you—because

my father was not there, and the calumnies you put about
regarding my mother—are they lies, also?''

My blade-comrade Seg Segutorio had been forced to kill a
few folk for these false and vile rumors about Delia. I'd
experienced horror when he'd told me—death for a few words!
Now, seeing the havoc they had wrought, these few words, I
could wish Seg had dispatched all the dispensers of lies and
calumnies regarding Delia. . . . Dayra had suffered, and I
had not known how she had been affected.

I croaked out—and Dayra turned her head to listen to me
even as Zankov spluttered and blasphemed on her other side!
—''Dayra—your mother is above reproach from anyone, she
cannot be touched by the stinks of offal like that.''

The effort of speaking nigh exhausted me. I could feel the
blood dripping down my face. I'd been sore wounded before,
far worse than these clumsy blows on the head, and I'd
recover well enough. But I needed to be alive and vigorous
right now. Right at this moment I needed all the strength and
willpower I could muster. This schemer Zankov had to be
unmasked, and now. Dayra could not be expected to change
her mind about the conduct of her life in an instant. The
painful process would take time. She had to be convinced and
then when she had thought it all through for herself and seen
the truth, why, then she would make the decision.

All I could do was hope Pando got here in time.

And—I could go on through the dizziness and put in what
arguments I could, explain, keep calm—keep calm!—and try
to make Dayra's agonizing reappraisal an experience that
would not destroy her. That, I shuddered to think, was a real
danger. . . . But, was it? Would a daughter of Delia's be
shattered? I took heart. No—not while the Ice Floes of Sicce
exuded their chill breath!

Intermittently I heard Dayra trying to question Zankov, and
he slid away from the quizzing and harped on the great
enterprise and his powerful friends and the treasure they had
entrusted to him to pay for the ships that would carry the army
to Vallia. I struggled to listen and learn of this, although I
cursed the fellow and willed Dayra to press her inquiries.

''The Lord Farris?'' shouted Zankov, answering one of her
questions at last. ''Yes, he was there. When I see him he will
tell you the truth, him and Lykon Crimahan both!''

Spluttering, I coughed out: ''Lykon Crimahan! I did not
speak of him, Zankov, so how—?''

"It is common knowledge—"

"It is not common knowledge. Lykon Crimahan, the Kov of Forli, returned to his kovnate and fought the aragorn and the slavemasters. He was no friend to me. But now he is loyal, and he saw you slay the emperor. . . ."

"He saw you, you cramph!"

"I think," I said to Dayra, "that unless Crimahan is very careful, if this fellow here is let free, these words have signed Crimahan's death warrant."

"He and Farris, all of you!" shrieked Zankov.

Dayra turned those gorgeous brown Vallian eyes on me. I could see her mother there. "And you truly joined the Lemmites and wore the silver mask to rescue the sacrifice and burn the temple?"

"You saw me carrying the child to safety. The temple burned."

"Yes . . ."

"Did you, Dayra, become a Leem-Lover—?"

"I never was! D'you think I could—?"

"No, my daughter, no, I do not think you could."

"We'll see!" shouted Zankov. "You have betrayed me, Ros. I am finished with you! When my friends get here—"

"Or when the Zhantil masks return," I put in, hard.

We hung there, the three of us, breathing hoarsely. This Zankov, for all his villainy, had courage. And I saw what the plan was against Vallia, the thoughts ringing in my head. They would land the enterprise in Delphond—my Delia's Delphond!—and march to cut off my lad Drak. They'd catch him between two armies, crush him, and then turn like leems on the capital of Vondium. It all fitted together. And Zankov had the money to pay for it all. A deal of that gold had gone to Strom Murgon, that was clear. They were all in it. Pompino's actions and mine against the Leem Lovers had been, also, against the foes of Vallia.

It all fit.

And I was strung up like a bird in the kitchen to be plucked, stuffed and roasted. . . .

The time dripped away. Zankov kept on railing against Dayra, and she protested that she must have time to think and he made it perfectly plain that if she was not wholeheartedly for him then she was against him. He became more malevolent. He was confident. He knew the strength of the forces arrayed on his side.

The sound of iron-shod sandals, the crash of the bolts on the cell door brought a cry of triumph to his lips.

Eagerly, I looked, aching to see the golden masks appear, and Pando, and to have this ghastly ordeal over.

"Now you will see!" he crowed. "The silver leem-masks will destroy you forever, Dray Prescot!"

And I said in all my stupid arrogance: "And the golden zhantil-masks will rid the world of you, Zankov!"

We three stared in awful fascination as the door opened.

The wood creaked back. Torchlight flared brilliantly.

In that eye-watering radiance as the door opened—we stared—warriors broke in—in that brilliance the wink and glitter of silver overpowered in the stinking stone cell.

CHAPTER EIGHTEEN

Of the spitting of Ros Delphor

"Cut me down! Cut me down!"

Zankov's voice cracked with triumph.

The silver-masks rushed in and then halted at the sight before them. One jumped as though stung when Zankov shouted, and leaped forward, dagger lifted. He slashed the bonds and as the thongs fell free so Zankov collapsed forward onto his knees. He breathed in huge gasps. Wiry, vigorous, alive, he wore the green breechclout drawn up tightly.

Green is a perfectly ordinary color for a Vallian, and Zankov was Vallian, if nothing else. Dark blue is the color Vallians shun, to my sorrow. Pale blue is acceptable in seacoast provinces, and the old Vallian Air Service used to wear dark blue and orange in a fashion that did not last upwards of ten seasons. So, the importance of colors was not lost on me as Zankov shoved up, turning lithely, fighting the cramps, to gloat upon us, and I recognized that, yes, indeed, green in all the evil connotations of that otherwise admirable color was fit garb for him.

An Ift wearing the leem mask reached up his dagger to cut Dayra free.

Zankov knocked him aside.

"Give me the dagger, and stand away, rast!"

The Ift obeyed instantly.

Zankov took the dagger and fronted Dayra. He laughed; his eyes were very merry.

"Hurry, notor, there is not much time," said a fellow whose dark beard sprouted around the edges of his leem mask.

"There is time for this, Handroi." Zankov spoke in his thin and bitter voice and yet he was filled with elation. "You are a fool," he told Dayra. "You have failed me. I have suspected you for some time past, and now I know your allegiance to Lem the Silver Leem was mere make-believe. Well, shishi, think on this, before I kill you. You have a sister, you have two sisters, and a niece. When you are dead and gone wandering the Ice Floes imagine me, wed to Lela, or to Velia. Either will do. Or, if they fail me, I shall wed your niece, Didi. All are in the line of succession. And, all the others, all, will be dead and gone and mouldering!"

With that, triumphantly, he lifted the dagger to strike out the life of my daughter Dayra.

She spat in his face.

Now, if I repeat that I am Dray Prescot, Lord of Strombor and Krozair of Zy, too often, you may well think of me as a braggart. But this repetition arises from humility that life has afforded me so much. I do not boast. I state facts that mean a great deal. The bonds cut into my wrists. My head still felt as though it had been battered around a camp of my Clansmen in Segesthes. But, just because, I had to try.

The bonds broke—at last. Of course, as I fell in a heap to the stone, I expected to die at once. That mattered little—save for one or two items of unfinished business—but Zankov would not dagger the life from my daughter while I lived and could prevent it. And, if I thought of my daughter Velia, the first Velia, as I staggered up and bundled all any old how into Zankov, that, too, I think you will understand. . . .

I butted him a thwack in the ribs and he bowled over like a ponsho brought down by a leem. The dagger remained fast clenched in his fist, and I couldn't reach it. It was vitally necessary to roll over and over, away from the expected slash of blade or shaft of arrow.

"Father!" screamed Dayra.

Zankov, screeching, staggered up, the dagger glittering. Beyond him a fellow in a leem mask lifted his short bow. The arrow head centered on me and I dived aside, pivoted, put a foot into Zankov's green breechclout. His face joined that color scheme.

He fell away and a bulky Brokelsh rushed, sword uplifted, and I twisted him over my shoulder so that his head and the leem-mask hit the floor with an almighty thwack. Blood spurted—but the damned sword skittered across the stone flags, and I reared up to dodge the next arrow or front the next attacker.

The chances were not entirely hopeless. . . . Frantic action, constant movement, swift, savage and sudden . . .

Two more leem-masks dropped, broken, and my fingers reached for the hilt of a thraxter. In the corner of my eye a blurred rush—Dayra's passionate yell: "Your back!"—a twist, a vicious thrust of the sword—blood gushing over my wrist—a blow sending me staggering sideways—a recovery and sight of a silver-masked Rapa lifting his bow. Off balance, I tried to twist to avoid the shaft. The Rapa did not loose. He swiveled sideways. An arrow stood in the center of his back. He fell forward onto his beak, bent within the mask.

The heavy tramp of footfalls and a voice, a booming bull voice just finishing saying . . . "Trample all over 'em!"

Yet, despite that Pompino and Cap'n Murkizon and Quendur the Ripper and Larghos the Flatch bustled in, roaring, laying about them with the deadly flicker of steel, the first into the cell was Tipp the Kaktu.

Instantly, belting an inopportune Fristle over the furry head to make his whiskers wilt, I leaped for Dayra. The thraxter sliced bloodily through the bonds. She fell against my chest, and I held her, held her, as she trembled.

"Listen, daughter. Call me Jak. I am just Jak. Remember—"

"Jak the Drang?"

"No. Just Jak—sometimes Jak the Shot."

She recovered with the swift catlike ability that must have kept her alive in many a perilous situation when there was no mother or father to keep an eye on her.

"And me—Jak?"

"A friend. We have both been accustomed to using aliases. Are you still Ros?"

"Yes. But not the Claw—"

"Very well." The uproar bellowing away, as Pompino's fellows from *Tuscurs Maiden* and Tipp the Kaktu who had watched me and brought the crew here, fighting mad, sorted out the Lemmites, formed a chorus to Dayra and my quick words. "Yes—then you must be Ros the Radiant—"

"No. Delphor. Ros Delphor."

"As you wish—" A body with its head hanging and the silver mask slashed across tumbled past. "I'll have to help the lads now—"

"You said I am to be a friend. It won't be as easy or as quick as that."

"No. But it will—Ros Delphor!"

And I went roaring harum-scarum into the fight and, lo! it was all over.

Pompino brushed up his whiskers and stared around.

"By the tangled and nit-infested locks of the Divine Lady of Belschutz! What a mangy crew!"

Cap'n Murkizon's axe glimmered darkly with blood. Pompino said to me: "You are unharmed, Jak?" Then he laughed. "I seem to be saying that with distressing frequency, by Horato the Potent!" He stared at Dayra.

She stalked arrogantly across the floor, kicking bodies out of the way, ripped off a few capes and cloaks and things until she found a decent gray cape to swing about her shoulders. With a gray tunic—with only a few spots of blood—to go under the cloak, and a thraxter in her right fist and a dagger in her left, she paced back. She moved with the lethal grace of a hunting leem, and—as I thought in my admiration for this woman who was my daughter—with the nobility of a zhantil.

I made the Pappattu quickly.

"Scauro Pompino the Iarvin. Ros Delphor." And the others, swiftly, for we had to get clear of this place, and there were certain acts I had to perform this night before I could think that this adventure was over.

Together, we hurried from the cell. Needless to say I'd clothed and armed myself. We climbed stairs, and as we went I made it my business to say to Tipp the Kaktu: "My deepest thanks, Tipp the Kaktu."

Without the leem mask his face showed quick, intelligent appreciation of events. His nose was on the thin side; but his mouth was finely formed. "Naghan Raerdu is a generous paymaster. Also, he is very sudden. And, again, I do not care for people who chop up children."

With those sentiments, I fancied, we had the beating of the Lemmites.

We saw no more masks, either silver or golden, as we went through the house, apart from masks upon corpses. Stopping, I bent and freed the leather latchings of a golden zhantil mask from a dead man. He looked peaceful enough lying in his own blood. I stowed it away with a fine silver mask in the pouch taken from a fellow whose swag belly held more than the pouch. We pushed open the last door and so walked out onto the streets of Port Marsilus under the radiance of the Moons.

Among all the twisted corpses—and, believe me, I'd looked with attentive care—not one revealed the thin and bitter features of Zankov.

When I asked, Larghos the Flatch said, crossly: "That one. I shot, but a hulking Brokelsh got in the way and took the shaft in an eye. When I looked again this fellow—Zankov? —was gone."

"We'll blatter him yet!" boomed Murkizon, cheerfully. He mentioned the Divine Lady of Belschutz, and added: "That sort run hardly upon their noose."

Ros the Claw, Ros Delphor, said nothing.

I said to Tipp the Kaktu, and I own I felt concern: "Monsi the Bosom? She is safe—you both got out of the fires in the cellars?" He saw my concern. "And the child?"

"Yes, Jak. And the child."

"Thank the good Pandrite."

Dayra favored me with a swift liquid upward glance; again, she said nothing. Pandrite, a chief god of Pandahem, sat oddly on the lips of a Vallian. In a bunch, desperadoes, all of us, we moved along the street, our cloaks and capes flaring in the night breeze.

The glow in the sky suffused drifting clouds with orange; of flames, nothing, and of smoke, none in the night. The temple, that had been the Playhouse of the Singing Lotus, had not taken long to burn to the ground. But, by Krun, she must have made a splendid spectacle when she roared in fury!

Moderating our progress now we were away, we still kept a sharp lookout. Pompino fell in on my other side. He glanced across at Dayra, at ease and most gallant in his haughty Khibil way.

"My lady. Where may we have the honor of escorting you?" And then, before she could answer: "You appear to be friendly with our Jak, which he does not deserve. Perhaps you would care to favor us with an account of your acquaintance, although, of course, one would not press. . . ."

Jesting though he was, he struck shrewdly.

Dayra did not flinch.

"I give you thanks for your timely rescue, kot—horter Pompino. Jak claims friendship with me; I am not sure I give mine so freely."

"Aha!" exclaimed Pompino, bubbling now with the aftereffects of the fight in his blood. "I knew it! I always said he kept secrets too well. You see, my lady—"

I broke in. "Some secrets—like secret wine drinkers, and some not so secret, like Herry Tarkness, of the great spirit and dedications, steeling themselves to face the edge—some secrets remain so, and, therefore, by definition, cannot be known."

He eyed me and licked his lips and did not brush up his moustaches. "The point is, Jak, we are collecting a great harem of womenfolk, and what are we to do with them all?"

"The children could always join your two pair of twins and Ashti of the Jungle."

Abruptly, he slapped his thigh, laughing. "Capital. And my dear lady wife would welcome them, too, for her ideas encompass far greater imaginative leaps than that."

"As for the ladies—Nalfi and Ros for the moment—they will do what they will to do."

"I will to see about Zankov," said Dayra. She spoke with a rasp. "Jak—you heard him talk of the treasure?"

I was there, already, ten leaps ahead. I nodded. But it would be boorish to tell Dayra her own plans.

"Treasure?" said Pompino, bristling up.

I had to say, gently: "My lady Ros—if treasure is in the wind I must warn you these lads have sticky fingers."

"They may take it all, for me, provided they take it from those who possess it now, and those who covet it for gain."

"Well, that last category covers the crew, for a start."

But, for all the banter, we were deadly serious. And Dayra was shrewd enough to see she did not have to spell it out.

"How many do we have to knock over?" Pompino transparently gained in good humor. "For I realize the generality of this army they're hiring would not be privy to the secret whereabouts of the pay chests."

"No one trusts anyone. Zankov admitted—back there—he had lost his trust in me." She sounded hard, determined, not bitter or resigned; but changed. Oh, yes, Dayra had changed in those traumatic hours. I was not fool enough to imagine that the change would encompass my good graces, not just yet, anyway. She went on: "Like any undertaking of this sort, they set up a complicated series of transactions. They used agents and tools of accomplice. Kov Colun Mogper of Mursham, which is in Menaham and therefore suspicious to these Pandaheem, had a hand in it. He worked with Strom Murgon."

"But the treasure?" persisted Pompino.

"I do not know where Zankov got it from. He fell out with his master, the Hyr Notor, and when he died Zankov seemed relieved of a great burden. But it is certain sure Zankov could never lay his hands on so much gold. There is someone—or some group of people—anxious to harm Vallia—"

"Anxious to open the gate to plunder and slavery," I put in, quickly. Dayra might be an accomplished agent in Vallia; here in Pandahem she would have to be more careful. Already, she'd said "kot" for koter, the Vallian word for horter, and now she was showing a lively concern over the island empire that, to most Pandaheem, could sink into the sea to general joy and thanksgiving.

As though echoing these unpleasant thoughts of mine, Pompino said: "That might be a capital adventure."

Casually, being careful, I said: "Better to lay our hands on the treasure now. That is real and within our grasp."

"Aye. You are right, Jak. By Horato the Potent! What it would be to return home with gold enough to make my lady wife blink—maybe then the gold might match her ambitions." He considered. Then: "No. No, I do not think gold enough exists for *that*."

"I," quoth Dayra with great firmness, "am starving hungry."

"And I!"

While on Kregen some taverns stay open all night, not in general being irked by licensing regulations, we deemed it prudent not to patronize a public eating place. To the best of our knowledge no one spied on us as we hurried into the Zhantil Palace. Our friends were relieved to see we were still alive. The temple had blazed awesomely. Some of Pando's property had burned along with it, and Pompino and I exchanged glances. That problem was for the future. Just when young Pando would get into Port Marsilus remained unknown. Framco had not returned, and this was perfectly understandable; there was no message from him.

Tipp the Kaktu had disappeared en route here—gone home, clearly. He and Monsi would not know who I was, if Naghan Raerdu exercized his usual caution. Only my daughter Dayra was aware of my true situation; and, as you may imagine, there were very many things we had to talk about—very many, by Zair!

Also, you may imagine my relief when no one had heard or seen the Vallian ambassador, Strazab Larghos ti Therminsax. Naghan Raerdu must have shuffled him off successfully in some other way than involving Captain Linson and the ship. *Tuscurs Maiden*, I gathered, had pushed off from the jetty and moored up a few hundred paces offshore. A sensible precaution, that. . . .

We ate hugely, plundering Constanchoin's best, and drank moderately, refreshing ourselves, and then we slept ready for the morrow's exertions. Like the day that had gone, tomorrow would be a big day. . . .

We stood to as the mists of dawn curled silvery vapors above the battlements and the twin suns began their daily shafting of emerald and ruby light across the world. There was time only for the Fristle ord-Deldar, Naghan the Pellendur, to shriek out a single warning.

The main gate simply erupted as the iron-headed ram burst through. Smashing the splintered wreckage aside, leaping ferally into the palace, armored men shocked into instant combat with the guards. The clang of steel and the hideous uproar of battle told us we were abruptly faced with mortal danger. Men swarmed into the palace, the Brown and Silvers brandishing weapons and seeking to destroy all within and take back the Vadni Dafni—for, striking magnificently in the warriors' van, Strom Murgon led that devastating onslaught.

CHAPTER NINETEEN

Sheathed Talons . . . ?

In a twinkling Deldar Naghan the Pellendur's men were tumbled back from the gate and the first courtyard. Rushing up I was in time to join the defense as we sought to hold the inner wall. The uproar flowered to the rising suns.

Arrows shafted in; but the overhang prevented them from striking down upon us. That first abrupt onslaught was held— somehow—and we gained a breathing space. When the next attack came an odd thing happened.

Now, as you know, I am not one of your fighting men who believe they must have one special weapon in battle. Any paktun who depends on a particular sword is likely, if he goes adventuring, to be parted from it smartly. If, then, he feels incapable of fighting well with another weapon—oh, no! Oh, no. Your true paktun will fight with whatever comes to hand, a master of any weapon.

I own that I have gone to some lengths to retain a particular Krozair longsword, or a matched set of rapier and main gauche. But not to extreme lengths, by Zair . . .

So, as we fought, I used a thraxter. The stout weapon, shorter and fuller than a rapier, served well in the crude bash of the melée. A warrior, brave undoubtedly, tried to get at me over the wall, and I cut him down. His companion, a moltingur, tried to stick me from the side. I blocked the blow and, even as I struck back, recognized the weapons the man wielded. They were the rapier and main gauche I'd had from Captain Nath Periklain in *Schydan Imperial*, the very matching set I'd lost when the zhantil-masks knocked me over. Without hesitation I trompled the moltingur down—in turn, in turn!—and

162

snatched the weapons. The fellow wore my belts, also. In the next few moments, as we drove back that assault, I was able to drag him in by the proboscis and strip the leather from him.

Pompino said: "You're getting fussy, Jak." Then he saw the weapons, recognized them, and said: "You know what you told me—"

"Aye. But, right now we are like rats in a trap."

"True. But you must admit we are trapped with as bonny a bunch of fighting men as you could wish."

"I'm past being choosy in whose company I die."

"Ha! By Horato the Potent, you speak sooth. And, my friend, I'd like to know how this Murgon knew and why he chose to attack now."

"Spies, Pompino, spies. They get everywhere."

"We can hold them in that chamber with the zhantils painted along the walls—for a time. . . .

"I'll tell you one thing that is no longer a puzzle. This rapier and dagger were taken from me by the zhantil-masked people. Now they turn up here with Strom Murgon. That means that moltingur was a leem-mask who slew the zhantil-faces."

"And they roar out into the open—and here they come again!"

So, once more we went at it, tinker fashion, hammering them back. Just how many men Murgon would commit we had no way of knowing. We did know that he'd have more men than we did. Also, through his lavish dispersal of the funds provided by Zankov, he'd have no trouble from the ordinary folk of the city. No doubt they fancied they'd be better off under Murgon than serving Pando. I did not share that opinion. . . .

As we battled and then drew back, using all the tricks of which we were masters to delay the foe, everyone became aware that we were never going to halt Murgon until he had destroyed us all. The odd little thought occurred to me that one was entitled to wonder what Zankov would think of this use of his money. . . .

The booming roar of Cap'n Murkizon as he exhorted us to: "Hit 'em, knock 'em down, tromple all over 'em!" heartened us. The two varterist sisters, Wilma the Shot and Alwim the Eye, highly displeased there were no ballistae they could shoot, got stuck in with bows and then cold steel. Rondas the Bold, in his element, fought magnificently. Nath Kemchug, dour, fought as only Chuliks can fight. Quendur the Ripper, like quicksilver, slashed now here, now there, battling back. Larghos the Flatch shot superbly—I even fancied Seg might have nodded a quiet approval. Chandarlie the Gut had a gigantic boarding pike and this dripped red. As for Lisa the Empoin, despite Quendur's entreaties, she stood shoulder to shoulder with us in this fight to the death. The Lady Nalfi was not with us and for the sake of Larghos the Flatch we welcomed her absence.

In a quick breathing space as the enemy pulled back and the remnants of the Fristle guard joined us, with Naghan the Pellendur shaking the drops from his scimitar, Pompino spoke in a fretful way, as though affronted. That this, in the midst of battle, was highly amusing was almost—almost but not quite—lost on my comrade.

"We're trapped here, Jak—and for what? We do not have to hold the palace, for Pandrite's sake!"

"True. Murgon can bring so many men he'll push us back until there is nowhere left."

"It will be dead men and women who reach there, that place at the end," said Rondas the Bold. He whiffled a finger through his facial feathers. "But I shall not reach that end. I shall charge into them, going forward—"

"Yes, Rondas," I cut in, "admirable. But wait a few murs first. Strike with us, together, that is our strength."

"Normally, yes—but this is not your usual battle."

They had all missed my meaning.

Pompino, I knew, although he talked of retreating until we were all slaughtered in some hole or corner, would instantly seize the other course. He would, even though it meant us all rushing out to what appeared certain death. Each one of us would believe that he or she would scrape through somehow.

So I spoke the obvious words, and they all agreed.

"Although," said Lisa the Empoin, "and remember I stick with Quendur—although this Kov Pando ought to be here soon. I stayed in the palace, and they talked of nothing else."

"My heart," said Quendur, gently—and with the blood splashed gorily upon him— "Do not put too much store by a miraculous rescue—"

"You know me, Quendur, by now! I merely pointed out what I had heard—onker!"

So, we were all in good heart.

In good heart to rush out upon our sudden deaths.

Constanchoin was told to take all his people and the slaves and those who could not fight and find some secure place where they might bargain for their lives. At that, a number of sturdy slaves volunteered to join us, and we provided them with weapons, to the horror of the good Constanchoin. He would, we felt, strike a bargain with Strom Murgon.

The best place to make the break lay toward a side entrance. Naghan knew the palace. In furtherance of these preparations we had pulled back swiftly, abandoning a whole block of the building within the courtyard, and barricading doors and windows behind us. We collected in the ground floor hall of what we were told was the Nathium Cupola. That lofted many stories above our heads. We prepared to rush out.

Someone called in excited shock. Heads turned.

Through the distant clangor as Murgon's men broke down our improvised barricades, through the buzz of the people, through the nervously clinked sounds of steel against iron, that voice lifted high.

"Mindi the Mad!"

She was there, standing as before, head lowered and her pale blue gown depending in its straight folds into that neat circle about her feet. She stood against a small and insignificant door leading to a slave's cleaning room. She lifted her head. Her hand rose, a forefinger beckoned.

Naghan yelled: "Mindi!" Then he rounded on us. "She is a witch and she knows many strange things—"

As Mindi beckoned again, I said: "And she knows a secret way out of the palace, that is clear."

"Aye!"

They roared out, now, most of them, yelling: "Show us, Mindi, show us!" And: "Lead us to safety, Mindi!"

Rondas looked thoroughly put out. Murkizon whistled his axe about.

"Now then, you two!" and Pompino spoke with barbs in his tongue. "No fighting without cause—remember where we are going and what to do, and then think again!"

"Aye, you are right, Horter Pompino, although I was set upon the last great fight—"

"Not today. Let us follow this Mindi the Mad."

So, that is what we did. We trooped along through the

slave's cleaning room and down stairways and along flang-infested corridors and so, after a goodly distance, came to a blank end to a side corridor. The pale insubstantial specter beckoned us.

We looked at the blank masonry, dripping and green with lichen, and our torches struck sparks from nitre specks.

"Is this it!" demanded some.

The dead-end corridor contained a broken chest to the side, holding rusted iron, and the place stank of rotting vegetation, a dank, stagnant stink.

Pompino brushed up his reddish whiskers and stepped forward. No haughty and smart Khibil, his manner proclaimed, could be beaten by a small mystery like this—no, by Horato the Potent!

Cap'n Murkizon let rip a bellow. "The lever to open the secret block is here, in this rusty iron." He stalked over to the broken chest. "It is obvious!" With that, he bent to grasp a projecting rod of orange-rusted iron.

With a liquid flash of blue the spectral form of Mindi the Mad reared before Murkizon. He staggered back. One arm flung up to protect himself and the other groped futilely for his axe.

Mindi pointed up. She stabbed up twice, and then brought her palm down, flat and squashing. Her face reflected the greatest alarm.

It was clear—as Pompino acidly pointed out.

"Had you pulled that lever, Cap'n—a great block of stone would have dropped on you—and us! Squash!"

Cap'n Murkizon stood back. He did not mention the Divine Lady of Belschutz.

Mindi the Mad pointed to a certain junction of masonry where a finger hole showed, black and oozing water. Into this Pompino stuck a finger. He did so with great aplomb. He might have had it bitten off, and he knew it. He twisted. With a groaning like a miser paying out gold, a doorway-sized block of stone revolved before us. The stink gushed out, gagging us.

Quietly, Dayra said to me: "I think I like your Khibil friend very much—for a Khibil and a friend of yours."

People pushed through the opening. Dayra and I stood aside as the crocodile of children went along. We'd brought them with us when a chance of escape favored by Mindi had presented itself. Caring for them were Natalini, Sharmin, Tinli and Suli.

One little girl's slipper fell off and she was too scared and too pushed along by the others to stop for it. I bent and picked it up.

"If we leave any signs Murgon will know where we've gone."

And—I swear it!—even as I said this we heard the first sounds from the maze of corridors at our backs. The tread of iron-studded sandals, the clink of spear or sword against stone, told us we had to hurry. A small group remained to the last, ready to bash anyone who tried to stop us. Rondas was still in half a mind to rush out to the last great fight; we did not quite drag him into the opening; but he was highly reluctant. As for me, I had greater schemes afoot than enjoying a bout of sword-fighting in the cellars, by Krun!

All the same, I managed to persuade Pompino to go on and sort out what lay ahead while I brought up the rear. So, it chanced that I was the last to go through into that dark opening and Dayra the penultimate.

A wooden horizontal bar across the inside of the slab afforded purchase to close it. I put a hand to this, Dayra stood at my side and helped. The slab began to revolve to close us off in secret and, far off down that main tunnel the sounds hastened on and a gleam of light struck into the nitre flecking the walls, reflected like an accusing host of eyes.

I stopped shutting the slab.

"What's up now?" demanded Dayra, still pushing on.

"Wait a moment, Ros." With that I turned sideways and slid through the narrow crack. I reached down to the certain junction of masonry where a finger hole showed. From it I drew out a palm's length of ribbon. Water stained the ribbon darkly, but the stripe of zig-zag silver down the center had reflected that accusing flicker of torchlight. Dayra's whistle of surprise was stifled instantly. I stuffed the ribbon into my flap-pouch, squeezed back into the opening and together we closed the slab.

The stink really got up my nostrils, and Dayra said: "By Vox! What a pestilential place!"

I said: "Use Pandrite, or Chusto or Chozputz—"

We crept along a narrow and slimy ledge with the sounds of the others before us and the erratic light of their torches to prevent us from stepping into the sewer at our side.

"Chusto?" said Dayra. "Chozputz? I've never heard—"

"Nor has anyone else. I made them up."

"Oh!"

"And we have someone in our midst who leaves ribbons to mark where we went."

"You have no suspicions?"

"None. It is probably one of the slaves we armed and brought along. Or, possibly, one of Naghan's guards. They seek to earn a disreputable coin or two from a grateful Murgon."

"They will earn something a little different from me, by Vo—Chusto!—when they are unmasked."

"When."

The small sewer led into a medium-sized sewer which led to a large sewer. The striking fact was the stinks did not improve or lessen; the folk of Port Marsilus were median in their ablutional functions. Scurrying claws fled from us; we met no fearsome monsters and I was mightily thankful for that. I thought of the girl children and the way their new dresses were being ruined. At last we reached a manhole where Pompino's fiercely whiskered face peered down, and he said: "Come on, Jak! We're waiting for you! Oh—my lady Ros—here, take my hand."

With great gallantry he assisted her up. We were in a shadowed shed racked with implements like shovels and brooms and water-carrying equipment. So we could wash some of the muck off before we started out into the daytime streets of the city.

"To skulk off from a fight does not please me," Pompino said. "But the greater good demands this dishonor."

"Gold demands it," I pointed out—with little pleasure.

"Lead us to the gold," quoth Cap'n Murkizon. "I fancy we know what to do with it after those pestilential sewers."

"Beng Dikkane will wax fat," said Larghos, his arm protectingly around the lady Nalfi. She looked disheveled and unhappy.

We decided not to split up to slink through the city but to go in a bold body down to the docks. Dayra guided us. We met no one who offered to stop us; we guessed word of our presence would quickly reach Murgon. We just had to beat him for speed.

At the jetty the children were ferried out to *Tuscurs Maiden* with the lady Nalfi and some of the slaves who had escaped with us and were not fighters. Then we went along to where Zankov's ship, the swordship *Igukwa Valjid*, lay moored.

The watch saw us coming, of course, and attempted to resist. But with gold in the nostrils of our fellows we were not to be denied. The watch either went overboard or fled. Dayra knew exactly where the chests were stored; the iron bars presented no problem to gold-hungry rascals like us, and we began to pass the strong iron-bound lenken chests aloft.

About the time we had a sizable pile at the jetty and the first boatload had gone across to *Tuscurs Maiden*, the sentries shouted the alarm.

Mounted men galloped down onto the stones of the jetty, shrieking, shirling swords and slanting lances. We formed to meet them and that first impetuous charge was shot to pieces.

"There will be more of the rasts," panted Pompino, shaking his bow. He shouted back over his shoulder. "Hurry up, there! Get the chests aboard!"

"Quidang!"

The next attack combined a few kreutzin with the cavalry so that we shot and then came to handstrokes. Still we had the beating of these disorganized attacks. When Murgon and Zankov brought the full weight of their new army to bear it would be a different story. By this time the holes we had punctured in the bottom of *Igukwa Valjid* had admitted water enough to bring her deck level with the waves. A pity we could not have seized her and pulled her out; that was not on in our circumstances. We braced for the next onslaught and saw that off, and then there remained but the one pile of boxes, a ship's boatload.

All this time Dayra had placed the balass box she'd brought from Zankov's vessel by her feet on the dock. She did not move from that spot overmuch as she shot with the precision taught by Seg Segutorio. The bows from *Tuscurs Maiden* were the short compound reflex bows of Pandahem, with a few crossbows; with them we wrought great execution. But our time was running out.

I said to Dayra in a pause in the fighting: "Do you go with this last load of chests, Ros."

"I think—Jak—I will remain for a while yet."

As she spoke she looked at her balass box and then searchingly at the files of soldiers trotting out at the far end of the jetty. Her face lit up. I whirled.

He was there, leading on a group of men, Zankov, arrogant, brittle thin, nervous, yet filled with courage. I marked him and shot, and missed, and Dayra laughed.

"I do not think that one is yours, Jak."

"I'm glad Seg didn't see that."

Zankov rushed on at the head of his men. Larghos the Flatch reeled back with an arrow in his shoulder, whereat he cursed wrathfully. Rondas the Bold's mail was slashed and dangling. Nath Kemchug's Chulik pigtail gleamed with blood from a headwound. Cap'n Murkizon whistled his axe ferociously.

I said: "Mayhap we had best leave this last pile of boxes."

"I'm not leaving the gold for this mangy pack!" roared Murkizon.

Working like demons the men hefted the chests into the boat. The second boat pulled frantically for the shore to take us off. We might still do it. The Suns glittered on the water, gulls screeched and winged overhead, the air scented sweet with the sweetness of Kregen—it was good to be alive and futile to die for a handful of gold. But gold is gold and people are people; there is no gainsaying that on two worlds. . . .

The front rank of soldiers hit us and we battled back. We halted them and sent them reeling and someone screeched: "The gold is loaded! The boat is here!"

"Time to go!" roared Pompino. "No arguments, anyone!"

We knew what he meant right enough.

"They come in again!" yelled Rondas. "Hai, jikai!"

Ros bent to her bronze-bound balass box. From its velvet-lined interior she took her Claw, the shining razor-sharp Talons, and strapped them up on her left arm. Now she was a Taloned Demoness, a Sister of the Rose, one who could slash the face from an opponent and stick another with her rapier.

We jumped into a last mad affray, a jumbled affair of leaping and ducking, of slashing and hacking. We were pressed back, and a slave, brave with his new-won freedom and his spear, died under our feet. I felt the rage at the waste and pressed in ruthlessly. Ros the Claw, slashing, slicing, merciless, cut the face from a fellow and instantly swirled to take the side of a face from another. How her wicked Talons raked in! How they smashed in and twisted and left merely a red wrecked pudding!

With horrified disbelief I saw she was down. In a twinkling she slipped on spilled blood and took a vicious glancing blow

from a thraxter. Instantly I dashed the brains from the fellow
before me and hurdled his body and reached and scooped up
my daughter. Ghastly visions of Velia floated before my
eyes—I would not lose two daughters, not while I lived!

Zankov rushed me. His sword blurred. He would have
gutted me then and there, but I managed to twist and kick him
in the shins. He did not howl but staggered back. His thin and
bitter face shone with effort, his eyes were wide and drugged
and hating. He gathered himself for the final spring when he
anticipated he would finish us once and for all.

A broken axe haft whirred past his head. He ducked in
reflex action. A broad, barrel-like form hurtled past. Arms
spread wide, red face a Zim-set of fury, that compact thunder-
bolt of muscle crashed into Zankov.

". . . of Belschutz!" Massive arms wrapped about the thin
and brittle form.

"Back to the boat!" screamed Pompino. "Bratch!"

I did not hesitate. Oh, no, not me, not puissant Dray
Prescot with a wounded daughter in my arms! I simply scuttled for the boat and the waiting arms of the crew. I saw
Dayra safely into the boat and then turned back, sword out,
ready once more to hurl into the fray.

I saw. Zankov was bent across Cap'n Murkizon's knee.
The barrel body strained as a woodcutter casually strains to
break a branch for the fire. I do not believe Cap'n Murkizon
needed great strength or pressure. He jerked his arms
downwards. Zankov stiffened and went limp. He drooped.
Murkizon threw Zankov away and ducked back, haring for
the boat. Arrows fleeted past, feathering the first of those
who tried to follow.

We all bundled into the boat. Covered by arrows we pulled
for *Tuscurs Maiden*. We were all flushed, wrought-up. I bent
to Dayra. Her eyes opened.

"It is nothing," she said, most acidly. "A worse knock is
suffered in training—"

"Lie still, Ros Delphor, lie still."

As we neared the vessel her canvas rose. Captain Linson
was all prepared to go—no doubt he'd have gone if we hadn't
reached him in time. The boat hooked on and we were
hoisted bodily from the water. *Tuscurs Maiden* heeled and
headed out to sea.

Wearing an untidy yellow bandage around her head, Dayra
insisted on staying on deck. I joyed in having her at my side,

and trembled, yes, trembled in terror at what lay ahead for us in our prickly relationship. I could not expect to be received back as a dear and doting father in the blink of an eyelid. Also, by Zair, the young miss needed to be thoroughly conversant with the magnitude of her follies.

Pompino said: "Without pay, the captains of what ships Murgon has will never chase us. By Horato the Potent! We've hamstrung him finely!"

Certainly, no movement could be observed among the small scatter of shipping. *Tuscurs Maiden* sailed splendidly, carrying us well out to sea.

Mantig the Screw, one of the few apims in Framco the Tranzer's guard detail, reported in. He'd been sent with the message, and reaching the Zhantil Palace to find it besieged, had very sensibly gone on to *Tuscurs Maiden* to find us. A sharp-set young man, with a pointy look to his face—his nose was not exactly screw-shaped, but the general suggestion could not be denied—he delivered the message briskly.

"The cadade informs you that the Kovneva Tilda is safe at Plaxing. Kov Pando is with her. He is aware of the situation—

"Is he, by thunder!"

"The kov has with him the Mytham twins and Mindi the Mad, who keeps his intelligence."

"That explains that, then," said Pompino.

I was amused. Pompino, who like me was a kregoinye, working for the superhuman and supernatural Star Lords took their incredible powers perfectly matter-of-factly. But when it came to a witch performing a little lesser magic the short hairs bristled!

Naghan the Pellendur, dourly, said: "And I'll wager, by Numi-Hyrjiv the Golden Splendor, that unhanged rascal Twayne Gullik played both ends against the middle. He's loyal again because Kov Pando is with him."

"A fellow to be watched," observed Pompino.

The breeze tautened our canvas and the bluff bows smashed through the billows. The stout lenken chests were stowed below, and Cap'n Murkizon and Nath Kemchug, with Rondas the Bold and others of our friends, oversaw the stowage with exactness.

Cap'n Murkizon gave his opinion that the few swordships in port might follow for the gold. This would not worry us once we were well out into the offing. When Murkizon joined us, Dayra looked at him searchingly. He huffed and harrumphed, and then said: "I think his backbone was broken clear through, my lady; but he was not dead."

Dayra said to me: "I think I will go below, now,—Jak."

At the head of the companionway she halted and looked back. "Call me if there is a fight." She went below. We had a great deal to clear up; but, first, another important matter had to be dealt with.

"Gold," said Pompino, "equals dead men and women."

If in the ordinary way a mercenary received a silver piece a day, less if he was an Och, more if he was a Pachak or a Chulik—or a Khibil!—and if Murgon had recruited something like thirty or forty thousand men, with ships to transport them and ration allowances, plus the mounts for the cavalry, then we might expect to find a treasure of considerable size. How long the enemies of Vallia expected the campaign to last with their own gold before they could subsist from the Vallian countryside, must remain conjectural. Pompino was confident we had laid our hands on the equivalent of two hundred thousand gold pieces, for much of the treasure would have to be in silver coins. This treasure would be shared out among us according to the usual customs. We would have to set reliable watches and sleep with our swords naked at our sides.

Just where all this gold was coming from I could not know for sure. I had a terrible belief that I did know. Well, if I was right, then the future, dark though it might be, held also the promise of vivid action and headlong adventure, together with intrigue and peril enough to frizzle the scales from a dinosaur.

All that had to wait. Now I could luxuriate in the thoughts I had been keeping at bay and now was unable any longer to resist.

When I saw Delia! By Zair! What a story to tell her— Dayra, the fierce and ferocious taloned miss, the merciless Ros the Claw, our little Dayra—at last true to Vallia and to herself. Yet this was not a facile example of the return of the Prodigal Daughter, oh, no. Very much it was the return and redemption of a Prodigal Parent—for Delia had always retained Dayra's love, of that I was very sure, despite what I had seen to the contrary in times past.

If I could win my own daughter's affection, if I could sheathe those Deadly Talons—wouldn't *that* be a thing to tell Delia?

Don't miss the great novels of Dray Prescot on Kregen, world of Antares!

PHILIP K. DICK

"The greatest American novelist of the second half of the 20th Century."

—*Norman Spinrad*

"A genius . . . He writes it the way he sees it and it is the quality, the clarity of his Vision that makes him great."

—*Thomas M. Disch*

"The most consistently brilliant science fiction writer in the world."

—*John Brunner*

PHILIP K. DICK

In print again, in DAW Books' special memorial editions:

- ☐ **WE CAN BUILD YOU** (#UE1793—$2.50)
- ☐ **THE THREE STIGMATA OF PALMER ELDTRITCH**
  (#UE1810—$2.50)
- ☐ **A MAZE OF DEATH** (#UE1830—$2.50)
- ☐ **UBIK** (#UE1859—$2.50)
- ☐ **DEUS IRAE** (#UE1887—$2.50)
- ☐ **NOW WAIT FOR LAST YEAR** (#UE1654—$2.50)
- ☐ **FLOW MY TEARS, THE POLICEMAN SAID**
  (#UE1624—$2.25)